SOPHOMORE SUMMER

THE HIGH SCHOOL SUMMER SERIES
BOOK ONE

CHASE TATUM

1

It's the last day of school, and we're finally at one of my all-time favorite traditions: yearbook signing. Sure, it's textbook cliché, and yeah, everyone's probably copying and pasting compliments from one yearbook to another. But let's not kid ourselves: There's something great about these sappy, short, and sometimes sweet messages from kids that you just spent most of your days with. I like to think of it as my school year's highlight reel, filled with graffiti-like doodles, inside jokes, and shout-outs from that one teacher who actually made math fun. For me, yearbook signing is the high school equivalent of a season finale—epic and unmissable.

My first year at Cascade Prep, the private school I attend, is almost done, and let's be real—even though it wasn't the worst year, no one really likes being a freshman in high school. New school, new faces, and the upperclassmen act like you're invisible. Lucky for me, this year of school is in the rearview mirror, and I am shedding the "freshman" label and stepping into my sophomore summer.

I am making my way back from a yearbook signature collection spree from some of my favorite teachers and staff at school this year. Morgan and Celeste, my two best friends, think I'm crazy for letting teachers sign my yearbook. But they're also the ones who unearthed my past yearbooks from middle school and grade school and read over the teachers' notes. So, who's the real crazy here, huh?

I'm weaving through the leftover crowd of mostly freshmen still waiting for their rides when I spot my friends, as usual, hanging out on our favorite hill overlooking the soccer field.

Walking toward my friends hits me—life can change so much in a year. When I started this year at Cascade Prep, it was just me, my two best friends, and a handful of familiar faces from junior high. It felt daunting to walk into class and see so many new people.

I was always the girl in middle school who was the friendly face in the hallway, holding doors and sharing smiles; any guy from my middle school could vouch for my kindness. But none would ever say, "Oh yeah, Noli and I are tight." Why? Because despite my friendly demeanor and genuine interest in people, I've never had a boyfriend or even a first kiss. And if I'm laying all my cards on the table? Boys, especially the older ones at Cascade Prep, absolutely terrified me during my freshman year.

Take Celeste's older brother, for instance. Whenever I'm at her house, and he is there, I feel like an anthropologist studying an intriguing new species—not because he's some wild creature, but because boys are simply a different breed. They act, talk, and hang out differently. As a girl with only two younger sisters, my experience with boys is, well, limited.

The memory from a sleepover at Celeste's house in seventh grade still makes me cringe. We were deep into a karaoke showdown, and I was mid-chorus, fully embracing my inner Selena Gomez when her older brother Carter sauntered in. I froze, my voice catching in my throat. I had a huge crush on Carter and was mortified to be caught acting like such a kid. Let's be real, though; I was a kid.

Amused, Carter quipped, "Forget the words?"

Panicking, I blurted out, "Nope, just really have to pee," and dashed out of the room like my life depended on it. I tried to figure out if I could crawl through their bathroom window and escape as I heard Carter's laughter filtering through the door, followed by Celeste's voice chastising him for teasing me.

Ugh, even thinking about it right now makes me cringe. But it also makes me realize why I am so lucky to have my two best friends. Celeste has always been so protective of me, and that's not the only thing I love about her. In fact, there's so much more than meets the eye.

So that's me with guys. I'm obsessed with always having a crush, but I have zero experience when it comes to flirting, getting guys to notice me, or even having guys as friends. Lucky for me, I didn't need to fill the friend roster trying to get anyone's attention because I have Celeste and Morgan.

When people first meet Celeste, they often put her in the 'quiet' or 'introverted' category. But that couldn't be further from the truth. Beneath her reserved exterior lies a wise soul that I lovingly call a "wisdom witch," trapped in the body of a teenager. Celeste isn't just comfortable in her own skin; she exudes a level of self-confidence that most people twice her age haven't achieved.

But what's even more astonishing? Celeste is a literary prodigy. Destined, I'm convinced, to win a Nobel Prize in Literature someday. Under a well-guarded fake name, she's already published several novels, with one soaring to the heights of the New York Times best-seller list just last year. This monumental achievement is a closely guarded secret, known only to a privileged few—her parents, her writing agent, Carter, and me. Celeste didn't think our other best friend, Morgan, could keep her secret safe, so we never openly talked about her being this big-time mega-author.

Celeste is our group's resident conspiracy theorist. She's the one who can make boring conversations about school seem like an episode from an espionage thriller. I swear, Celeste could have a second career as a detective; she notices the little details that the rest of us miss and somehow weaves them into stories that are so compelling it's hard to dismiss them as just something my best friend came up with.

Like last year, when she first brought up the idea that Mr. Smith, the band teacher, was having an affair with the school's lunch lady, a woman significantly older than him. We laughed it off as another one of Celeste's wild theories. But Celeste wouldn't let it go, pointing out that Mr. Smith was the only one who ever got an extra dessert every lunch. To our utter disbelief, by the end of the year, the rumor had spiraled out of control, and it turned out Celeste had been right all along.

In stark contrast to Celeste is Morgan—she's effervescent, energetic, and always at the heart of any excitement. If there's no party happening, trust Morgan to kick one into gear. Morgan has this incredible ability to engage anyone in conversation, leaving them feeling like they're the center of her universe. She has a way of being friends with everyone while also keeping her private life fully guarded. I suspect it's a skill she learned while her parents were getting a divorce.

Morgan's parents divorced when she was just ten, and her dad moved across the country from Utah to New York. Since then, her life has been a constant shuffle: school years with her mom in Utah and major holidays and summer breaks in the Big Apple. She keeps a tight lid on her feelings about the divorce and the constant travel, but I can tell it's a strain on her. As much as I try to empathize, our family couldn't be more different, so sometimes it's hard to understand what she's going through. But I do know Morgan, and I would do anything for her.

Morgan often acts as the spark that propels me out of my comfort zone. She's a near-constant presence in our home, almost like an honorary sister in our already bustling, almost all-female household. With her mom frequently out of town for work and deeply involved in the local mountain biking community—a hobby Morgan can't stand—she prefers the lively chaos of our home to the solitude of her own. There's something about our loud household that appeals to her. Maybe it's the warmth, the way my parents treat her like one of their daughters, the non-stop action, or it's just the assurance that she's part of something big, comforting, and constant.

I adore having Morgan around so much, especially because she helps diffuse the constant energy of my younger sisters, Poppy and Jazzy. Anyone who's dealt with younger sisters knows they can be a handful; mine are no exception. Morgan steps in as a sort of second big sister, expertly diverting some of that sibling pressure away from me. Her presence has become so woven into our daily lives that it's hard to imagine our household without her.

I round out the third member of this bestie group. People always get my name wrong. My sisters and I are all named after flowers. I am Magnolia, or Noli, to my friends. I have been called Maggie, Mags, and even Magatha. UGH. I hated my name when I was little, but I feel like my name finally grew on me in middle school. Kids stopped being as mean about it and started to say how cool my name was.

Like I said, I have two younger sisters, a mom and dad, who are both heavily involved in the community, their work, and, of course, raising us girls. I have two main passions in life. Golf and wake surfing, and lucky for me, I live in the best neighborhood for both of these things.

We live in a gated community that was built right on a man-made lake that was specifically designed for wake surfing and water-skiing. Behind the lake is the country club that our family is a member of. It has a gorgeous 18-hole golf course that I golf at daily.

I spend a ton of time outside between my two favorite hobbies, but when I can't be outside, I usually scroll through Spotify to make epic playlists for every mood/moment of my life or read.

The biggest regret of my life up to this point was cutting my hair too short right before my freshman year started. I watched a movie where the leading character had her hair cut between her shoulders and the bottom of her ear lobe. I thought it was so cute, and I wanted something cute and a little more grown-up since I was going into high school. So I took the picture to a salon and showed the girl what

I wanted. She said she for sure could do it, but after she chopped off five inches of my hair, she couldn't get it even. I ended up with my hair cut just above the top of my ears, and I cried for at least a week.

My hair is growing out, but I swear I will never cut my hair short again. I made Celeste and Morgan swear to me that if I ever told them I wanted to cut my hair short they will smack me right across the face and remind me what a bad idea short hair is.

Bound together since fifth grade, Celeste, Morgan, and I make up a trio that's as mismatched as it is inseparable. Our personalities may be as different as night and day, but we've made a pact always to have each other's backs and keep the good times rolling, no matter what life throws our way, even bad haircuts.

I don't know what I would have done without Morgan and Celeste on the first day of freshman year. The night before school started, my nerves were in overdrive. The maze of hallways of a new school kept racing around in my mind, and I worried that I would get lost. I also worried that my class schedule would separate me from Celeste and Morgan, and that they would be off making new friends and I would end up sitting behind the school on a metal trash can eating my lunch alone. Amidst my spiraling anxiety, I was texting my friends, and they were doing their best to anchor me back to reality.

I had been sending them messages about how I would literally die if I couldn't find them for lunch when I started getting texts from both of them at the same time.

> Morgan: Cool it Noli, we'll find you in the morning. We can pick a lunch spot to meet at. K?

> Celeste: You know she's gonna be up all night thinking about eating her lunch on a garbage can.

> Celeste: Maybe Carter will eat lunch with her! ;)

Me: Mock me all you want, but it's so true.
Please, please, PLEASE can we find a place
to eat lunch right now? I don't think I will
sleep tonight if we don't.

Me: UGH…I forgot I would see Carter at
school OMG

Celeste: Don't worry, he doesn't want to be
seen with freshies

Morgan: Too bad, I was hoping he would be
my bf this year ;)

Me: gross

Morgan: Magnolia wishes Carter would
sweep you off your feet and be your first
kiss.

Celeste: enough of that! He's my brother

Me: I can't think about kissing Carter right
now….REMEMBER?!!! SCHOOL? LUNCH?
EATING ALONE ON A GARBAGE
CAN?????????????

Morgan: fine. Let's meet at the hilltop by the
soccer field.

Morgan: does her royal highness accept?

Me: YES! Thank you guys.

The next day, I had successfully navigated the first part of the
school, and finally, the lunch bell rang, and I beelined it to the desig-
nated spot. As I made my way to the hill, I saw an unexpected sight.
Our spot had been taken. A group of guys, with one girl who looked
vaguely familiar from my math class, were sitting right where my

friends and I had decided to eat lunch. I pulled out my phone to text my friends when I spotted Morgan and Celeste. They were right there, sitting with the guys.

I hesitated, my steps slowing as I approached. A wave of uncertainty washed over me, undercutting the sense of relief that should have come from seeing my friends.

It was Morgan who caught sight of me first. "Hey, Noli! Get over here! Meet my new besties," she shouted, waving me over with an enthusiasm that only Morgan would get meeting new people. Morgan loves being with new people and hearing all about them, especially guys. I shouldn't be surprised, but I slowly walked toward the group, not knowing what to expect.

I stopped when I got to them, waiting for one of my friends to explain to me why we were going to eat lunch with strange boys. Morgan started talking while smiling at the guys, "Turns out these guys had the same idea about this being the ultimate lunch spot. Neither of us was willing to budge, so, you know, in the grand spirit of high school diplomacy, we decided—why not mix and mingle?"

As I met her gaze, I couldn't help but shoot her a skeptical look, which I hoped conveyed an entire paragraph's worth of annoyance. I didn't want to spend another anxiety-filled hour trying to get to know new people and gauge if I was doing a good job. I just wanted to relax with my friends and hope that the first-day butterflies would go away for a moment. I could tell that wasn't an option, so I joined the group after letting out a small sigh.

I tried to think of something funny to say. Something that would convey to the group that I was cool while also letting my friends know that I absolutely did not want to eat lunch with these people. My cheeks flushed a warm shade of embarrassment as the collective eyes of the group pivoted in my direction, and I said nothing.

Just then, one of the guys sprang to his feet. He seemed to tower over me despite my higher vantage point on the hill. "I'm Noah," he announced, his face contorted into a grin that could only be described as goofily endearing. "If we're gonna be best friends, might as well hug it out."

He enveloped me in a bear hug that was both mortifying and oddly comforting. Laughter erupted around us.

Another guy slapped Noah's leg, admonishing, "Dude, seriously, cut it out. You're making it weird. She'll bail if you keep this up."

I peeked out from the bear hug, and my eyes met his—Xander, sitting casually next to Morgan, was the one talking. I was caught off guard by his impossibly long eyelashes—why did guys get those?—and piercing blue eyes. His lips, plush and tantalizing, reminded me of that heartthrob from my favorite movie. I'd never been kissed, but staring at those lips, it was all too easy to drift into a daydream.

Snapping back to reality, I realized I'd been openly ogling him. My cheeks flushed a hot shade of crimson. Desperate to escape the spotlight of my own embarrassment, I found myself retreating back into the strange sanctuary of Noah's lingering hug.

Noah's hug served as a curious refuge from my self-inflicted embarrassment. The warmth in his arms diffused through me, making me feel as if I've known him for years instead of seconds. He held onto me just a beat longer than what was normal, as though he sensed that I wasn't quite ready to face the scrutiny of a group filled with fresh faces. Finally mustering the courage to look up, I greeted him with a smile that felt more genuine than any I'd offered that day —cautiously averting my eyes from Xander's all-too-tempting lips. "I'm Magnolia," I offered, "but you can call me Noli. Stoked to hear we are new best friends."

Noah's grin was practically luminous. "Anytime, Noli." Noah's gaze stayed on me. It was strange. Most guys our age don't actually look into your eyes, they usually stare down at their phones, or even worse, they stare at your chest. Noah didn't. He looked into my eyes, then said, "I know where I know you from! You are the golfer, girl!! You spanked all of us guys at that open tournament last fall."

He didn't seem bugged like most golfing guys my age that I play.

He seemed genuinely impressed. I couldn't help but smile back at Noah.

And just like that, in the span of a single lunch break on the first day of freshman year, my social universe expanded in the most unexpected way. Our trio—Morgan, Celeste, and I—seamlessly merged with Noah, Xander, Evan, Chris, and his girlfriend Addy. They came as a package deal, each one adding a unique flavor to our new group dynamic.

It was as if an unspoken agreement had been made before the end of the first day of school that this would be our friend group freshman year. And who could've guessed that being friends with boys could be so fun? Their laughter was contagious, their outlook refreshingly light-hearted, and their supply of absurdly adventurous ideas ensured that life was anything but monotonous.

Before we all became friends, Celeste, Morgan, and I could easily spend hours just lounging by the pool or paddleboarding at the lake behind my house, getting lost in chatter. But with the arrival of this motley crew, our hanging out now came with adrenaline-filled adventures, dumb jokes, and unforgettable memories.

As I head toward my cluster of friends for the last time as a freshman on the final day of school, I find myself appreciating the awesomeness of having these friends in my life. And it still blows my mind that being friends with guys really was so easy.

"Hey!" I say once I'm within earshot of everyone. The group opens up, allowing me to take my usual spot, snug between Noah and Xander.

Morgan teases, "Managed to get the lunch lady to sign your yearbook?"

I scrunch up my nose in playful distaste, retorting, "Grace is a wonderful lady, and I'm actually bummed I didn't get her to sign my yearbook. She's not here today."

Noah throws an arm around me. "It's cool how you make time for all the old people that work at the school. I bet it brightens their day. Though, Noli, it is 'sus' that you have them sign your yearbook."

Looking up at Noah, I counter, "Is 'sus' still even a thing?"

Xander joins in. "NOBODY is using 'sus.' Not even my little brother."

But Noah, still with his arm slung over my shoulder, remains resolute. "I'll never quit 'sus.'" He smiles wide at me, and I can't help but to snort my laughter at him.

Noah has unquestionably become my new favorite friend this year. We have grown close, and he feels more like a best friend than a guy I just met this year at school.

He'll call me at the most random times during the day, diving straight into a conversation as though we'd been chatting for hours. He's unabashedly candid, voicing his thoughts without a hint of restraint. Morgan says it annoys her sometimes, but it is the thing I like about Noah. I'm never left guessing about his thoughts or what's happening in his world.

Noah is my only friend who plays golf. He made the JV team, and I made the Varsity team. We went to several golf tournaments, and it was such a breath of fresh air to be with Noah and have a friend to golf with. It also helps that he also doesn't care that I am a better golfer than he is, which most guys in high school are completely pissed about.

Before Noah and I started golfing together, I wouldn't talk to any other players, and I got the nickname the "Ice Queen" on the course. It's not that I am stuck up or witchy or anything like that. It's just that I get so nervous trying to come up with what to say, and my goal coach said it was best if I focus on my game. With Noah, I actually have fun playing.

My dad always takes golf more seriously than I do. He doesn't approve or fully appreciate our goofy approach. Despite my dad's vision of me becoming a professional golfer one day, in truth, I love golf, but not THAT much. Honestly, I started golfing to satisfy my parents and conveniently dodge joining my sisters in a dance studio. Don't get me wrong, I am good at it. But I don't want to play professionally for the rest of my life.

I'm lost in thought of sun-soaked afternoons on the golf course with Noah and going wake surfing as much as possible with my friends when my yearbook is abruptly snatched from my grip. "Haven't signed this yet," Xander says, his captivating blue eyes locking on to mine.

A surge of exhilaration sweeps over me; Xander has a way of making me become hyper-aware of everything. I flashback to that fateful first day of freshman year when our eyes met, and my crush on him was instant. I have fallen hard for Xander, and it's not just that he reminds me of my Hollywood crush. It's the way he laughs and the way he is always coming up with these crazy stories and trying to outdo everyone. Some guys might be annoying, but with Xander, it's cute. I'm far from alone; practically every girl in our school has a crush on him.

His allure is undeniable. He's the epitome of universal appeal— beloved by guys, desired by girls. He possesses this extraordinary ability to make you feel like you're the only person in the room worth his time. There's something almost magical about his gaze; it's as if he knows precisely the impact he has in an effortless way that leaves you spellbound. Xander knows he is cute, too. He is an incessant flirt, and he knows how to do it in a way that makes me question if maybe he took a class on how to flirt to make every single girl fall in love with the way he does it.

My crush on Xander has lasted all year, but I'm fairly certain he doesn't know. The reality that I am friends—actual friends—with the most sought-after guy in our grade is nothing short of surreal. I tell myself that being friends with him is enough because I am positive I would never have a chance at being his girlfriend. Even upperclassmen aren't immune to being swept up in his gaze and feeling utterly smitten by him. Xander had a senior girl ask him to do one of the dances this year.

Of course, I had to tell Morgan and Celeste about my secret crush on Xander. They were like, "Been there, done that. Time to move on." But moving on isn't that easy when you're friends with the guy you're crushing on and when he keeps doing the most adorable/hot things daily. I mean, how do you turn off those feelings when you see him all the time?

Whenever I catch Xander's eye, my heart goes from zero to sixty. It's not like an all-the-time thing, but when he's actually focused on me, I get this wave of butterflies that's hard to ignore. Something about him sticks to me, and I can't shake it off.

Xander has my yearbook in his hands, and he is still giving me one of those famous flirty looks when he says, "Hang on, be right back,"

He walks over to the school stairs and sits down like he's got something major to write.

I'm not gonna lie; I'm curious. Like, why does he need all that space and privacy just to sign a yearbook? Apparently, I'm not the only one who's wondering.

Noah yells after Xander, "Bruh, what are you doing with that yearbook? Planning to write your autobiography in there?"

Xander continues writing, offering no reply to Noah's jest. Noah looks back at me with his eyebrows raised and shrugs his shoulders. I'm no "Noah Expert," but I have a feeling he may know what this is all about.

I don't want to let anyone know how curious I am about what Xander's writing in my yearbook, so I steer the convo back to the group. "Any big summer plans?" I toss out, trying to sound as chill as possible.

Each friend spills about their summer, and it's clear we're all going in different directions. Morgan's heading to the Hamptons to hang with her dad—a trip she's both amped and anxious about. Celeste mentions "writing camp," but I know that's code for her family renting a lakeside house in Wisconsin where she'll be writing her next big novel. Noah's off to live the ranch life with his Idaho cousins. Chris and Evan are going to church camp down in Texas. And Addy? She's all booked with dance competitions and expos, and, oh yeah, she's even scored a killer dance photoshoot. It sounds like I am the only one sticking around here for the summer.

I glance over at Xander. He is crumpling a piece of paper up and throwing it away in the trash can as he walks back to our group. He gives Noah a slight nod and slides my yearbook into my hands. Xander bends down and gets close enough for me to feel his warm breath on my ear. "Wait until you're home to read it," he murmurs. My cheeks feel like they're on fire, and my curiosity is like a raging inferno. What on earth did he write?

I want to rush home right then, lock myself away, and find out what Xander's message says. I'm so deep in my thoughts, pondering over what Xander might have inscribed, that I barely notice the silence. It's only when I glance up that I find everyone's eyes fixed on me. They may have caught that love-struck expression I have plastered on my face. I'm busted!

Celeste swoops to my rescue. "Noli, Addy wants to know about your summer plans."

Caught off guard, I respond, "Oh man, I totally zoned out." I flash a quick grin to indicate my return to the present conversation and explain, "Not much on my agenda. A couple of golf tournaments, lots of lake time, and our family friends visit us during the Fourth of July week. After that, I've got a golf camp I am going to. That's about it."

Trying to seem casual, I turn to Xander. "Your turn. What's summer looking like for you?"

"I got accepted into this insane soccer camp at the REAL soccer stadium." He grins. "It's supposed to be super intense, guys coming in from all over. After that, I'm working at a dude ranch down south. Mom says it'll look good on college apps."

And just that fast—my mind drifts off again. This time, my mind flashes to Xander being a cowboy at a dude ranch. I picture him in snug jeans and a fitted plaid shirt, topped with a cowboy hat that somehow makes him even more irresistible. I can see him straddling a horse, looking all rugged, and...*Okay, Noli, snap out of it!* If I keep staring at him with these starry eyes, I'm sure Noah is going to call me out.

Just as I'm teetering on the brink of actually drooling over Xander and us getting married, my mom's car rolls up—perfect timing. I give quick hugs to Morgan, Celeste, and Addy, reminding them of our sleepover tonight.

"No peeking in your yearbook!" Celeste shouts, wagging her finger at me.

Usually, I can promise her I won't, but today is different. There is a personal note from Xander in that yearbook that I can't wait to read. I shoot a thumbs-up in Celeste's direction and turn away without saying anything.

I'm about to dash off to my mom's car when Noah chimes in, "Whoa, whoa! You're not escaping without a hug."

Laughing, I pretend to bolt, fully aware he's right behind me. True to form, he catches up and wraps me in a bear hug so tight it's almost bone-crushing. "Remember, it's only weird if you make it weird."

Nestling into the comfort of his embrace, I shoot back, "Your hugs aren't what's weird. You are."

Noah's laughter vibrates through me as he lets go. He says, "I am going to miss you this summer. Don't forget to read my message, ok?"

I assure him I will read it tonight. What is it with these guys and their yearbook messages? I glance back at Evan, Chris, and Xander, waving my final goodbyes. Evan and Chris return the wave with a casual nod. Xander, however, locks eyes with me, winks, and grins. "I'll text you later," he promises.

Wait, did Xander wink at me? Sure, he's known for those little flirtatious winks, but never has one been directed at me. As I make my way to my mom's car, my mind starts to churn with summer possibilities. When I hop in the car, I glance back, Xander is back to holding court with the group, but Noah is facing the car, watching me go.

Initially, I thought my summer was going to be filled with big group hangouts—maybe our days on the lake with some wake surfing. But as quickly as that idea forms, it shrinks. No one is going to be here all summer. As much of a bummer as that is, I realize something. I'm not that sad about most of the group not being here. My mind is zeroing in on Xander.

Who am I kidding? A group hangout sounds fun, but the idea of spending one-on-one time with Xander sounds way better. Sure, he is going to soccer camp and the dude ranch, but there has got to be time that we can spend some of the summer together. What if that is my summer? What if this sophomore summer isn't about making memories with this new group of friends, but what if it's all about Xander and me?

The moment I slide into the car, my mind starts to play a highlight reel of what just happened. First, Xander takes my yearbook and writes for seven minutes something so secretive that I'm not allowed to read it until I'm home. Yes, I counted the agonizing seven minutes it took him to write. Then, he teases me with a whisper, promising a text later, and caps it off with a wink. It's as if the boundaries of our friendship are blurring ever so slightly. Could it be? Has Xander finally stopped seeing me as just another friend? The possibility sends an electric charge through me.

As my mom pulls away from the curb, my heart pounds with brand-new excitement. I can't help but think that maybe, just maybe, this will be the summer when the sparks between Xander and me ignite into something more.

2

Ever since Morgan, Celeste, and I became besties, we've had this tradition: an epic sleepover on the last day of school. It's basically our version of New Year's Eve—complete with all of the best foods, staying up WAY too late, and celebrating the closing of a chapter of our lives. There is also one golden rule that we've all sworn to; we made a pact not to read our yearbooks until we're together that night. We love being able to read our yearbooks together and being able to see each other's reactions and gossip about kids from school. We are so serious about this rule that we even made up a consequence if any of us broke it. Break the rule? You're taking a midnight skinny dip. Sounds scandalous, right? Okay, maybe for some people, it's not that scandalous. Morgan has skinny-dipped several times, but me? Nope, I would rather die than have my friends see me naked.

This year, we've got a newcomer in the mix: Addy. She slid into our girl squad like she has always been there, so leaving her out would be all kinds of wrong. Addy's like the doppelganger of my little sister, Jazzy—long-legged, graceful, and deceptively tough. They both might look like delicate dance flowers, but trust me, their competitive spirit is no joke. Dancing isn't just a hobby for them; it's a battlefield.

At first, Morgan wasn't too sure about Addy. She was a little intimidated, but when I said, "Imagine she's just an older Jazzy," Morgan finally understood Addy a bit better, and now they're great friends. Don't get me wrong; the OG trio of Morgan, Celeste, and I still have our moments, especially since Addy's often off doing her dance thing. But when she's around, whether at school or chilling with the guys, the vibes are always good.

As Mom drives me home, she's in full interrogation mode—every parent's favorite last-day-of-school ritual. She keeps throwing me questions about the last day of school and about the sleepover tonight. But my brain's checked out, playing and replaying the day's events, especially Xander's curveballs. My answers to Mom's questions are auto-pilot level. "Yeah." "No." "Mmm-hmm." Honestly, I'd give anything for a mental "mute button" right now, just so I could drown in my Xander-centric thoughts without interruption.

"What are we thinking for food tonight?" Mom asks, glancing over at me as she steers the car. It's our turn to host the sleepover this year, after all.

"Pizza," I answer automatically, barely investing a second's thought into it.

Mom gives me a "Really?" kind of hum. "Hmm."

"What about having Dad set up the outdoor screen for a movie?" she suggests, her voice full of enthusiasm. Mom lives for this stuff—making every gathering at our place an Instagrammable event.

"Nah," I sigh deeply, half out of exhaustion and half to emphasize my point.

She inhales sharply. I brace myself; I know what's coming.

"Look, I get it. Our house might not seem like a big deal to you," she says, "but your friends love it. The pool, the fire pit, the hot tub, that pickle ball court you barely use, and the tricked-out basement— your friends are always having fun and wanting to hang out here.

And don't even get me started on how much they beg you to take the boat out for wake surfing because we live on a lake."

She's not wrong. My mom's pretty much the hostess with the mostest, and my friends love being at our house. And let's be real, the boys basically think my mom's a saint. The pantry's always stocked with enough snacks to feed a small army, and if she ever hears anyone even mention something that she can make, bake, or create, she will do it.

My mom continues her pitch, shifting into what I recognize as her professional negotiating tone. "Besides, don't you think Morgan would love an outdoor movie? It's her only chance before she leaves for the summer." She exhales, her eyes meeting mine. "I can't imagine how her mom feels, not being able to see her for so long."

Talk of Morgan's life due to her parents' divorce always turns the mood. I hate it when people bring that subject up; Morgan despises discussing it. I usually find a way to redirect conversations away from it. It's a small gesture but one that spares her from judgment or pity, both of which she hates.

Mom is still talking, but honestly, I just want her to stop—stop talking about Morgan, stop talking in general—so I can retreat back into my daydreams about Xander. I've got the ultimate trump card, a surefire way to steer the conversation back into a realm where I'm comfortable. Despite my mom's prowess in the art of negotiation— she does it for a living, after all—I have my own knack for steering situations while letting her think she's won.

"Mom, you know how I'm a disaster when it comes to planning get-togethers," I begin, my tone as earnest as I can muster. "Would you mind taking care of the preparations for the sleepover? I trust you'll make it awesome."

My mom practically buzzes with excitement at the challenge. "Oh, I've got some great ideas! A balloon arch might be a stretch on short notice, but I'm sure we've got some party supplies stashed somewhere."

A balloon arch? Seriously? Only my mom would think of something so extra for a simple sleepover.

"That sounds fantastic, Mom," I affirm, my voice giving me away. But it doesn't matter; I've won this round, even if she thinks she's holding all the cards.

For the rest of the ride home, my mom is quiet as she mentally assembles an itinerary that I'm sure will be way too elaborate for just a sleepover. But Morgan and Celeste have always enjoyed the flair. They're used to it, and it keeps them entertained. And, as much as it usually annoys me or leaves me red-faced, if it keeps my mom occupied and out of my business right now, then that's a victory in my book.

The moment the garage door closes behind us, Mom bolts from the Tesla, striding purposefully toward her home office—a space we've affectionately dubbed the 'command center.' She'll be lost in her planning frenzy for the remainder of the night, orchestrating the over-the-top sleepover.

With my sisters away at their end-of-year bashes and Dad still glued to his desk at work, the house is blissfully empty. Alone at last, the privacy I need to get into the Xander note is finally mine. Sure, I made that pact to save my yearbook's revelations for the sleepover, but come on—this is Xander we're talking about! My curiosity is reaching unbearable levels. I need to see what he wrote, and I need to see it now.

Bypassing my usual post-school ritual—out of the uniform, bag on the hook, and a snack in the kitchen—I race upstairs, still in my uniform, throw my bag on the floor, and plop onto my bed, the yearbook clenched in my excited grasp. I rifle through the pages from the start, my eyes scanning for the unique flourishes of Xander's handwriting, the exaggerated 'X' he uses like a personal emblem. My stomach somersaults as each page flips until—there it is! The oversized 'X' right where I knew it would be.

A tide of giddy, nervous energy floods my veins, making my hands shake as I skim over the message. It's long-ish, not quite the novella that Celeste annually pens in my yearbook, but substantial, especially for a guy. My eyes dart through the words, on high alert for tell-tale words like "love" or "boyfriend." One word stands out, and I let out an involuntary, joyous squeak. But I haven't grasped the whole message yet, and I catch myself. "Slow down, Noli. Breathe." Taking a moment to center myself, I start again from the top of Xander's note, this time committed to absorbing every single word.

> "Noli-
> One of the best things about the school year was
>   meeting you. You are such an amazing friend. I
>   love having you around. Your laugh lights me up
>   every time I hear it. I don't know how to go a
>   whole summer without seeing you. The experi-
>   ences that we are going to have together are what
>   I know I will look back on and remember my
>   entire life. Can't wait to make more memories
>   with you. Xander"

I pore over the note, digesting every word and nuance. I read it over and over again. The message is perfect phrases put together that make my heart flutter, but I also feel a nagging hint of disappointment that there's no grand declaration of love or a plea to be his girlfriend. The word "love" that I spotted earlier refers to him loving my company. I decide to set aside the disappointment and revel in the positivity. Blushing, grinning, and squealing excitedly, I daydream about what the rest of our high school years could be like. Xander and me, together. Xander and I walking hand in hand down the hallways at school. Xander leaning down to kiss me at lunch.

As I am grinning broadly, studying his handwritten note, something that I had missed in my previous twenty read-throughs catches my eye. Tucked away before his bold 'X' signature, Xander has scribbled a tiny 'XO.' It's so small I almost didn't notice it. But it's there! Hugs AND kisses!

With a high-pitched squeal, I fall back onto my bed, the yearbook tossed aside. It's happening. Xander and I are destined to be together. He's going to be my boyfriend, my first kiss! It seems so surreal, yet this is exactly how it's supposed to be. The urge to text my friends and spill all about the note gnaws at me.

Then it hits me—my friends. Morgan, Celeste, and Addy will be flipping through my yearbook tonight. They'll read Xander's deeply personal message to me. The note he intended for my eyes only. If I text them now, they'll know I broke the pact we made not to read the yearbook until our sleepover. They would be livid, and there's the additional humiliation of facing the skinny-dipping consequence we all agreed upon for anyone who broke the pact.

A knot tightens in my stomach, and my heart feels like it's lodged in my throat. This is not okay. With all of my friends taking off for the summer tomorrow, I don't want our last sleepover to end up with them upset with me. Xander's note needs to stay a secret, a treasure just for me, and yet I can't betray my friends by revealing that I've already read it. My mind is a whirlpool of competing emotions: exhilaration at Xander's words, terror at the idea of betraying my friends, and a gut-wrenching indecisiveness that grips me. What am I going to do?

Just as I'm teetering on the edge of an emotional cliff, a stroke of cunning hits me. It's risky, but it might just work. Xander's note is isolated, carefully written on the backside of a blank Freshman title page. With trembling hands, I reach for the scissors on my desk.

The scissors feel heavier than usual as I position them along the edge of the page. Before I chicken out, I grab the paper and start cutting. Each snip sounds like a drumroll in my ears; each cut shredding a tiny piece of my conscience. I pause, half done, heart pounding as I think of the permanent change I'm about to make. It feels like I'm cheating on my friends for a guy, and it feels so wrong.

Suddenly, the door handle jiggles—someone's coming in! Panic grips me. I hurriedly stash the scissors under a pile of books, my pulse skyrocketing. The door swings open. It's my mom holding a tray of freshly baked cookies.

"Thought you might like a snack while you're...uh, relaxing." She scans the room, missing the yearbook on my bed. I can tell she isn't thrilled that I haven't changed and that my backpack is thrown on the floor.

I hop up and go to pick up my backpack. I start to grab clothes from my closet to change into. I don't want her to linger anymore and ask questions. I smile as I make my way to my bathroom.

"Thanks, Mom," I manage to say, my voice strangled.

She leaves, satisfied that I am not just scrolling on my phone, unaware of what I have really been up to, and I exhale a breath I didn't know I was holding. The close call sends my heart racing but also solidifies my resolve. I finish the deed with newfound urgency, the scissors cutting through the last strands of paper like it's severing the last threads of my innocence.

If my friends ever discover this, they might just strangle me. But at this moment, the cut page in my hand feels like a piece of stolen treasure, guilty yet thrilling. It's done. I've crossed a line, but in my turbulent teenage life, crossing lines seems to be part of the journey.

Once I manage to free the page, I look at the void I've created in the yearbook. It's a clean cut. No one would notice unless they were deliberately searching for it. But just as I'm about to exhale in relief, another realization pierces me—I'm not done. I need to replace Xander's message with a new one, and it has to pass for Xander's handwriting. My friends knew he'd taken his time writing; Evan had even mentioned it. The absence of a longer message would set off alarm bells.

I dig through my backpack that I just hung up, pulling out a piece of scrap paper from my worn-out freshman notebook. It feels like a relic, how do notebooks and textbooks do that? One minute, they are part of your everyday existence, and a moment later, they are obsolete, used-up things that you will never look at again.

My eyes dart between Xander's original note and the blank paper before me. I practice the quirks of his handwriting—the way he loops his 'y,' the uniqueness of his 'X,' and the sharp angles of his characters. My hand aches, my mind races, but finally, I think I've got it.

For a moment, I hesitate, my pen hovering above the blank page in my yearbook. What am I doing? Is this the person I want to be? Seriously? This really isn't that big of a deal, but I feel like I am in too deep.

My hand trembles and I take a deep breath as I put pen to paper. This is it. There's no turning back now. I begin to write, mimicking Xander's style as best as I can. Each stroke feels like a little betrayal—of my friends, of Xander, and even of myself. But as I finish the last line and cap my pen, a complex mixture of relief and fear washes over me.

> "Noli, Thanks for being my friend this year. That was
> rad."

SHOOT. Xander never says rad, but it's too late, I wrote it in pen, and I can't take it back. I keep writing,

> "So glad you got to play golf. Also, thanks for having
> us over at your house this year. I really really liked
> wake surfing and eating your mom's food. Hope
> you have a great summer. Maybe we can play
> Connect Four on our phones while I am gone. See
> you next year."

Dang it! Another mistake. The only people you say, "See you next year" are the people you had a class with but don't really know. I can't believe I keep messing up! The entire message is dumb, and Xander would never write something like this. I need to end this note before I say something that will for sure give me away, like YOLO. I sign it perfectly with his signature and curse inwardly at the silly mistakes I made.

I've done it. Whether that makes me cunning or deceitful, I can't say. All I know is that I've ventured into a moral gray area, a no-man's land where the only signposts are my own instincts and fears.

My heart is still racing from my covert operation when I hear Mom's voice carrying up the stairs, "NOLI! Morgan's here!" The suddenness of her arrival jolts me back to reality. A quick glance at the clock confirms it's half-past five already. How did time slip away from me so fast? Probably because my heart and mind were tangled up in Xander's every word.

It's a split-second pivot, from the private world of my thoughts to being with my friends. "Snap out of it, Noli," I whisper to myself. The original note, now my secret treasure, quickly finds a hiding spot in my pillowcase.

Just then, Morgan bursts into my room, rolling in her arsenal of bags as if she's moving in for a month. I laugh way too loud, and have to remind myself to calm down. Morgan furrows her brows at my loud laugh and starts to throw bags on the ground. I steady myself and turn my attention to Morgan and her pile of bags. "Seriously, Morgan? Planning to move in?"

"Hey, a girl's gotta have options!" she retorts, dumping her carry-on filled with 'casual wear,' hanging her garment bag of 'preferred outfits,' and plopping down a duffel bag bursting with shoes and accessories. I am used to her usual three bag, but it seems like they have multiplied.

I can't help but laugh. "You know, we should probably consider adding a wing to the house just for your sleepover stuff."

With a dramatic flourish that only Morgan can pull off, she drops onto my bed. "Honestly, I would love to live here full-time. I even talked to your dad about it. But he said I'd have to change my name to a flower to fit in with the family theme. So what do you think suits me more, Delphinium or Buttercup?"

It has been a family tradition for decades in my mom's family that all of the women are named flower names. My mom's name is Lily. I'm Magnolia, and my sisters are Jasmine and Poppy.

"I think you'd be more like a... Primrose," I try to answer, but Morgan is already on to her next thought.

"Speaking of things in bloom, I've got more blooming bags because I'm hoping you'll be my summer storage unit," Morgan says, gesturing to her luggage empire. I do a quick count—she's right. Instead of her usual trio of bags, there are six.

"Of course, that's fine." I nod, taking in the new pieces of luggage. Normally, Morgan stashes her belongings in our guest room, her second home really. But with Jack's family coming this summer, that space is off-limits. "We'll just have to keep them in the downstairs basement for you."

"I really can't have Mom snooping through my stuff when I'm with Dad," she confides.

Of course. Morgan is worried that her mom will start cleaning up her room, get rid of tons of stuff she didn't want to get rid of, and probably find some stuff that Morgan doesn't want found. I realize too that this is the first time Morgan is actually talking about spending the summer with her dad.

Morgan's dad is a touchy subject. The divorce, his move across the country, the semi-estranged relationship—each is a conversational landmine. My mind races, searching for the right words, I never know exactly what to say. Last summer when she mentioned her dad, I said something about how much fun it would be to go on shopping sprees in New York City, and she blew up at me and said maybe I should try and have a dad only show up for you with a credit card for a couple of weeks and see how it feels. Of course, I said sorry, she said sorry, and then we didn't talk about it again. Now, I am wondering if I should ignore the whole topic or acknowledge her summer, when salvation arrives in the form of Celeste.

"Whoa, moving in or just staying overnight?" Celeste jokes as she saunters into my room, casting a glance at Morgan's luggage collection. Celeste walks in carrying nothing but a chic Prada handbag, which probably holds little more than a toothbrush, AirPods, a swimsuit, and a single change of underwear.

Morgan chuckles. "I had to pack extra for you, you psycho. What kind of person shows up to a sleepover with just a handbag?"

Celeste shoots her a sly grin. "The kind that has friends with well-stocked closets."

She's not wrong. Celeste knows she can always borrow from me or Morgan. And that's the beauty of our friendship—we always have each other's backs. Whether it's borrowing clothes or supporting each other. We may not be a carbon copy group of friends, the "Three Musketeers" kind, but our love for each other is the glue that keeps our mismatched pieces together.

We are all lounging around talking about the new movie coming out when Addy bursts through the door, fashionably late and apologizing. She was just booked for another modeling gig tomorrow and had to make sure she had everything she needed since she will be going straight from the sleepover to the photoshoot.

As Addy plops down, we quickly brief her on the sacred tradition of our yearbook sleepover: each of us reads every message written in our yearbooks, we all talk about how our year went, the people that wrote in our yearbooks, and generally just how school was. My mom is our snack supplier and cruise director of the evening's events. When we get bored or when we are done reading all of the yearbook entries, she is always ready for the next event.

I look over at Addy after we have explained everything to her. She is excited to be here and was so touched that we included her. It makes me happy to have her here. Sometimes I feel it's hard to talk to her at school without her boyfriend, Chris, always butting in with his opinions or answering for Addy. It's girls only tonight, and as much as I would love Xander to be here, I'm pumped that Chris and Evan aren't.

I glance out my window and catch sight of a balloon arch in our school colors, carefully erected in the backyard, along with a setup for an outdoor movie. My mom is nowhere in sight, but I have a feeling she's lurking among the bushes, possibly tweaking some string lights or adjusting one of her custom diffusers.

"Wow, your mom went all out," Addy observes, following my gaze.

Morgan nods. "Mom—err, Lily—always knows how to throw a party."

"Yeah," I chuckle as I start to tell Addy a story about my mom that Celeste and Morgan already know. "You should've seen her when we went to Disneyland as kids. We were on this ride that pumped out different scents at key moments, and she became obsessed with 'scentscaping.' It's like she's DJ-ing an event, but with fragrances."

"That's so cool," Addy comments. "Like, the atmosphere really changes with the right scent, you know?"

I nod. "Exactly. She even had these diffusers custom-made to look like rocks and plants. It's her secret weapon for the legendary parties she hosts. The whole neighborhood can't figure out how she does it."

After marveling at my mom's knack for party planning, we bring our focus back to the main event: our yearbook sleepover. Since Addy is the newest addition to our tight-knit group, she's the first up in the reading ritual.

As she opens her yearbook, I can't help but feel curious. I wonder what her yearbook will reveal about her, what different messages will reveal about her relationships at school. Who liked her enough to sign her yearbook, what they wrote,, and what we'll learn about her life beyond our circle. You can learn a lot about someone by what other people write in their yearbook. Each message is like a snapshot, not just of her year, but of all our personal lives and interactions.

She reads the first couple, and they are like any other yearbook entry from random kids,

"YOLO 801-226-12-3"

"Can't wait to see you next year."
"HAGS"
"It was fun to have a class with you."
"Loved getting to know you."
"OMG...You are the sweetest!"
"OMG...You are so pretty. SERIOUSLY!"

We're all laughing over the fact that Hailey has been writing the same thing in everyone's yearbooks since the 7th grade:

"We have our memories. Now let's go make the future."

The irony of it strikes us—the recycled messages contrast with the theme of 'making new memories.' It's so ridiculous that it's poetic.

But then, abruptly, Addy stops reading. Her face flushes a deep red, her eyes locking onto a spot on the page. The room's atmosphere shifts; it's like we can all sense the electric charge of secrets begging to come out..

"Do I have to read all of the yearbook messages?" Addy stammers, her voice tinged with vulnerability.

Morgan leans forward, her eyes gleaming. She has a love for other people's drama, and she can smell a story brewing. "It's a requirement," she says, not even trying to hide her excitement. "If you're too embarrassed to read it, one of us will read it for you."

Addy covers her face with her hands, obviously embarrassed with what someone wrote in her yearbook. Morgan can't contain herself and lets out an excited squeal, practically vibrating in her seat.

I start laughing, but it's a nervous laughter, aware that we're teetering on the edge of a really good revelation. Celeste glances at me, arching an elegant brow, and says, "Well, looks like we're about to start an episode of *Gossip Girl*—unscripted and live."

Gossip Girl is our collective TV obsession, an old-school drama we all fell in love with after I convinced everyone it was far superior to *Outer Banks*—a series I couldn't watch at home thanks to Mom's rules. After binge-watching a few episodes of *Outer Banks* at Celeste's house, we were all in unanimous agreement: *Gossip Girl* trumps all when it comes to capturing the rollercoaster of teenage emotions.

Celeste has this habit of declaring real-life drama as episodes of our very own *Gossip Girl*, a nod to the show's intricate webs of secrets and betrayals. As we all hold our collective breath, waiting for Addy to reveal the hidden message in her yearbook, I can see the gears turning in Celeste's head. Her eyes gleam as she imagines the explosive plot twists that could unfold. Secret love affairs? Evil twins masquerading as schoolmates? I think of all of the crazy possibilities if this were Serena reading something out of her yearbook to Blair Waldorf. We aren't in New York and our friend group is definitely not from Constance Private School. We are just normal kids attending Cascade Prep in Utah.

I realize that the message is probably bland, and silly, but for a brief second, I wonder what it would be like to have Blair and Serena as friends instead of Addy, Celeste, and Morgan. It would be a lot different than the things we think are big deals around here. My thought evaporates as Addy exhales deeply, finally pulling her hands away from her face and we all realize she is crying. .

"Addy!" I exclaim, rushing to her side and wrapping my arm around her. "What type of message is making you cry? Did someone write something mean?"

Morgan chimes in, "It wouldn't be the first time some jerk writes something jerky. If someone's messed with you, I'm down for a little house-egging."

Celeste adds, "Or perhaps we can murder their pets?"

Addy stares at Celeste, eyes wide and shocked that she just mentioned murder.

Celeste grins. "Too much?"

We all break into laughter at how twisted Celeste got and how fast she took it there. Count on Celeste to lighten the mood in the darkest way.

Addy sniffles and sighs. "It's not what someone else wrote," she admits hesitantly. "It's something I did this year that's haunting me."

Haunting? So dramatic and I wonder if maybe we are reaching Gossip Girl status with this revelation. My mind races through the possibilities. What could Addy have possibly done? She's not one for scandal. If it were Morgan, sure, but Addy?

Celeste leans forward, locking eyes with Addy. "The unspoken rule of yearbook sleepover night is: What happens in this room stays in this room. Your secrets are safe with us."

We nod in agreement, and Morgan adds, "You're in a trust circle here."

Addy sighs deeply. "All right. If you all promise to keep this between us."

We all shout, "PROMISE!" almost too eagerly.

Wiping away her tears, Addy opens her yearbook, takes another deep breath, and begins to read:

> "'But, soft! What light through yonder window
> breaks? It is the east, and Juliet is the sun.' Being a
> TA with you in the library was the greatest thing
> about the year. It was fun getting to recite Romeo
> and Juliet with you. 'Good night, good night!
> parting is such sweet sorrow, That I shall say
> good night till it be morrow.'—Max"

As Addy slams her yearbook shut and collapses onto the bed, a heavy tension hangs in the air. Max is a junior and is hardly the guy you'd associate with high school drama. He's a bookish, polite, and so low-key you'd forget he's even there.

"I can't believe he would write that!" Addy's voice trembles, teetering on the edge of fresh tears.

Celeste joins in, somewhat innocently, "Yeah, what a dick move."

Morgan chuckles, always entertained when Celeste tries to use slang. But her laughter is short-lived, because none of us can really figure out what the big deal is. Max wrote some lines from Romeo and Juliet, who cares?

Just when I'm about to ask Addy what the big deal is about Max's note, she drops a revelation that would make even the juiciest episode of *Gossip Girl* pale in comparison.

Taking a shaky breath, she confesses, "I can't believe how much I made out with him this year. If Chris found out, he would kill me."

Our collective jaws hit the floor. Morgan springs up from her seat. "Are you kidding me? You? Addy! You have been hooking up with Max?"

Addy groans, sinking further into her emotional abyss. "Yes, okay? I don't even know how it happened. Well, that's not true—I do. Max turned out to be really nice and surprisingly funny, and SO romantic. We got close, like real close, during our TA sessions in the library."

I knew that Addy was a TA in the library. They usually save TA for the seniors, but no one would sign up to help in the library, so Addy decided to use that period to TA and catch up on her homework.

It does surprise me that Max talked enough to Addy that she got to know him. I don't think I have ever seen Max say more than a sentence to anyone at school. I know he's a junior, and we are all freshmen, but our school is small, so we get to know who everyone is at school pretty quickly.

Addy continues telling us what happened. "One day we were putting books back and he asked me what my favorite book was. I confessed my love for Romeo and Juliet. Instantly, without even needing to look it up, he recited the final lines Romeo utters to Juliet. Most people have never read Romeo and Juliet, let alone know it well enough to recite it by memory. Oh, and the way he said it." Addy pauses, and it's like she is back in that moment. She has this small smile on her lips.

"UGH...," She continues, coming back to the present. "Even thinking about it gets me completely smitten. In that moment, something just...shifted within me. I practically pounced on him right there in the L-N aisle of the library, and we ended up kissing for what felt like an eternity." Addy drops her head in her hands, once again embarrassed at the secret.

I'm both shocked and impressed. I had no inkling that Addy was making out with anyone. Even though she and Chris have been together for quite a while, theirs is what we dubbed an "elementary relationship." They started dating back when they were in junior high, so up until now, they have only had these random short kisses.

Morgan is itching for more details and asks, "So, how long has this been happening?"

Peeking out from behind her hands, Addy finally sits upright. "Just after Christmas break. Every time it happens, I swear I won't do it again, but he reels me back in with his ridiculous poetry or those enticing looks across the book stacks."

Celeste bursts into laughter, her eyes gleaming with a mix of delight. "Oh, Addy, you've got yourself into a real-life romantic tragedy. What are you going to do now?"

Addy looks at each of us, her eyes stopping at me. "I don't know," she says, her voice tinged with vulnerability. "That's the worst part. Every time I look at Chris, I feel like I'm betraying him, but when I'm with Max, it feels like...like I'm where I'm supposed to be."

Morgan leans in, her eyes wide. "So, are you going to break up with Chris?"

"Break up with Chris for Max?" Addy seems to ponder the idea for a moment, then shakes her head. "No, that's not an option. Max and I, we're just an illusion created by poetic lines and secluded corners of the library. But Chris, he's my reality, and sometimes reality is where you need to be, no matter how enchanting the illusion is."

Okay. I'm no expert in relationships, but to think that Addy is already grappling with concepts like settling and illusions versus reality. I mean, we're just freshmen in high school! This should be a time for experimentation, for finding out who we are—not settling for "good enough."

"Okay, spill," I say, unable to curb my curiosity. "Tell us what it's like making out with Max."

Addy's cheeks flare a bright crimson, making me question my question. Did I push too far? Do I sound way too eager to hear what it feels like to kiss someone? I start to feel awkward when Morgan speaks up.

Morgan interjects, "How about we give Addy a break? She can reveal her makeout details after we've all gone through the rest of the yearbooks. We have all night to hear about how well Max, "the poetry nerd," can kiss."

Addy seems relieved to move past the Max bombshell. She flips through the remaining pages of her yearbook, but nothing else catches our attention like Max's poetic message. Even Chris's comment is flat and uninspiring:

"Hey babe, great year. -Chris."

Morgan can't resist after hearing Chris' yearbook note. She looks at Addy and says, "Honestly, that message alone is breakup material. He's no Romeo, that's for sure." We all break into laughter. I look over at Addy. Maybe Cascade Prep is more Gossip Girl than I thought.

After Addy finishes reading her yearbook to us, we decide it's time for a snack. I swear, it's as if my mom has a sixth sense for our hunger or maybe a camera on us because she has perfect timing. She has prepared a lavish charcuterie board when we get down to the kitchen. It's sitting on the kitchen counter, next to an array of chilled beverages and bowls of ice. Mom is, of course, absent. Her knack for creating memorable atmospheres often works best behind the scenes, but I can't help but wonder what she is working on right now. Maybe a band will show up?

As we grab the food and drinks and make our way back to my room, I can't help but start to feel nervous about reading my yearbook. I haven't thought about Xander's message all evening, but it will soon be my turn. I hope I have done a good enough job that my lie won't be spotted and called out.

"So who's next?" Morgan asks, clutching her yearbook tightly as if it were a sacred text.

I leaf through the yearbook, the glossy pages reflecting the overhead light in my bedroom. I try not to make eye contact with any of my friends. I don't feel ready to see if my little spy mission has worked. My heart skips a beat when Celeste announces, "Noli's turn."

3

I play it cool—or at least I try to. With a practiced casualness trying to push down my rising anxiety, I open my yearbook that is sitting on my lap and start from the beginning. Thoughts swirl through my mind: What if the secret in my yearbook betrays me? I'm not sure if I'm more afraid of being found out or the consequence of lying to my friends.

With a shaky hand, I flip open to the first page, where I've always had my teachers sign my yearbook. This is a great place to start; nothing too crazy here, and my friends usually zone out while I read the teacher's notes. I can work on steadying my voice and my breathing. I clear my throat, my eyes scanning the inscriptions. "Miss Norris wrote..."

Morgan jumps in, the playful cynic in her at full throttle. "Oh, get ready, Addy! We're about to dive into the world of boring sentiments from Noli's teachers."

Ever the optimist, Addy chimes in, "I think it's sweet that Noli likes her teachers enough to let them be a part of her yearbook."

Her words warm me and help calm the butterflies in my stomach, "Thank you, Addy," I reply, touched by her understanding and grateful that I can make my way through these messages before I have to try my hand at lying to my friends.

My friends are engrossed in their snack-fest, uncaring as I read through the predictable praises and 'have a great summer' notes from my teachers. Morgan and Addy engage in an impromptu game of 'catch the grape,' where Morgan tries to catch grapes that Addy throws in the air. Their antics are endearing but annoying; it's as if my yearbook is just a snack break for them.

Taking this as my cue, I decide to skip the remaining teacher comments and plunge into the heart of the yearbook—the student messages. As soon as I switch, I catch Morgan's eye. She abruptly stops her grape-catching game, clearly tuned in now.

The air in the room shifts subtly, charged with a mix of curiosity from them and nervousness from me. They sense it, too; this is where the real drama resides. This is where friendships are celebrated, crushes are subtly confessed, and personal jokes are immortalized. It's also where secrets could potentially spill out, just like they did with Addy.

I take a deep breath, feeling as if I'm standing on the edge of a cliff, peering into the abyss. How far down does this rabbit hole go? I tighten my grip on the yearbook; its weight seems to have doubled, heavy with secrets I don't want my friends to know. The scent of fresh ink and glossed paper fills my nostrils, mingled with a trace of something deeper—fear that my friends may find me out, maybe, or regret that I know I am about to lie to them.

With my heart pounding a rhythmic drumbeat of apprehension in my ears, I read the first student comment. It's a deceptively simple note from Maren, a girl I had a few classes with. "Noli, you're so sweet! Have an awesome summer!" Her message is bland, and honestly, this is what most of the yearbook messages sound like.

I see Xander's fake message and stare at it, not ready to read it yet. I just know they will be on to me. I feel Morgan's eyes on me, her expression a curious mix of eagerness and unspoken understanding.

"Whenever you're ready," she says bored. She has no idea what I'm about to do.

I can't do it! I chicken out from reading the fake message from Xander. I scan the page for someone else's message to read and find Noah. Phew. I let out a sigh of relief. It's just Noah. This one will be safe.

> "Hey Noli, I can't believe we have only known each other since the beginning of this year. It feels like you and I have been friends forever. You are seriously one of my favorite people to be around, and you get bonus points for giving the best hugs. I feel like you get me and it has been rad to have someone like you as a friend. Sad I won't be able to see you this summer, but make sure to text me like crazy. Like stalker crazy, ok?—everyone else<Noah"

As I finish reading I say, "I freaking love that kid," and I start to read the next yearbook message from some random person when, Morgan stops me, "NO WAY. We're definitely not gliding past that message! We need a discussion."

Addy's mouth is agape as if she's surprised, and Celeste nods in agreement with Morgan. I feel like I've missed something.

"What?" I question the group.

"Addy," Morgan says, looking in Addy's direction, "Read the message Noah wrote in your yearbook again so Magnolia Jane can hear the difference between a regular Noah note and HER Noah note."

Morgan says my full name to get my attention. Addy flips through her yearbook and locates the page Noah wrote on. She recites,

> "Stay cool, dance hard. -everyone else<Noah"

All eyes are trained on me expectantly.

A blush creeps onto my cheeks. They're trying to say that Noah's yearbook message holds some deeper meaning. I don't want to hear it. Noah and I are just awesome friends. If only they knew what Xander wrote.

"Noah and I are just friends like that," I respond, trying to assure them that we haven't unearthed the next juicy gossip.

I can tell that I'm not persuading anyone. "MAGNOLIA! You're utterly oblivious." Morgan launches into full-on drama mode.

"I knew it! He's been totally into you since you two went to the golf tournament in Palm Springs over Spring Break," she exclaims. I'm attempting to disregard Morgan, but now even Celeste is bobbing her head in agreement.

Celeste is my most level-headed and observant friend, and it shocks me to see her in agreement with Morgan. Even the sweet and usually non-interfering Addy is nodding her head.

"What?!" I'm literally blown away that they all believe Noah has a thing for me. "He doesn't see me that way. We're just good friends. That's it."

Celeste chimes in, "Noli, I don't know why you're so blind when it comes to Noah. He doesn't just like you; he's smitten with you."

My cheeks color again, and I'm unable to process what they're saying. Not Noah. It's not about Noah. It's about Xander. It's always been about Xander. From the moment I first met Xander, it's always been him. It's almost as if Celeste is reading my mind.

Celeste points out, "You've had such tunnel vision for Xander that you've failed to see what else is happening around you." I feel a wave of irritation at Celeste's flat-out reference to my crush on Xander. Addy is not privy to my deep crush on him, but considering she's now part of our girl squad, I figure I shouldn't be too bothered.

Addy joins in, "Noah never hugs any of us. He greets us with high fives and fist bumps and teases us every now and then. However, when you're around, he's exceptionally attentive. He watches you, listens to you, and is always ready to take care of you. It's genuinely cute. I would be thrilled if Chris would be half as attentive to me as Noah is to you."

I remember being at school earlier in the day, and I remember how Noah watched me approach our group of friends. He was the first one to see me, almost like he had been waiting and watching. Before I even got to our group, he met me with an enthusiastic hug. Noah was the one to create space for me within the circle. Noah is always the one who asks me about how I'm doing or asks my opinions of things we are talking about.

"Not to mention the most adorable thing ever that Noah does for you," Morgan says.

I try and think about the adorable things Noah does for me, but my mind is blank. I still can't connect the dots that Noah has a crush on me. Morgan reads my blank stare.

"DUH Noli, remember how you are always cold but never bring a sweatshirt? Noah started to carry around a sweatshirt in his backpack for you. Whenever you would get cold in biology, he would pull out the sweatshirt and ask you, "Do you want your sweatshirt?" Noah was totally sweet to do that. I realize how much space an extra sweatshirt would take up in his backpack and realize that he always had it for me.

"It was seriously the CUTEST thing ever!!" Morgan is practically yelling at me. "He called it YOUR sweatshirt." She lets out a sigh.

"I once asked him if I could borrow the sweatshirt, thinking it was like a community sweatshirt. He told me no because he worried you would want it later." Morgan is telling me this like it is hard proof that Noah is in love with me.

I know my friends want me to launch into a monologue about Noah, but I just can't. It's Noah we are talking about. I like him too much as my guy BFF, and to gossip about him or to fake like this could be a thing.

"This is getting way too conspiracy theory for me, and I'm not really up for Celeste's take on how Noah is my one true love. Let's get back to my yearbook." I say, wanting to move on.

I glance at Celeste, whose lips are pursed. I can tell she's armed with a well-researched 'proof' about Noah and me, complete with dates, times, and events. For a moment, she looks like she's about to unleash it all, but then she restrains herself as I quickly change the subject.

I scan my yearbook for another entry to read, hoping to divert the conversation from the precarious edge of revelations about Noah. Then my eyes land on McKinley's note on the same page as Noah's. Ah, perfect.

"Let's read what McKinley wrote," I announce, immediately catching Morgan's attention.

I read a short note from McKinley, a girl we have been attending school with since junior high. She writes that we need to get together this summer at the country club and that she wants to get our nails done together and have lunch sometime.

Morgan's reaction is instantaneous, and her exaggerated outrage is as amusing as it is predictable. She firmly believes McKinley is a manipulating puppet master who has been scheming to take over Morgan's role in our friend group. It's a level of paranoia that borders on hilarious, but it's not completely baseless.

Still, I've never had a personal issue with McKinley, so I've always remained neutral. But reading her note now promises to be an entertaining spectacle, and it will effectively steer us away from the topic of Noah and his yearbook message, which, I have to admit, was really sweet.

Morgan's animated freakout against McKinley eventually winds down, and I half-heartedly promise not to accept any summer hangout invitations, my eyes flit to the empty space where Xander's note used to be. I skim past it, my heart pounding.

Miraculously, no one seems to notice my anxiety as they are still stuck on Noah's yearbook message and McKinley's wanting to hang out this summer. A tidal wave of relief floods over me. I've just sidestepped a proverbial landmine and escaped unscathed. I allow myself a silent exhale, relieved as if I've pulled off a grand heist. My shoulders loosen, and I get back into the sea of yearbook messages.

We are all in the middle of laughing over a series of comments from the boys' golf team.

"You're a pretty good golfer, see you on the green,"

they've written practically in unison. Our school has no girls' golf team, so I practice on the boys' varsity team. The irony in the yearbook messages is palpable—I don't just hold my own; I crush most of them on the course. Only two of the ten boys on the team can claim to be in my league.

At first, I was mortified that I had to play with the boys, but it has actually been a huge advantage for me. It's a running joke that the coach needed me to join the team to help him teach the boys how to play golf. He singles me out as the example of technique and how to stay focused, much to the boys' chagrin. The level of their barely concealed annoyance delights me every time.

We have just read the last dumb message from the golf team when I suddenly feel a renewed surge of anxiety as my eyes rest on the place where Xander's note should be. Fabricating a quick lie in my head, I prepare to read the 'fictitious' note from him. "Here's what Xander wrote in my yearbook," I say, my voice slightly quivering yet steady.

The room fills with a synchronized, elongated "Oooooooh" in unison. They all know about my year-long crush on Xander, and I know they will want to talk about whatever he wrote. The air in the room grows thick with anticipation, and I can almost hear our collective heartbeat. Here goes nothing.

"Noli,
Thanks for being my friend this year. That was rad. So
    glad you got to play golf. Also, thanks for having
    us over at your house this year. I really really liked

> wake surfing and eating your mom's food. Hope
> you have a great summer. Maybe we can play
> Connect Four on our phones while I am gone. See
> you next year."

I'm studying my decent forgery of Xander's signature, quite satisfied with how convincingly I've recreated it, when I realize that a strange silence has fallen. I glance up to find the girls all wearing peculiar expressions. Addy appears uncomfortable, Celeste emanates sympathy, and Morgan looks furious. Once again, I feel like I'm trailing behind, unable to catch up with their shared understanding. Can they see through my fabricated message? Will they confront me about it?

Unsure of how to react or what to say, I remain motionless, letting the silence extend until Celeste finally breaks it. "I'm sorry, Noli."

"Sorry for what?" I ask, genuinely confused.

"Sorry that Xander's a total jerk and doesn't see you the way Noah does," Morgan fires back. She seems deeply upset, and I can't comprehend why.

Their gazes are making me realize I screwed up big time. The message didn't hit the way it was supposed to. I can feel something brewing. I just don't know what it is. What are they making this fake message from Xander mean?

"I know we usually don't do this, but I think we need to jump ahead and read what Xander wrote in my yearbook." Morgan is going over and grabbing her yearbook, and she's right; we never read our yearbooks out of turn.

She flips to a page and says, "This is what Xander wrote in my yearbook:

"Morgan-
One of the best things about the school year was
    meeting you. You are such an amazing friend. I love

having you around. Your laugh lights me up every
time I hear it. I don't know how to go a whole
summer without seeing you. The experiences that
we are going to have together are what I know I will
look back on and remember my entire life. Can't
wait to make more memories with you. Xander"

As she finishes reading, my face turns ashen. A gut-wrenching wave of nausea overtakes me. Every word echoes painfully in my ears because they're the same words, word for word, that Xander wrote in my yearbook. The real message. Words that I obsessed over, that filled me with a heady mix of hope and exhilaration. Words that I had snipped out of my yearbook to treasure.

As my trembling hands clutch the yearbook, my eyes lock with Morgan's. Her gaze is ablaze with complex emotions, and my heart drops. My most intimate secret has been unwittingly unveiled. The fantasy I had orchestrated in my mind is crumbling, and now I face the mortifying reality that my infatuation is painfully one-sided.

Just then, Addy interjects softly, "Xander began writing in my yearbook earlier today but stopped when he saw you approaching. This is how far he got with mine." She shows me the unfinished message:

"Addy: One of the best things about this school year
was..."

Suddenly, it dawns on me that I've been blind to the obvious: Xander's attention may not be what I had thought. The original message that I thought was so special is the same thing he wrote in all of my friend's yearbooks.

I forged a fake message that has now singled me out for how general it is. I don't know what I am more upset about. That I may have to fess up to the fake note, or the fact that the message I was trying to keep so private is an exact copy message in so many other yearbooks.

My friends mistake my shocked silence for heartbreak. Morgan rushes to my side, wrapping her arms around me. "Xander isn't worth it," she reassures me, her words missing the point entirely. I fight to hold back tears.

My cheeks flush crimson as Celeste picks up my yearbook and scrutinizes the note a bit too closely. I can feel the walls closing in on me, my embarrassment reaching its apex. My carefully crafted narrative is falling apart, leaving me exposed in front of the very people from whom I'd wanted to hide my deepest insecurities.

The gravity of Xander's betrayal—because that's what it feels like now, a betrayal—settles around me like a shroud. I suddenly realize that Xander could have written the same sweet-nothings to every girl in the school. My dreams for a love-filled sophomore year are collapsing into ashes before my eyes. How naïve was I to read into every text, every wink, when all this time, they were likely a part of his larger script? A script written not just for me but for any girl willing to believe they were special in his eyes. The realization gut-punches me: I've been just another face in a crowd of smitten girls. And the thought nauseates me.

Morgan rants about Xander, but now it's tinged with an under-tone of 'I told you so.' Addy, ever the quiet supporter, rubs my back as if trying to massage away the anguish. And there's Celeste, peering at me as though she's trying to figure something out. Without warning, Celeste stands up and says, "Morgan, Addy, could you go ask Lily to make some of her famous fries? They're Noli's favorite."

The proposition seems out of place since we literally have loads of food in front of us, but I welcome the excuse to get some space from my friends for a moment. Addy, grateful for the distraction, springs up. Morgan locks eyes with Celeste, who subtly nods as if passing on some unspoken message. Intrigued but too drained to probe, I watch them leave my room as I listen to Morgan telling Addy how my mom's fries are literal therapy.

My room suddenly feels too big and too small all at once. Too big for my now-shrunken daydreams of Xander and I together and too small to contain the expanding balloon of my humiliation. I'm alone with Celeste, and the atmosphere hangs heavy, burdened by the weight of newly exposed vulnerabilities.

Can you break a crush? Because that's exactly what it feels like. Xander has broken my crush on him.

I find comfort in Celeste's calming presence. While Morgan is an exciting whirlwind, Celeste is the grounding force, my safe harbor. She is also incredibly smart and picks up on subtle hints. I recognize that sending Morgan and Addy on a wild goose chase for fries is a tactical move; it would distract our friends and buy us the time we need to talk alone.

Once I am sure Morgan and Addy are completely out of earshot, the dam breaks. I'm not sniffling or softly weeping; rather, it feels like someone has switched on a tap, and the water just flows uncontrollably down my cheeks.

Celeste doesn't rush to my side. She merely sits where she is, observing in silence. It's not awkward, considering that's just who Celeste is—she exudes a serene aura like she's well-equipped to handle this big emotional outburst.

When the faucet finally turns off, I wipe my eyes and say, "The yearbook message that I read from Xander is a fake. Xander didn't write it."

Celeste says, "I know. From the looks of your yearbook, I am going to take a wild guess that Xander wrote his actual message on the back of the Freshman intro page."

I don't know how she does that. I can never lie or get away with anything with her.

I let out a big breath. "Yep, that's exactly where he wrote it."

"Want to tell me why you took it out and faked a note?" Celeste asks.

Celeste would be fine if I said no. She wouldn't push me, but after the past couple of minutes and the anxiety I have been feeling all evening, I feel like it's time to relieve myself of this weight, and honestly, I could use an outside perspective on this.

"I was so excited when Xander took my yearbook and walked away from the group," I start. "I even timed how long he had it." I can't believe I am admitting this, but I know Celeste won't judge me.

"When he gave my yearbook back to me, he told me I couldn't read it until I got home and even winked at me when I left." I let out a sigh. This all sounds so silly saying it out loud to Celeste.

"Even before I left the school, I knew I was going to come home and read his message. I just couldn't help it."

I take the real message from Xander out of my pillowcase and show her how it was the EXACT note that Morgan read from her yearbook and how embarrassed I am thinking that his message meant something more than it obviously does.

Celeste listens to me and nods occasionally. I wear out all my words talking about Xander, how I had built up this whole summer of us together, and what it would feel like starting our sophomore year with Xander as my boyfriend. I talk so much that I instantly feel exhausted. Celeste says, "I can't believe I'm about to say this because I hate it when my mom says it to me, but do you want my advice, or did you just need someone to listen to you?"

Celeste's mom is a therapist and says things like that to her all of the time. I know it annoys her, but I think her mom is rad, and right now, I am so grateful that Celeste is saying the same thing to me.

"I think I need advice. I don't know what to do," I admit. Despite feeling utterly drained and emotionally spent, I feel a sense of relief wash over me. There's a strange comfort in admitting that I don't know what to do. Celeste nods and starts in.

"First, I think you should understand that what Xander did hurts. It doesn't feel great being led on, especially when it's by someone you want to like you and see you as something more than a friend," she says, her voice calm and soothing.

"That's exactly how I feel, led on," I say, glad that she understands. I realize I was worried she would tell me I was being silly and this is all on me. And yes, I did build the whole thing up, but it was Xander who was acting like this was something more.

She continues, "And second, I want you to consider something. You've been so focused on Xander that you may be missing out on other opportunities around you."

"Like Noah?" I ask, my voice barely above a whisper.

"Yeah, like Noah. Or maybe someone else entirely. The point is, don't let Xander's incessant flirting with you and everyone else AND your huge crush keep you from getting to know more people. We've had such a great time this year with our new group of friends," Celeste continues. "Imagine how much more exciting it will be to keep meeting new people and experience different things."

I nod, taking in her words. Celeste has this knack for making even the complicated seem simple. "Xander's good-looking, charming, fun. But he's also immature and, honestly, way too much of a flirt. The thing is, he's not quite boyfriend material. He's the type of guy you hook up with and then get talked about all around school. He has totally hooked up with McKinley, Camry, and Kennedy just this year."

I feel a jolt of surprise. "What? I had no idea. Why didn't anyone tell me?"

Celeste looks apologetic. "I thought you knew. McKinley was talking about it one day, and I assumed word had gotten around. I'm really sorry, Noli."

I shake my head, my eyes wet again. "Why do I feel so dumb?"

"You're not dumb for having a crush Noli," Celeste says, offering me a comforting touch on the shoulder. "I think it has helped you only see the good in Xander. Don't let his actions change who you are."

Silence fills the room as I process everything. My mind shifts to earlier moments I had ignored. Signs I should've picked up on—Xander's covert exchanges with McKinley and Kennedy, and when I saw Camry's name on his phone and he quickly turned his screen around.. I'd been willfully blind, swept up in a fantasy that clouded my judgment.

"I can't believe how infatuated I have been," I finally admit, flopping back onto my bed. "You know how he and I play Connect Four on our phones? I would actually let him win because when he won, he'd text me more."

"I even intentionally had a bad golf game when he came with Noah and me so I wouldn't intimidate him," I continue, the realization making my stomach churn. My golf coach is always telling me to never change my performance based on who I am playing. It is now hitting me how I have totally done this with Xander.

"Look," Celeste interjects my thoughts gently, "Xander's not a bad guy. I actually love having him as a friend, but I don't think he is dating material. I mean, look at you. You just admitted that you would change stuff about yourself just to get his attention. I'm not sure that's how it's supposed to be"

I can't help but laugh a little, thinking of how I would never let Noah win at golf just so that he could feel good about himself. I think about Xander again and admit to Celeste, "I definitely haven't been my best self around him." I feel like I have to confess this last thing to her, "I can't tell you the number of times I have planned my entire summer and sophomore year around us being an item. I even thought about quitting golf so we could spend more time together once we were a thing"

Celeste grins, clearly entertained. "Noli, we all let our imaginations run wild sometimes. The key is not letting it take over your reality. Why would you want to be with someone if you can't be your bright, brilliant, butt-kicking self?"

Celeste's words are the wake-up call I needed. I need to confront what is really going on. I was trying to be different, so a guy gave me some attention. I also had been spending my time crushing on a guy who wasn't at all interested in me.

"I guess it's time to crush the crush," I say, more as a commitment to myself than as a statement.

"Sometimes that's the best thing to do," Celeste agrees. "You'll be better for it, trust me."

And just like that, the weight lifts a little. I'm not entirely okay, but I can see how I will be. I couldn't have asked for a better friend to guide me through this emotional maze. With Celeste by my side, I start to feel like I'm going to be fine.

With a grateful nod, I urge Celeste to go downstairs and give my mom a hand with the fries. "I'll join you guys in a bit," I tell her, planning to freshen up before making my way downstairs for some fries. Once she's gone, I head to the bathroom, making an internal pact: no more tears over Xander. That chapter is closed; he won't be my summer romance, first kiss, or sophomore boyfriend.

The rest of the evening unfolds much like any other yearbook sleepover we've had. The only difference is that my friends spare me the ritualistic reading of the rest of my yearbook messages. I slip my yearbook under my pillow and vow to myself that I won't look at it again for a long time.

We skip to Morgan, regaling us with her yearbook drama as we eat my mom's heavenly fries. The night is exactly what I need, with lots of laughter, gossip, food, and finally, an outdoor movie by the pool. Celeste keeps the secret of the faked Xander message to herself, and for that, I'm grateful. But I also realize I have a certain sleepover rule to uphold.

As the movie plays and my friends lounge by the pool, I discreetly slip away to the outdoor bathroom. I undress, taking a deep breath to steady myself. My parents are out picking up my sisters from their parties. I glance out the bathroom window toward the lake for a quick scan to make sure there are no late-night boaters. When I see that the coast is clear, I make my bold move. Bursting from the bathroom naked, I shout, "Cannonball!" and make a full-moon plunge into the pool's deep end. The yelps and cheers from my friends reach me even underwater.

Resurfacing, I catch Morgan's bewildered expression. "Who are you, and what have you done with my buttoned-up bestie?" she exclaims.

Amidst the laughter, Addy quips about my need for a full-body tan to remedy my 'luminous lunar glow.' Celeste smiles knowingly but doesn't spill the beans to Morgan and Addy about how she knows why I just jumped in the pool naked. I can tell she respects my audacious move, not because she would've made me do it but because it adheres to our yearbook sleepover rule.

The water hugs me, washing away lingering insecurities and awkwardness. I feel both exposed and free; somehow, it's the most confident I've felt all day.

Morgan doesn't need any convincing to do anything crazy. She is naked and jumping in the pool in no time, and Celeste and Addy soon follow. It's fun doing something daring with my friends, but it doesn't feel that bold as soon as we do it. It just feels like we are swimming together in my pool at midnight. But I know it's a sign that we are growing up. I love these friends, and I'm grateful that they are here tonight, even if it feels like one of my worst nights.

We finally call it a night around 3 a.m., each of us emotionally and physically spent. The next morning—or late morning—my mom has prepared an elaborate breakfast spread. We eat at a snail's pace, savoring each bite as if delaying the meal could somehow postpone our summer separations. We hate being away from each other all summer, so we try to make this sleepover last as long as possible.

By early afternoon, Addy departs for her photo shoot, her bags packed and her spirit buoyant. She hugs us all and tells us how much it meant to her to be included in our sleepover. We vow one more time to keep her Max makeouts a secret. She still hasn't decided what to do about the whole Max/Chris thing.

Morgan follows shortly after, her mom swooping in to whisk her away to the airport for a summer with her dad. Tearful goodbyes are said, and I still can't process that I won't see her all summer. I watch as she turns from her bubbly, crazy Morgan self that she is with us to the guarded, moody Morgan that she is with her mom. Hopefully, her summer with her dad will be better.

Celeste lingers, providing a brief window for a private conversation. We talk about her real summer plans. She's actually spending her vacation working on her highly-anticipated next book. The pressure from her publisher to produce a masterpiece is intense. She has the idea for the book and has the outline complete, but she says she is nervous the "spark" to write just won't be there this summer. I remind her that she has said this for her past two books, and it never happens. She's grateful for the reminder.

After we talk about the book, Celeste changes the subject, "What about you? How are you feeling today about all of the Xander stuff?"

I let out a deep breath. "I have some lingering regrets over the whole Xander fiasco last night. I should have been honest with you guys. I shouldn't have read the message on my own. I just keep thinking that if I would have waited for our yearbook sleepover to read it, this whole thing wouldn't have happened."

I continue, "Sure, I would have been embarrassed for a second, but I wouldn't have lied to you all, been worried all night, or had such emotional outbursts."

She listens and tells me there is no use wishing for the past to be different. Then she lays on her parting words, "I just can't wait to see who the lucky guy is that you choose to be with."

"I see your Jedi mind trick," I say, grinning. "I will be the one CHOOSING to like a guy that is into me too."

She taps her nose knowingly, affirming my insight.

Once she's gone, the weight of the summer ahead sinks in, pressing on the fresh wound left by Xander. I tell my mom I need some more rest. I was supposed to spend the day obsessing over texts and yearbook messages from Xander. Instead, I cry in solitude, my yearbook not seeing the light of day.

By the time the hunger pangs and sounds of my family's laughter drift up from downstairs, it's evening. They're celebrating the start of summer with a BBQ, a family tradition aimed at setting the tone for the coming months. Regardless of how the summer unfolds, I realize this will be a summer etched into my memory as the summer I grow up. It already feels so different than any summer before.

My phone vibrates as I get up to join my family's festivities. It's Xander. I feel a familiar flush of resentment, but then I recall Celeste's words: Xander could still be a good friend. Taking a deep breath, I resolve to begin this new chapter in our friendship—one where my heart isn't on the line, and I don't downplay who I am in order to get his attention.

I open the text.

> Xander: How was the sleepover?

> Me: It was good

I keep it short. I am trying to be a good friend, but really I want to tell him off and delete his number.

> Xander: Noah wanted to come try to
> convince your mom to let us sleepover too.
> HAHAHA

I am smiling at the thought of Noah trying to convince my mom to let him sleep over. My mom loves Noah the most out of all the guys. He is always helping clean up and makes it a point to find my mom and dad before he leaves to say thank you. I laugh to myself, thinking that Noah may actually be able to convince my mom to let him be part of the yearbook sleepover.

> Xander: Did you read my note? ;)

The mention of Xander's note snaps me back to reality. My cheeks get hot, and I am glad that Xander isn't here to see it. I want to be his friend, and I also want to stand up for myself. In a moment when I am feeling brave and a little pissed off, I send off my message.

> Me: Yep, I got your note. The same note you
> wrote probably to every girl in our grade.
> Classy.

I should probably regret sending it, but I don't. I want to call him out on it and let him know that I am on to him. I see the bubble on my text thread with Xander that tells me he is texting me. It takes a minute, and then another text comes through.

> Xander: You caught me! I did write the same
> message to almost all of the girls. It was just
> easier that way. Should have figured you
> girls would talk. HAHA

I am a tad bit relieved to see that he at least confessed, but still really bugged that he did it in the first place. I am going to put my phone on "do not disturb" when I get another text from Xander.

> Xander: But I wasn't talking about my
> yearbook message. I was talking about the
> note that I wrote you that I tucked into the
> back of your yearbook.

> Xander: Did you get THAT note?

My fingers freeze above my phone screen. Time seems to slow for a moment as my thoughts rush to catch up with what Xander has just texted. I thought I had him figured out, slotted into that all-too-familiar category of insincere high school boys. This is new information. What does the note say? I find myself rushing back to crush zone, and I have to remind myself that he could have written a note to other girls, too.

Xander had tucked another note into my yearbook—a note just for me? Can I be sure? Confusion, disbelief, and a kernel of hope wrestle within me.

Me: Wait. What? There was another note?

I scroll up and down the text thread with Xander as if doing so could help make sense of this new twist. The bubbles on the screen indicate he's responding, and my pulse quickens. I almost don't want him to reply, afraid his next message will either mend my broken heart or shatter it completely.

Xander: Yes, silly girl, there's another note.

Xander: It's not something I did for everyone, just you.

It's almost like he can hear my thoughts. The weight of his words hits me hard. This isn't the Xander who writes flirty messages for mass consumption; this is a Xander who chose to say something privately to me. I suddenly remember my unread yearbook and my mind screams at me to run and find this mysterious note.

But I hesitate for a moment. Is this just another stunt? Is this Xander toying with me? Could it send me spiraling back into doubt and regret? OR is this real?

Taking a deep breath, I craft my next message carefully.

Me: I didn't see that. Oops…I'll find it.

Putting my phone on the bed, I walk cautiously over to the yearbook. It feels different now—no longer the object that brought me so much hurt last night, but a book that is holding something uniquely meant for me. As I open the back cover, my hands slightly tremble.

There it is, a folded piece of paper tucked securely in the back. I can't believe it. Xander actually did write a note for me. He really was writing something just for me in that seven minutes he was sitting on the steps at school.

I carefully unfold it and start to read, my heart pounding in my chest. Regardless of what this note says, I know one thing: This is a pivotal moment, a crossroads that will undoubtedly shape what comes next.

This isn't just a revelation about Xander. It's a revelation about me, about us, about what could be next. I haven't even read the note and am back to clutching onto my crush on Xander. Well, that wasn't long.

My mind flashes to my friends' faces last night as I read the fake They were so embarrassed and sad for me. What Celeste said about Xander kissing all the girls from school also makes its way into my thoughts, and I slam the door on all of it. Xander wrote me a personal note. Xander, the Xander is texting me and wanting to know what I think about this note. I have to give all of my attention to him. As I read the first line of the note, I can't help but feel like this summer may hold even more surprises than I could have ever imagined.

> Noli-
> I really like you, and I am hoping that you like me. Is it
>> crazy that I just started off with that? I wrote it
>> before I lost my nerve and didn't tell you. I'm
>> feeling brave because I won't see you all summer,
>> but I can't go any longer without telling you. You
>> are one of the most amazing girls I know. I have
>> liked you since the beginning of the year, but I
>> don't want to ruin our new awesome friendship.
> You make me happy every single time I see you. You
>> get close by, and I can't help but notice you and
>> want to be next to you. I would do anything to
>> hear your laugh and see you smile. I love
>> spending time with you wake surfing. There is
>> something so cute about when you try a new trick
>> and are so focused that you stick your tongue out.
> The very best part about us is hugging you. I love your
>> hugs and get lost thinking that maybe someday

you will be mine, and those hugs will mean something more. I don't know what will happen after
you get this, but I just wanted you to know.

My eyes glide over the handwritten lines of the note, and a whirlwind of emotions unfurls within me. Each word feels like a zing
inside me, each sentence like a whisper in my ear from Xander like he
did yesterday. I can't help but go through the moments I have filed
away in my mind where Xander was paying attention to me.

His note is proof. He is interested in me. I can't believe he noticed
me all this time. A bit of doubt is floating in my mind, but I am also
filled with excitement, maybe even elation, at the revelation that
Xander has feelings for me. I look back at the mention of wake
surfing and how detailed the mention of me sticking out my tongue
is when I try a new trick. I remember the times we would go boating,
and I would glance at Xander when I went surfing to see if he was
watching. Every single time he wasn't. He was always on his phone,
goofing around with our friends or dancing to the music, but obviously, he had been noticing me the whole time.

I read the last lines of the note again,

*"I love your hugs and get lost thinking that maybe
someday you will be mine, and those hugs will mean
something more."*

I think back to when I hugged Xander. Nothing comes to mind,
but I do know that we have occasionally given those random side
hugs when we have seen each other. I had no idea they meant so
much to him. I instantly wish he was here so I could actually give
him a hug or maybe something more.

How is this even possible? I sit back and clutch the note tightly in
my hands. So many signs led me to believe Xander had put me in the
'just friends' category. But now, this note, vulnerable, sincere, and
kind of intimate, changes everything.

I think back to my earlier conversation with Celeste. I know that Xander is putting out there that he likes me and hopes we can be more than friends, but that doesn't erase the fact that he has been kissing those other girls from school. As much as I want to text him back and tell him that I like him too, something holds me back.

I can't leave him hanging, and I know I need to text something back.

> Me: Just read the note. Seriously the
> sweetest thing I have ever gotten.

> Me: But I need some time to think about it.

> Me: Is that ok?

I hit send, and part of me feels like I just jumped off a cliff. I'm not sure what I want to do. I wish my friends weren't flying all over the country so I could call them and tell them what happened. I guess I'm on my own. This could be the summer. A turning point in my life. I'm unsure what will happen, but I know I need to tell my friends. I can't let this actual note from Xander be the thing I lie to my friends about.

Before I can send my text to the group chat with the girls, my phone buzzes and I see another text from Xander.

> Xander: Take all the time you need.

> Xander: I wouldn't have told you all this if I
> didn't think our friendship could handle it.
> No pressure.

> Xander: I want to text you while I'm at
> soccer camp.

A thrill goes through my body. Xander and I have never texted separately from our friend group chat. I can't believe he wants to text just me, but then I think back to the note. I can't help but smile to myself.

Me: Of course

Xander: Better watch out!

Xander: You may just fall in love with me ;)

I don't even know what to say to that! I send a heart-eye emoji and put my phone on silent. I don't know if I can handle any more revelations tonight. I place the note back in my yearbook, and a sense of satisfaction washes over me. Regardless of what happens, one thing is clear. Xander likes me. This is shaping up to be a summer I will never forget.

4

Me to the group chat: Don't freak out. This
just happened and I wanted you to know.

I send them a picture of the note from Xander. I also send a couple of screenshots of my texts with Xander.

Instant message from Morgan: EWWWW
NOOOOOOOOOOOOOOOOOOOOO

Addy: Girl, I think Morgan is right. He made
out with all those girls at school. You have
no idea if he wrote this to other girls. Just
move on. XO.

Morgan: I swear I am getting back on the
plane and coming back to Utah. Promise me
you won't text him.

Celeste: Remember what I told you right
before I left. You choose. But make sure you
are choosing someone who is choosing you.

Me: Are you not all reading the note I am
reading?!!! He likes me!

Morgan: No, like hell no.

I want to send them a video explaining why this is so different. I want my friends to be on the same page as me. I want them to be as excited as I am.

Morgan: Okay, how about we compromise?
You can text him, but you can't see him until
after the Fourth of July, and absolutely DO
NOT SEND HIM nudes.

The mention of me sending nudes to anyone has me laugh out loud. I would never. I could barely be naked in front of my best friends, let alone send nudes to a guy.

Me: Deal

The mention of the Fourth of July reminds me that my family is downstairs having their start of summer BBQ. Whew, this summer is already turning out to be the most interesting summer I have ever had.

Hearing my dad's voice reverberate up the stairs the next morning pulls me out of my sleepy haze. "Noli," he calls.

I groan softly; this is supposed to be my summer, meaning lazy mornings and late wake-ups, at least in my ideal world. But the reality in our household is different. Dad's practically an evangelist when it comes to early morning tee times and rigorous golf practice. He even hired Coach Gus, a retired pro, to elevate my game. So even when it's not my scheduled day for official coaching, he wants me at the golf course.

His voice amplifies, breaking my train of thought. "Magnolia Jane!" Ah, the full name—Dad's not messing around now. Springing out of bed, I dart to the top of the stairs to show him I'm not ignoring him.

"Morning, Dad. What's up?" My heart sinks a little when I realize I'll probably be spending my entire day at the golf course, possibly for a 36-hole marathon. I love to golf; I just don't want to golf all day.

To my surprise, he's in his gym clothes, not his golf clothes, and he's grinning. "Up and at 'em, Noli. Get dressed. You're coming to the airport with me."

Curious, I ask him, "Why are we going to the airport?"

He doesn't look up from his phone as he responds, "We're picking up Jack."

I frown in confusion. Jack? As in Jack Foster, our family friend who I have grown up with since I was a baby? That Jack? It's only two weeks into June. The Fosters always visit in July. And we never pick them up. They always rent a car. Something must be going on here; this is all different from our usual "Foster Fun Fest."

"Why are the Fosters coming into town in June?" I ask.

"Baby girl, go get ready!" Dad retorts. I can tell he's growing impatient with my incessant questioning and is also distracted by whatever is occupying his attention on his phone.

As I turn to get dressed, I'm still puzzled as to why the Fosters are showing up a whole month earlier than usual. Dad finally responds as I walk back into my room, "The Fosters aren't coming into town. Just Jack."

This is quite the revelation. Jack has never come to visit by himself. I pivot and dash back into my room, hastily grabbing a top off my floor and my favorite pair of cut-off jean shorts. Why would Jack come alone? I wonder. Jack is an only child of Jill and Jeremy Foster. He is our honorary brother, and before last year, I deemed him my favorite friend of the summer. We grew up having adventures, getting into trouble, and growing up together.

It's hard thinking of Jack. Part of me remembers the turmoil of last summer and how we were both such jerks to one another. I debate whether I even want to see him, but the anticipation that Jack —just Jack—is coming here alone, and in June no less, ignites a spark of excitement in me. I definitely want to see why he is here.

Rushing toward the car, I notice my sandals are missing from their usual spot. Ugh. I'm almost certain Jazzy, my sister who is a year younger than me, must've taken them when she went out last night. Classic Jazzy move. Just as I'm about to storm upstairs and give her a piece of my mind, Dad strides past, urgency in his eyes.

"Let's go, we're running late," he announces.

I open my mouth to vent about Jazzy and my missing sandals, but Dad cuts me off, gesturing at my nearby slippers. "We're not even getting out of the car, just put on whatever's there."

So I opt for my ridiculously comfortable, albeit laughably childish, shark slippers. They're the kind of footwear that only someone who truly loves you can ignore. The moment my feet sink into the well-worn fuzz, a grin spreads across my face. Sure, they might be a bit juvenile, but there's a nostalgic charm to them that I can't resist. In fact, every time I wear them, I hear the iconic "Jaws" theme music crescendoing in my head. DAH NAH... DAH NAH... DAH NAH, DAH NAH, DAH NAH! I can't help but chuckle at my own little inside joke as I hop into the G Wagon beside Dad.

Riding shotgun next to my dad is always a favorite moment for me. While my friends use car rides as an excuse to create new Spotify lists and tune out their parents, I relish this undisturbed time with my dad. No golf talk. No distractions. No electronics. Just us—our little bubble away from the chaos of a family with my two younger sisters and a perpetually busy mom.

"Why's Jack coming so early? It's only June," I prod again as Dad reverses the G Wagon out of our garage.

He checks the rearview mirror before answering. "Jack got invited to a soccer camp at Real Salt Lake stadium. He's staying at the apartments right across from the stadium and will be training hard. Jeremy says this could lead to some more soccer opportunities for Jack."

Jack being in Utah for all of June, catches me off guard. I sift through recent conversations, trying to remember if Mom or Dad ever dropped this little bombshell. Nothing. "Uh, no one mentioned Jack would be in Utah for all of June. You know I'd remember that."

Dad offers an apologetic smile, "I'm sorry, Noli. With work and everything, it must've slipped my mind. Plus, it's not like it will impact you that much. He won't be staying with us."

I let him off the hook, but he adds, "He'll just be staying with us this weekend to acclimate to the altitude. After that, your mom will help him settle in at camp, and you'll see him again around the Fourth of July."

Acclimating to the altitude? Totally something that Jeremy, Jack's dad, would set up. Jeremy is meticulous to a fault, leaving no variable unchecked to give Jack the slightest edge with soccer. Dad and Jeremy have been buddies since high school. They're the type of friends that don't see each other all year, but when they get together, they still click like teenagers. Our families still choose to spend several weeks in July together. We have named it our "Foster Fun Fest." My youngest sister, Poppy loves Jack so much that she always included Jack on her family tree homework assignment as an "adopted brother." When Poppy's teacher called to ask my mom if she would be willing to come and speak to the class about the adoption process, my mom had to explain who Jack was to our family.

I chuckle at the thought of Poppy always including Jack as a brother in everything. I also can't help but laugh out loud at the thought of Jack "acclimating" to the altitude here in Utah. I turn to Dad and say, "We both know what 'acclimating' will actually involve, right?"

Dad's eyes twinkle as he grins. "Absolutely. Lounging by the pool, raiding our pantry, and late-night gaming. Maybe even cereal feasts at all hours of the night."

For as much as my dad pushes me in golf and my sister in dance, Jeremy is in a league of his own when it comes to parental intensity. When Jack's with us, he's not just getting a break from soccer; he's getting a break from the relentless treadmill of life that Jeremy has him on.

And if what we call 'routine' is Jack's idea of a vacation, I can't even imagine the gauntlet of commitments and responsibilities he must run through every day. But I know one thing: With Jack around, even if just for a weekend, this is going to get interesting. I get nervous thinking about where Jack and I left things last year. I was so mad at him, and he was such a jerk to me.

I get a text from Noah.

> Noah: Did you get the note that Xander gave you?

I can't believe that Xander has already told Noah about the note! I am embarrassed and a little bugged. But then I remember how quickly I wanted to call my friends last night and tell them everything. I guess it's fine that Noah knows.

> Me: Yeah, I read it last night.

> Noah: AND??????

I'm not sure how much I want to tell Noah. Noah is my friend, but he is also Xander's best friend. I don't want to gush to Noah about how I am feeling about this note and my crush on Xander. But I also don't want to be bratty and tell Noah to butt out.

> Me: Not sure what to think about the whole thing. I mean, maybe we should just stay friends, ya know?

I wait for a response from Noah, and I don't get a text back. Noah's silence makes me think he is talking to Xander, and I worry I may have just ruined it. The absence of those three little dots that signify a message is being typed is both a relief and a concern. I wonder why he can't text me back. Suddenly, my attention completely shifts.

We're nearing the airport when my dad's phone buzzes, and the caller ID on the car's screen flashes, "Jack." He hits the answer button on his screen and says, "Hey, buddy. Did you just land?"

Jack's voice comes through the speaker, and I find myself holding my breath as I hear his voice.

"Uh, yeah," Jack responds. "The plane just landed, and I'm heading to the baggage claim now. I'll be out as soon as I grab my bags."

My dad replies, "See you soon. Just text me what stop you're at."

They end the call, and I release my breath. I can't figure out why I feel this buzzing anticipation now that I'm about to see Jack. It wasn't always like this. When we were kids, the Fosters' arrival felt like the start of an awaited tradition. I wasn't ever nervous around him. But, we have some unresolved tension that will either make or break our friendship. I hadn't realized I would have to think about this so soon in the summer, but here I am, wondering if Jack and I are still friends.

I think back on all of our shared summers. Summer isn't summer without Jack spending time with our family during July. I can't remember the last time my July didn't start out with the Fosters. I'd be engrossed in a book or cooling off in the pool, and suddenly Jack would appear, and I would know the Foster Festival of Fun had started.

I never felt nervous or fluttery, it was more of a comfortable recognition, a feeling of something falling into its rightful place. Just like when mom brings out Christmas decorations, there's this sense of familiarity. tradition, and joy. Jack's presence brought the same kind of warmth.

But last summer, it was different. Jack showed up moody and not like himself. I morphed from being easygoing around Jack to feeling an acute awareness of him whenever he was near. I never knew if what I was going to say would be met with his icy glares or quick mean comments. He wasn't always like that, but it was enough to put me on edge. It was as if my senses had developed an all-new feature that constantly kept track of his whereabouts, and I was always trying to gauge if he was in a bad mood.

Celeste chalked Jack's moodiness up to puberty. She was probably right, but I wished he would flip that switch off so we could just go back to normal. Honestly, I wish I could place all the blame on him for last summer, but it wasn't just him. I was a total bratty snob to him. I just didn't know how to navigate his mood swings.

This change made our relationship feel uneven during his last visit. I was so preoccupied with our dynamic and how I was acting that I became overly sensitive to his usual teasing, something we'd done since we were kids. He would say something to tease me, I would overreact, he would tease me more, which made me overreact more, and then he would get moody, say something totally rude, and leave.

Even Jazzy noticed the shift in Jack's behavior, commenting on how he'd turned into a jerk. Poppy, however, seemed oblivious to the change. At ten years old, she wasn't quite adept at detecting subtle shifts in people's personalities. She saw everyone as the same people she had always known. To her, Jack was still the same fun-loving prankster, always ready for a wrestle and a laugh. A sigh escapes me as I remember how horribly things went the last time we saw each other. I need to shake off these thoughts. I hope this summer will be different.

I take a deep breath, repeating a mantra: "It's just Jack. The kid I've grown up with. The boy who's felt the need to update me on his romantic escapades every year since seventh grade. The friend I've comforted when he's broken down from the pressure of his dad. It's just Jack. The boy I shared a bed with when we were kids. He isn't some guy at school I need to impress or try to figure out. It's just Jack."

I let out a deep breath and tell myself again, "It's just Jack."

I must have said the last mantra out loud because my dad is pulling off the exit and asking, "You okay?"

"Yeah." I think about adding more, but with Dad, I don't have to. If I say yes, he believes me.

For half a second, I want to tell him what happened with Xander. Maybe if I talk about Xander, I can stop thinking about seeing Jack. Plus, Dad may have some different insight than my friends did. He was, in fact, a teenage boy at one point in his life. I quickly squash that idea. Jack will be in the car soon, and I don't trust that Dad can keep the Xander information to himself while we drive home. I would absolutely die if Dad talked about Xander in front of Jack.

A text comes through to my dad.

Jack: Stop 7.

We start making our way to stop seven, and I look out my window at the people pulling up to pick up their friends and family. Some people get out of the car and hug the person they are picking up. I watch a girl in her twenties jump out of the car, wrap her entire body around a man, and start making out with him. I see a man roll up and honk at his wife, who has four kids with her and five bags. He doesn't get out to help, and the wife starts yelling at him. Seeing that everyone greets their people in completely different ways fascinates me.

We are going past stop five when I start worrying about how to greet Jack. Do I get out of the car? Do I give him a hug? Should I stay in the car and wait until he says something to me?

Caught in my swirl of thoughts, I raise my gaze, and there he is. Jack. He stands there, headphones draped around his neck, a backpack hunched over one shoulder, and a duffle bag and roller luggage at his feet. He looks... different.

I remember him telling me he would shave his head if his high school team made the state finals. I am used to seeing Jack with floppy, dirty blonde hair that has a way of looking undone in the most perfectly done way. Because Jack stays with us, I know how long it takes him to make his hair look that way. His time in the bathroom in front of the mirror rivals Jazzy. As I look again at him, I realize that his team must've made it to finals because his hair is much shorter than I remember, cropped close but not completely buzzed.

When were the state finals? Early May? Makes sense that his hair has grown out a bit. It looks good. His short hair makes his deep green eyes show even better, and I can already see his dimples as he recognizes Dad's car.

As we pull up in front of Jack, I still haven't sorted out how to greet him, but there is something else that I can't sort out. Something else is different about him, but I can't figure it out. My dad is already out of the car, moving to help Jack with his luggage. I decide to follow suit, opening my door and stepping out. Dad and Jack are already by the trunk of the car, sharing a friendly hug.

"Hi Gavin," Jack greets my dad as he gives him a big hug. "Thanks for picking me up."

"No problem, buddy," Dad replies, stooping to pick up one of Jack's bags. It always amuses me how my dad calls Jack by the pet names most dads reserve for their six-year-old sons. Jack doesn't seem to mind, always joking that my dad uses all the boyish nicknames on him because he never had sons of his own.

"Ready to hit the road, Champ?" Dad asks Jack, his voice warm.

"Absolutely. Let's get going." Jack turns around, and we are suddenly facing each other.

Until this moment, I don't think Jack realized I was here. He gives me a thorough once-over before grinning broadly. "Well, if it isn't Noli in all her glory."

I can't help but roll my eyes at his familiar teasing. When we were kids, I would put on my favorite princess costume to eat breakfast when the Fosters were in town. Jill would always compliment me on how pretty I looked, and Jeremey would spring me around while teasing me, saying, "Here is Noli in all her glory." Jack picked it up and wouldn't ever let me live it down.

When we were thirteen, I wanted to look really good at the

annual hot air balloon fest that we go to every Fourth of July morning. I knew that my junior high crush would be there with his family, so I picked out a pretty dress that was way too overdone for the event. When Jack saw me, he started laughing and said, "Here is Noli in all her glory!"

Jeremy made him stop, but when we got to the balloon fest and I was talking to my crush, Jack, Jazzy, and Poppy started yelling, "NOLI'S GLORY! NOLI'S GLORY."

"Nice outfit," Jack says, staring at me at the airport. "How long did it take you to get it like that?"

What is he talking about? I look down at my outfit, and all of a sudden, I am filled with utter embarrassment. I completely forgot that the reason my tank top was on the floor was that I had gotten a huge red stain from helping my mom cut pounds of strawberries for our town's local Strawberry Days, which is going on right now. We had stayed up all night cutting hundreds of strawberries. My tank top had gotten so stained that it was probably ruined. But I was so exhausted from the night before that I had taken it off and fallen right into bed. I am mortified standing here in my strawberry-stained tank top and shark slippers.

Jack walks past me, not giving me a hug, and says, "Love the slippers."

He quickly turns back, gives me a once-over, smirks jumps in the front seat, and shuts the door. Such a Jack thing to do.

I haven't said anything to him. I can't think fast enough to come up with a retort. The only thing that keeps going through my mind is, "Jack is here." I slink into the backseat and count the minutes until we get home, and I can change. I still can't figure out what is different about him, but one thing's for sure, Jack is here.

We have been spending the summer with the Fosters since Jack and I were babies. When we were little, our parents would pick a different beach each year, and we would meet there for the Fourth of July and spend a couple of weeks playing on the beach and exploring the cute beach towns. A couple of years ago, Jazzy got into an intense ballet camp that she can't miss, so we have to stick around here for the summers so she can attend ballet camp. The Fosters decided that instead of missing out on our summers together, they would start coming to our house and spending the Fourth of July here.

It has become a yearly ritual we all look forward to. We don't need the sandy beaches or the lavish holiday resorts. Our backyard is honestly a mini paradise with a backdrop of a lake just yards beyond the yard and a golf course in the distance. Who would ever want to leave? It becomes even more magical during the Fourth of July, complete with fairy lights and the mouth-watering aroma of Dad's barbecue that wafts through the summer air. There is no need for my mom's crazy scent ambiance because it naturally smells of the best summer holiday. We set up tents and spend the night under the stars, taking turns sharing ghost stories. Jack always has the scariest ones, which he only tells after Poppy has gone to bed.

Jill, Jack's mom, comes early to help my mom with the preparations and joins her in her overplanning endeavors. Jeremy, Jack's dad, arrives a little later, and work often keeps him busy. The Fourth of July is the only time I've seen him let loose, join us in our water fights, and sing along to the pop songs blaring from the speakers. Fourth of July is my favorite.

Jack's intense soccer training schedule often keeps him occupied, and the Fourth of July marks a brief vacation, a moment to pause, breathe, and just be a teenager. He seems to love this freedom. We go to the annual hot air balloon festival on the morning of the Fourth and spend the day playing tag among the balloons and lying on our backs in the park, watching the balloons take flight. The dads always mysteriously go missing for a couple of hours, and when they return with caffeine for everyone, even Poppy, it completely blows my mind. That kid doesn't need an ounce of manufactured energy.

After the balloon festival, we headed home and went out on the lake. We spend hours wake surfing and having fun. The entire time the Fosters are here, it feels like one tradition after another. How could anyone not love the Fourth of July?

As I stare out the car window, I think back to summer at the beach when we were little kids. Jack and I used to love to play together, and we would spend hours making sand creations like turtles, castles, and dolphins. As soon as we were finished, we would act like we were some sort of natural disaster and completely ruin what we had just spent hours creating. Our moms always got mad because we wouldn't wait for them to come over and take a picture of our creation with us smiling in front of it. I smile, thinking about how fun it used to be. A furrow comes over my brow as the memories from beach vacations turn into thinking about last year's Fourth of July. Even though we were ruining sand creations, it felt like we both took to each other with as much gusto as we used to take to those sand castles. We were destructive, and I think we may have ruined our friendship. But seeing his smirk as he hopped into the front seat just now, I am hoping maybe not.

Last year. I was so excited to see him. I saw their car pull and greeted them at the front door. Jack walked into the house with his AirPods in, backpack slumped over his shoulder, and his soccer ball tucked under his arm. He gave me a head nod and went straight up to the guest room. I didn't see him until that night at dinner, and he only talked to me because his mom kicked him under the table. I was hurt and confused about what had changed.

All his free time was spent working out with his dad OR playing in the pool with my sisters. I felt like he didn't want to be my friend anymore. I pop back to reality and realize we have driven all the way home from the airport. I haven't said a word. Jack and Dad have spent the entire time catching up, and Dad keeps telling Jack how proud he is of him. It is sweet how much my dad loves Jack, but I want to remind him that he was a total jerk last summer and doesn't deserve any praise until he apologizes.

As we pull up to the house, my phone buzzes. I look down. It's a text from Xander.

Xander: Hey cute girl!

I notice immediately that he hasn't used my name. I wonder if it's copy/paste text that he has sent to all the girls at school. But I squash that thought. He likes me.

> Xander: What are you up to? I'm just getting
> ready for camp.

Xander sends me a pic of himself. He is sticking out his tongue and winking. It's a dumb pic, but it's also kind of cute. Before the whole yearbook fiasco, I would have stared at this pic for hours.

I quickly message back.

> Me: A friend from out of town just got here.
> Have fun at camp.

As I send it, Jack is grabbing his bags from the trunk of the car, and he says to me, "New boyfriend?"

Seriously? He doesn't talk to me all the way home, and now he wants to chat. I'm not in the mood after he made fun of my outfit; that honestly does look terrible.

I look back at him, say, "Maybe," and get out of the car. Before I talk to Jack again, I have to change out of these clothes. I dash upstairs before Jack can say anything else.

It takes me an eternity to choose an outfit that I like,, but I finally emerge from my room and come downstairs. Jack is already in the kitchen, deep in conversation with my mom.

As I come downstairs, I get another message from Xander.

> Xander: What?! No Pic :(

I didn't send a selfie with the last text. I smile. I quickly take a pic in the kitchen and send it off. I turn around, and Jack is staring at me.

I glare back and say, "What?" Jack just shrugs his shoulders and goes back to eating. Seeing him there reminds me of the one day last summer when things felt normal between us.

It was one of those mornings that has become etched into my memory without trying to be extraordinary. The sun had just risen, casting warm streaks of light through the kitchen window. The sound of sizzling bacon and crackling toast served as the background music. The aroma of fresh coffee mingled with maple syrup in the air, promising a great start to the day.

Jack and I sat at the breakfast table, each lost in our own worlds yet comfortably sharing the silence. You know how there's a type of silence that weighs you down? This was the opposite—a silence full of unspoken words and implicit understanding. I was taking a bite of my pancake when I felt the sudden invasion of Jack's foot nudging against mine under the table.

Jack knows my quirky pet peeve. Feet touching feet—it grosses me out to an unreasonable degree. I don't mind if someone is giving me a foot rub, but I seriously lose it when someone else's bare feet touch mine. So Jack put his foot on mine, and he did it to tease because that was Jack, irreverent and playfully infuriating. It didn't matter that I had yelled at him and called him a jerk because of how he lashed out at me the night before. It was just Jack being his normal old self again at breakfast.

Trying to maintain a composed face, I gingerly moved my foot away. But as relentless as always, Jack edged his foot closer, challenging my boundaries like only he could. Finally, I'd had enough. Jumping up from my chair, I looked at him and forcefully said with a mouthful of pancakes, "STOP IT, JACK!"

"Noli, I can't help it. I love you!" Jack declared, a mischievous grin stretching across his face.

"No, you monster!" I yelped, darting behind the kitchen island. My heart pounded not from fear but exhilaration, the kind that comes from the joyful chaos of friendship. We both laughed so hard it felt like the room was vibrating with our happiness.

But just as Jack lunged at me to put his foot on mine, his dad entered the kitchen, breaking the spell. At that moment, the old Jack I knew vanished as if a switch had been flipped. His face reverted to its stony default of the summer, and he slunk back to his chair, resuming his breakfast with robotic precision. It was as if the last few minutes had never happened, as if the laughter that had filled the room was just another morning mirage.

The memory of the first part of that morning brings a smile to my face, and I try not to get my hopes up that the playful Jack is the one who is staying with us this weekend and not the checked-out moody version from last summer.

Jack and I never talk or text much when we're apart. The most interaction we had outside of our summer visits was the year we both got our phones, exchanging sporadic texts and occasional Face-Time calls. This absence of constant contact has always been a part of our friendship, and it's never bothered me.

When summer rolls around, and we're reunited, it always feels like we've never been apart. Before last summer, there was never any awkwardness or those weird silences that sometimes happened with me and the boys. It's just...easy. We used to talk about anything and everything, and I could be my genuine self around him. I don't know how to explain it. He is really important to me, and I was crushed last summer when I felt like I had lost him.

Following the tense Fourth of July, when Jack and I hardly spoke, I found myself wanting to text him during the school year. I missed him and felt as though I'd been robbed of a summer with my best friend. I wanted to catch up on his life, hear about his school year, and know what had happened his freshman year. I couldn't believe he didn't even text me about making the championship with his soccer team.

I hate to admit it, but I even missed him telling me about the girls he liked and who he had hooked up with. I missed having my summer, Jack.

And now, here I am, standing in the heart of our kitchen, a silent observer of a conversation I desperately want to be a part of. I hear his voice—it's slightly deeper than before, but the cadence, the way he emphasizes certain words, is all too familiar. He's talking to my mom, sharing updates about school, soccer, and how his mom's doing. All things I wish he would've shared with me.

My mom glances up, her eyes meeting mine. There's a flash of understanding there as if she can read the turmoil in my soul. She knows how much Jack means to me; she's witnessed the arc of our friendship, from sandcastles to awkward teenage years. And she must sense how much I'm craving for this summer to heal the fractures from the last.

Mom knows how to hit the nail on the head sometimes, even if it's wrapped in silly phrasing. "Noli, Jack was just telling me about his freshman year. It sounds like you both had a glow-up!"

Jack spins to face me, his eyes stretched wide in mock horror, lips twitching as if holding back an avalanche of laughter. There it is—a sliver of the Jack I used to know. I break first, laughing openly, and Jack follows suit.

My mom has a knack for this. She is a professional negotiator and knows the power of words. I can tell she crafted this sentence exactly how she wanted to, with the cringe-worthy use of words only a mom could say. They have the power to draw us into a shared laugh. And she doesn't mind being the butt of the joke if it means it'll bring us closer together.

"Lily, I don't think what I did my freshmen year would be considered a glow-up, and from the looks of Noli this morning, I don't think she had a glow-up year either."

I've moved closer, standing within arm's length of Jack in the breakfast nook. That's when it hits me—I know what's different about Jack. The thing I couldn't figure out at the airport. Jack's taller than me. Last summer, our eyes were almost level, but now, for the first time ever, I'm looking up to meet his gaze.

We notice our height difference at the same moment. Jack puffs out his chest, and I see that mischievous glint in his eyes return. "Well, well, well. What do we have here? I guess there's a new sheriff in town," he adds, recalling our childhood game.

I laugh again at the reference to the game we used to play as kids.

We would pretend there was a sheriff and a bad guy. I never wanted to be the bad guy, so I told Jack that whoever was the tallest got to be the sheriff and wear the badge. Jack would beg to be the sheriff, but I held firm and told him I didn't make the rules; the tallest person always had to be sheriff. This kept me firmly in the position of sheriff, and Jack, Poppy, and Jazzy always had to be the bad guys.

Jack relishes this. "So, little missy, any short bad guys I should know about?"

As Jack parades around the kitchen with feigned authority, I can't help but smile back at this friendship we've just rekindled. I am so happy that things feel normal between us. I knew that last July was hard with Jack, but I don't think I realized until this moment how much I missed him. This silliness feels like the promise of having us back. I can't help myself, I lean in and give Jack a hug. Dang Noah and all his hugs during the school year! He must have rubbed off on me because here I am, standing in the kitchen, in front of my mom, hugging Jack.

Jack is a bit surprised too, but he hugs me back, and I swear he gets on his tiptoes so he can rest his fuzzy head on top of mine.

My mom is looking at both of us approvingly. I release Jack from the hug and stand back to look at him.

"You obviously have had a glow-up," I tease him. "Why else would you be wearing a shirt?" I tug at his shirt with my eyebrows raised.

Whenever Jack is at our house, he never wears a shirt unless we are going out to dinner or the very rare occasion that he would come and play a round of golf with me. It doesn't matter if he is lounging poolside, training with his dad, eating, pranking us, or playing video games, he never wears a shirt.

Jack raises his eyebrows at me, and his shirt is off in an instant. "Thanks for reminding me!"

He stretches his arms over his head, and I still can't believe how tall he has gotten. He looks around like a king coming back to his castle and says, "Feels good to be home."

Then he throws his shirt in my face. "UGH...Jack!" I say and throw it back to him.

My mom is beaming. I can tell that she is happy that Jack and I are getting along, and there is nothing my mom loves to hear more than when people tell her that our house feels like they are home.

Jack knows that too, and I can tell he is raking in the brownie points with my mom.

She comes over and pats Jack's arm. "You are home and can stay as long as you like."

He smiles. "Thanks, Lily."

Mom tells us she has things to do and is off to the command center.

Now it's just Jack and me. I am both relieved to be here, both of us looking at one another, and also a bit nervous. I'm not sure what is next. It feels like I was asked to dance at my first school dance. I am both excited and nervous.

Like any good partner, Jack takes the lead. "How was freshmen year?" he asks, and I can see a coy smile forming on his lips. "I need details about this glow-up."

I let out a small groan. "I will tell you, but can we stop calling it a glow-up?"

Jack laughs. "Absolutely not."

We sit on the barstools, Jack's shirt still off. I know for a fact it won't go back on until he gets in the car for soccer camp. Two years ago, when I sent a picture of Jack and me both holding sparklers to Morgan and Celeste, they freaked out and messaged me back about how hot they thought Jack was. It is one of those things that I know he is cute, but also, we are best friends, so it never occurred to me how cute he really is.

Jack has a way of always being confident but laid back. He has these interesting eyes that are hazel green most of the time unless he is tired or pissed. Then they turn a green that is almost brown. He is so toned and lean from the hours of conditioning and soccer, and I am pretty sure that whatever activity he tries, he is good at.

As I start to share stories about Cascade Prep and the friends I've made there, I find my eyes lingering on Jack's features longer than they used to. My friends weren't wrong; he's ridiculously good-looking. It's as if his presence has come into sharper focus for me, and I can't help but wonder how I could have been so blind to it before.

My thoughts are interrupted by high-pitched squeals from the doorway. "OMG! Jack!" It's Poppy and Jazzy bursting into the room like two miniature whirlwinds. They rush over to Jack and envelop him in hugs as if trying to squeeze out every drop of his newly discovered height into themselves.

"I can't believe you're here!" Jazzy screams, her eyes alight with a joy only a younger sister can muster.

Poppy chimes in, almost bouncing on her feet. "Are you going to stay forever?"

"Only for the weekend, Pops," Jack replies, using Poppy's nickname, his eyes meeting mine for a moment as if sharing an inside joke.

Watching them, a sense of familiarity and warmth fills the room, but also I'm a bit jealous. It's like they've seamlessly picked up from where they left off, and I'm on the sidelines. But then again, wasn't that Jack and me just a few moments ago, laughing, teasing, and connecting?

I shake off the awkwardness and join the conversation. "So we've got big plans for the weekend, Jack. Hope you're ready."

"I was born ready," he says, his eyes locking on to mine. There's a challenge there, a spark that makes me think of our countless wake surfing competitions over the years. The air is tinged with a newfound electricity, almost as if we've rediscovered something we didn't know we had lost.

As Poppy and Jazzy lead us toward the living room, chattering about showing Jack their dance competition videos, I can't help but feel a sense of excitement. There's a strange kind of magic in the air that promises a weekend of reconnection. But that's not quite right. It also feels like something new is happening too.

5

This weekend has seriously been the best. It's incredible how Jack's personality is different when his parents aren't around. The tension and weirdness from last summer seem to be completely gone. I never figured out what put Jack on edge last year, but maybe it doesn't matter now. All I want is to preserve this newfound fun in our friendship.

Jack has spent hours playing video games, squaring off against Poppy, and even convincing Jazzy and me to join in too. He has been lounging by the pool, wake surfing behind the boat, kicking his soccer ball around, and we even relieved one of our fondest childhood memories by sleeping on the trampoline, just like when we were little. I feel like I don't want this weekend to end.

Out on the boat, every evening, Jack has been perfecting his wake surfing skills while also helping me out. He has been offering tips and tricks he picked up on YouTube. His eyes twinkle as he critiques my form, and I find myself distracted by the droplets of water tracing paths down his tanned chiseled chest, his wet hair sticking up, not quite long enough to make it to his forehead yet, and I can't help it, I am obsessed with his legs. Has he always had that many muscles?

His new height has given him an unanticipated masculinity, trans-forming him from boy to man in ways that I find distracting.

We tie the boat to our dock as dusk settles in on his last night with us, and we build a fire to chase away the chill that we all have after being on the water. Everything is perfect. It feels like a time bubble that I don't want to leave. It's late on Sunday; tomorrow, he's off to soccer camp. I'm excited for him, but part of me wishes he could stay with us. I even try to convince him to go to camp during the day and spend the night back here. But he says part of camp is getting to know the other players, and I know he's right. A knot forms in my gut at the thought that this magical weekend is going to end soon. What if that's all I get with Jack? One magical weekend that disappears as soon as Jack leaves?

Jack and I find ourselves keeping the fire going as we gaze at the stars. The house is dark and silent, with Poppy and Jazzy tucked in for the night and my parents already in bed. Though I have a golf game in the morning, sleep is the furthest thing from my mind. I can't shake the anxiety that things might revert to the strange tension of last summer once Jack leaves.

A sigh escapes my lips, prompting Jack to turn toward me. "What was that for?"

Trying to mask my worry, I give him a flimsy excuse: "Nothing, just...breathing."

He laughs, but his eyes stay fixed on me, curious and penetrating. He lets out a very exaggerated breath and sighs heavily. "Don't mind me," his voice high-pitched as he imitates me. "I'm just breathing."

I roll my eyes and throw a marshmallow at him. Jack has always been good at reading me. He knows there is something else on my mind. This feels like a pivotal moment, a great time to maybe talk about what happened last summer. And just as I muster the courage to speak, Jack moves from his side of the firepit and comes and sits right by me. His tongue licks his lips lightly, and he leans into me. He reaches his hand close to my face. His fingertips lightly caress my cheek. The touch is electrifying, unlike anything he's ever done before. I look over at him and meet his gaze, and in the moonlight, I'm struck by the mosaic of greens in his eyes.

He gives me a smile and says, "You had leftover marshmallow on your cheek."

I am embarrassed that I have been sitting here for who knows how long with marshmallow on my cheek.

I roll my eyes, trying to mask my red cheeks, and say, "I was saving that for later."

He gives a small laugh, but then he touches my face again, this time a light touch on my nose. I hope I don't have marshmallow on my nose, too, but then I look at his eyes. Jack wasn't touching me this time to remove food. What is going on? I stay still and just look into his eyes.

"Are you ready to tell me what that sigh was about?" he asks softly, his voice imbued with a seriousness I've rarely heard from him.

This feels intimate. Not like anything Jack and I have had with each other before. Desire rushes through me as I want him closer than he is. I want to touch him back. I want us to be something more. But I hold it back, reminding myself that I've been down this path before, mistaking intimacy for something more. Xander had taught me that lesson well. As much as I want to lose myself in this moment with Jack, I remind myself that this is Jack. Just Jack. I remind myself that Jack isn't Xander. Xander is the one who sent me that sweet note. Xander is the one who likes me.

The note. I haven't thought about it at all since Jack has been here. In fact, I haven't looked at my phone at all since Jack has been here. I wonder if I have any texts from Xander. I also feel bad about Noah. It felt like maybe telling him about the note from Xander was upsetting, but I never asked why. I can't think of any of this right now. Jack is here with me right now, and that's all that matters. I come back to what he asked me. I get brave for a couple of seconds and decide to go for it. I want to talk about last summer.

"I was just...thinking," I finally say, my voice tinged with vulnerability. "About how incredible this weekend has been and how I wish we could always be like this. I missed you, Jack. A lot. Especially last summer."

He falls silent, studying me as if he's piecing together a puzzle. Then he looks skyward, contemplative. "I'm sorry about last summer. It was...complicated."

And so the air shifts. We've crossed some invisible line. We are both admitting that last summer was a disaster. Part of me feels relief that Jack called it complicated. It's like he is admitting it wasn't just in my head. The words are out, lingering between us like the night air. But whatever happens next, one thing is certain: We've entered uncharted territory in our friendship, a place where we are vulnerable. And I know there's no turning back now.

Jack looks back into my eyes. He is staring at me. I can't tell if he is hurt or bothered. He starts, "If I'm being honest with you, it wasn't just me that ruined our summer last year. You were on some crazy pills or something. You kept taking everything so personally, and it felt like you were looking to find things that I was doing wrong. It was just a lot to be around, you know?"

It's funny how this whole time, I was thinking that I had ruined that summer and Jack was an accomplice. He was thinking the same thing about himself. But hearing him being so honest about what he experienced last summer stings. I know I wasn't always nice to him, but I always justified it in my head because he started it. As I think back on all of it, I hear how childish it sounds. I don't want to blame him for my crappy summer, and I can for sure see how my attitude was a contributing factor.

I want to tell him how sorry I am about my part in it, but before I can, Jack goes on, "I haven't told anyone this, and I'm not even sure your parents know. So can you promise it stays between us?"

He looks at me, and at that moment, I understand—he's about to share something big. I sit up and turn to face him, sitting cross-legged. I nod at him to show I'm his to share whatever he needs to.

"I won't tell anyone," I assure him.

Jack gives a nod of acknowledgment, pulls his chair closer to mine, and turns to face me. In the short amount of time Jack has been here, he is already getting an excellent tan. I try to stay focused on Jack's face and not his firm pecs that lead their way down to his washboard abs.

"Last year was really terrible. My parents...they separated for the first half of the year. They were trying to decide whether or not they wanted a divorce."

I'm stunned. What? Jill and Jeremy were going to get a divorce? I think back to the Fourth of July last year. I had no clue there were any problems, let alone they'd separated. I'm struggling to process this bombshell while trying to stay present and attentive to Jack.

I can tell that Jack is struggling to talk about it, but he continues. "So coming here during the Fourth of July felt...off. Mom and Dad didn't want any of you to worry or fuss over them. They didn't want to spend the whole week discussing the separation and having your parents get upset over it, so they asked me to act like everything was normal, like they were still together."

My mind flashes back to Jack last summer, his aloofness, his frosty demeanor. It all clicks into place. He's never been good at lying or pretending. I can't believe I was so blind and selfish. I thought that Jack's attitude was about me, and I was completely ignorant of his pain.

Without thinking, I reach out and rest my hand on his leg. "I'm so sorry, Jack. That must have sucked. How are your parents doing now?"

Jack rolls his eyes. "Apparently, they're more in love than ever now. Coming here for the Fourth of July was just what they needed. It reminded them why they were together in the first place. They decided to give it another shot and even had this weird commitment ceremony that just the three of us went to."

A wave of relief washes over me at the news that Jill and Jeremy aren't getting divorced. It would have been so hard to navigate our summers with only one of them. Or even worse, if they stopped coming altogether. I start thinking about what it would be like for my own parents to get a divorce, but luckily Jack's voice pulls me back from my thoughts.

"It was really tough not being able to talk about it with anyone. I was so pissed off at both of them." Jack looks away, and I can see the strain that keeping this secret has put on him. I'm not quite sure how to respond.

I think of Celeste's mom, the therapist, always having the right questions to ask. Channeling her, I ask Jack, "What helped you the most to get through all this?"

The question feels too mature coming from me, and I instantly regret it, wishing I could switch the topic. But then I notice the expression on Jack's face. It looks like he's on the brink of tears.

Part of me wants to bolt, to give him some space, but the bigger part is just scared that I won't be able to handle the situation. My mind jumps back to a time at Celeste's house when she cried in front of me. Her parents were there too. When she started crying, I thought she'd flee to her room, or maybe her dad would make an exit. But none of that happened. We all sat there, witnessing Celeste's tears, and her mom said, "It's completely okay to feel whatever you're feeling. We're right here to support you."

I tell myself, *"Support him, this is okay. He can cry."* I don't get uncomfortable. I ground into staying and being here for him.

I meet his gaze once more. His voice cracks as he starts speaking, "That's just it, Noli. I haven't... My parents are acting like last year didn't happen. They're in love, recommitted to each other, whatever that means. But up until last year, I thought my parents' relationship was indestructible. It wasn't; it isn't. And that scares me. They're pretending like nothing's changed, but I'm constantly on edge. I get worried whenever they seem annoyed with each other. I'm always on high alert when we're all together, trying to decipher if we're okay. If our family is okay. And I am so mad at them. They have forgiven each other, but they never asked me. They never asked me how their separation impacted me."

Jack starts to cry. I can tell he's been bottling this up for a long time. I reach out and squeeze his hand, and he grips mine tightly, not letting go. I'm unsure of what to do next.

I know that unburdening himself won't instantly resolve everything, and I also realize I'm probably not the best person for him to confide in about this. "You know, you can always talk to my mom or dad. They're here for you and for your parents," I tell him.

Jack sniffs and uses his free hand to wipe away the tears streaking down his face. "I've wanted to talk to them," he admits with a sigh of frustration. "My parents said I couldn't tell anyone. Like I said, they're acting like it never happened."

I'm annoyed at Jill and Jeremy for being so self-involved that they can't see how their actions have impacted Jack. It doesn't seem right that he can't share his own experiences with anyone. In my frustration, I blurt out, "Screw your parents! It's not right for them to make you go through this alone. You should be able to talk to someone. It might be their marriage, but it's your family too."

Jack lets go of my hand and leans back, laughing, "Magnolia Jane!" He uses my middle name when he's amused. "Did you just say 'screw'?"

He's teasing me, and I love seeing his playful side. He always acts as though he hasn't said worse. I miss feeling his hand in mine. Touching him feels exciting. I nudge him gently. "Maybe I did," I retort, welcoming the shift in tone. But even though it's nice to lighten the mood, I don't want us to lose track of our serious discussion. Only moments ago, he showed more pain than I've ever seen him. It doesn't feel right to gloss over that.

I make a bold move and still holding his hand, I stand up, and he does too. I walk us over to the pool and sit down so our feet are in the pool. I want to be close to him but not make it weird. We have sat like this countless times, and sitting this way, his face isn't as visible to me, but my mind races as I feel his warm body next to mine.

Jack doesn't move away from me. When we were kids, anytime Jack and I would be close together, he would playfully hold my hand

and tell me we were in love. He didn't do it because it was true, he did it to annoy me. As we sit here so close, I want to reach out and grab his hand and tell him that I love him. Not to annoy him, but because I feel it deeply right now. I love Jack so much, and seeing him hurt so much hurts me. If I try to do that right now, he will think I am teasing him.

My arms are stretched behind me, supporting me as I lean back, and he mirrors me, our hands lightly brushing against each other. Everything about this feels so normal, yet I am hyper-aware of every point of contact between us. Every slight graze of his skin sends sparks coursing through me. I debate with myself once more about talking to him about his parents. I want to be selfish, to focus on my feelings and wants. But if I truly care about Jack, I need to help him, to be there for him. It's not about what I want but what he needs.

I start before I lose my caring and concern for my friend and fall helplessly into my wants. "Jack, I know your parents said you can't talk to my family about what happened. But I can see how much this is still hurting. I think you should talk to my parents about it."

Before I forget, I add, "And I'm really sorry about how I acted last year. If I wasn't being so selfish, I may have been able to see that you were hurting."

It's like I am watching Jack relive last summer again. He gets tense, and a wave of emotion washes over his face. I don't want to spiral back to what he went through. I want to help him.

"I think you should talk to my dad," I suggest, trying to keep my voice steady. "My mom might, well, you know how she can be... but I know for a fact that my dad can handle anything you need to talk about." I turn to look at him, my eyes full of sincerity. "Seeing you in so much pain... it sucks, Jack. I know talking about it might not solve everything, but it can help, you know? Maybe it could even give you some ways to handle the anxiety that's been messing with you."

My words hang in the air, and I can only hope that he takes my advice to heart. He needs someone right now, and if I can help him find someone, then I'll feel like I am being the friend I should have been last summer.

"I don't know, Noli. How would I even start that conversation?" Jack questions, sounding unsure.

I sense his hesitation, and I instantly want to alleviate his worries. With a burst of energy, I stand up from our spot by the pool. I have to focus on taking care of Jack, even though I want to sit back down next to him and snuggle up close. "Don't worry about it, Jack. I can do it. I can start the conversation for you," I assure him.

He looks at me, a mix of hope and skepticism in his eyes, clearly uncertain about how this plan might pan out.

"Trust me," I say, trying to be supportive. "I got you," I tell him to stay put and dart into the house.

The house is quiet, lights out, and everyone sleeps soundly. My parents are strict about their sleeping habits, always chasing that ideal sleep environment to get the most restful night. But I'm confident that once I've explained the situation to my dad, he won't be upset about the disturbance. He cares deeply for Jack and his parents, just like I do, and he wants to help in any way he can.

I tiptoe through the hallway toward my parents' bedroom, careful to avoid the creaky floorboard. Their room is completely dark, not even a slice of moonlight illuminating the path to their bed. I take a deep breath, steeling myself for the conversation ahead. It's an odd feeling waking my dad up to have a heartfelt conversation with Jack, and I wonder what I should say, but if it helps Jack, it'll be worth every bit of discomfort.

I gently nudge my dad awake, and he's instantly alert. "What is it? Is everything okay?" he is way too alert to have just been woken up. My dad always tells us that when you become a parent, you get this new alarm clock activated in your body. Wherever your baby cries or your kids are out past curfew, the alarm sounds, and you are instantly wide awake. I guess it works when your friend's kid needs you too.

"It's about Jack," I tell him, trying to keep my voice steady.

At the mention of Jack, my dad immediately sits up, now even more wide awake. "Did he sneak out? Is he okay?" he rushes to ask, making me suppress a snicker at the thought of Jack sneaking out.

That is just so not Jack. "No, Dad. He didn't sneak out," I reassure him. "He needs someone to talk to." At this, my dad nods, understanding my unspoken plea.

"All right. Fill me in, but let's move out into the hallway. Don't want to disturb your mom." He picks up his shirt from the floor, and we silently tiptoe out of the room and into the dimly lit hallway.

I explain the situation to him, trying to keep my voice steady. "Jack's parents were separated and almost got a divorce last year before they came to our house for the Fourth of July. They are okay now, but they told Jack he couldn't tell anyone about what was happening. He's been keeping it in, dealing with it all on his own. It's taking a toll on him. He's not okay, Dad."

Dad lets out a long breath, and I can see the concern etched on his face. My dad is the best. He is always there for all of us. Even though he might not have expected to be woken up like this in the middle of the night, he's the type of person who's ready to step in when someone needs help, no matter the time or the circumstances.

"Okay," he says after a moment of contemplation. "Where is he now?" I tell him Jack is by the pool, and we walk together toward the back of the house.

Jack stands up as my dad makes his way to him. I stop at the doorway, not wanting to intrude on this conversation. Jack has an apprehensive expression on his face.

"Hey, tiger," my dad says, using his favorite nickname for Jack when he was younger. He gently gives Jack a small, understanding smile as he reaches out his arms for Jack.

Seeing this, Jack finally crumples into my dad's open arms. Dad holds him close as Jack starts to sob deeply. I decide to give them some privacy, quietly retreating into the family room. I opt to stay up, unable to fall asleep just yet. But lingering around them doesn't seem right either, so I pick up a book to pass the time. An hour later,

Dad and Jack walk back inside. My dad smiles warmly at me, his eyes tired but understanding. "We all should head to bed now," he suggests. Setting my book aside, I get up, nodding in agreement.

Jack and I move toward our rooms as my dad heads back to his room. Just as I'm about to disappear into mine, Jack's hand wraps around my waist gently, making me pause and turn to him. As I turn, he drops his hand from my waist and finds my hands. He interlocks our fingers together. We are standing in the hall holding hands as we face each other so close. This isn't like when we were kids. I know he isn't going to tell me he loves me in that teasing tone.

The way he touches me, it feels like he has done it before. But for me, this is all new. I still can't figure out what this means. But maybe, for now, I'm not supposed to figure it out. Jack starts talking. "Noli," he begins, a soft expression on his face, "thank you...for understanding what I needed even when I didn't. Talking to your dad...it really helped. You've always seemed to know what I need better than I do myself."

As he speaks, I can't help but notice how he seems better. He still looks tired, probably because of how late it is, but the heavyweight that seemed to be pressing down on him earlier tonight seems to have lightened. Seeing him relieved makes me happy. As I notice our linked fingers, a jolt of awareness runs through me. I love how my hands fit in his bigger ones, and once again, I am reminded that Jack isn't the kid I used to throw sand clumps at or race between hot air balloons with.

A wide grin spreads across my face as I tilt my head up to look at him. "Like I told you, I've got you." I let my gaze drop to our joined hands and then meet his eyes again, a serious note in my voice as I add, "And I always will."

In response, Jack draws me into a hug; his warm chest feels so good pressed against me, but then teasingly stretches himself up onto his tiptoes, his head coming to rest on top of mine. I can't help but giggle and lightly push him away, shaking my head. "Okay, okay, no need to keep reminding me you're taller."

As I move toward my room, I look back at him one last look. "Good night, Jack."

He's still standing there, a mischievous twinkle in his eyes, as he drawls out, "I think you mean to say, 'Good night, Sheriff.'" Mimicking the action of tipping an imaginary cowboy hat, he grins and adds, "Evening, ma'am," before sauntering off.

I retreat to my room, closing the door behind me. I can't help but replay the night's events, my thoughts occupied by Jack's laughter, his teasing, and the warmth of his hand in mine. It's a sensation so comforting, so familiar yet loaded with newfound feelings. Even with all of the hard from the evening, it felt good to be there for him and to be able to help him when he was hurting so badly.

Before I go to bed, I text the group chat with Morgan, Celeste, and Addy. I don't expect any of them to respond because it is so late where they all are across the country.

Me: Found a new crush. Crushing HARD

I get a message before I can even put my phone on silent and plug it into the charger.

Morgan: FINALLY! DYING. Tell us
everything.

Me: Too good to share tonight. Talk to you
girls in the morning.

I decide to leave them hanging. I want to keep Jack to myself tonight. In the morning, I can dish. I fall asleep with a smile on my face, a sweet exhaustion enveloping me. It's a sleep full of gentle dreams where Jack's laughter rings in my ears, where I see his eyes looking at me with an intensity that I've only begun to see from him tonight.

This is the first time I have not been dreaming of Xander in a long time, and it feels good to have another guy to think about. Even if it's a little weird because, well, it's Jack. It doesn't matter tonight, and I close my eyes, lost in the feeling of Jack's hand in mine.

When I wake up, the deafening silence lets me know that Jack is already gone to soccer camp. The silence of the house is too much. I already miss him. I remind myself that I probably have a dozen texts from my friends, and I go to pick up my phone. Before I do, my eyes fall upon a folded piece of paper resting on my phone. Picking it up, I unfold it to see Jack's familiar scrawl. A note. Jack was in my room this morning. He saw me sleeping. I wonder how I looked. I am too excited to get pulled off track. I open up the note.

> Roses are red; Violets are blue
>
> Soccer is fun, but not as much as hanging out
> with you.
>
> Can't wait for the Fourth; it's going to be a ball.
>
> Don't miss me too much.
>
> -Sherrif Jack

My heart is pounding with a rhythm that seems to echo Jack's name. My thoughts are lit up with the possibilities of what this could mean, of what our Fourth of July could look like. It is promising to be much better than last year. I smile to myself and see my phone light up. I grab it and see thirty missed texts. I'd better let my friends know before they go insane. I don't read anything and send a text to the group.

> Me: How do you all feel about Jack and I
> together?

Jack's openness last night has stirred something inside of me—something warm and fuzzy but also tinged with a pang of...guilt? Here was Jack, opening up his heart, trusting me with a secret he's carried for so long. I feel close to him in a way I haven't felt in years, and I know that this is the beginning of a different kind of friendship and maybe something else.

But even as I feel that warmth, my thoughts drift to Xander. How would I have felt if it were him sitting next to me tonight, sharing a vulnerable part of himself? His note showed me that there is a depth beneath his carefree persona, hints that he may just be the guy to explore things with. Would I have felt the same sense of closeness, of responsibility? My heart tugs in two directions, not quite ready to choose, and I swear at myself for even comparing the two situations. Tonight was about Jack, about our renewed friendship, and it's not fair to muddy that clarity with the fog of another guy.

It is so crazy to me that anyone can like more than one person at a time, but here I am experiencing it. My emotions are not bound to one guy. I guess the heart wants what it wants—often more than one thing or one person. It's a complicated knot that I don't yet know how to untangle. One thing is certain, though: This weekend has changed something fundamental in my relationship with Jack. Our friendship has matured. Maybe my mom was wrong. Maybe it isn't me or Jack that has had a glow-up. Maybe it's our relationship that has.

I owe it to myself and Jack and Xander to figure out exactly what I'm feeling. Emotional honesty isn't just about being transparent with others; it starts with being honest with yourself. And right now, that's exactly what I need to do.

6

As the days of June tick by, a juggling act unfolds in my life. My phone has two distinct ringtones, one for Jack and one for Xander. Each has me erupting into a different type of emotion when it goes off. My heart warms when I hear Jack's, and I feel myself smiling. It's like a hug you've been waiting for. But when Xander's tone chimes, it's like a flash from a flare has gone off in me. I get nervous, and I never know what to expect. Sometimes, there is intense flirtation, but other times, it's almost like Xander is bored.

His texts aren't daily rituals like Jack's; they're more like a random surprise that comes in without warning. Unlike Jack's sentimental GIFs, Xander's messages are more direct, infused with flirtation, and sometimes edged with audacity. There's a thrill in that, a spontaneity that leaves me both energized and always doubting myself.

But along with the thrill comes a layer of confusion. Xander may be bolder in his texting advances, but a flicker of uncertainty accompanies his brazenness. He'll ask for selfies, and when I oblige, he'll compliment me before subtly hinting at wanting something more daring. This push-and-pull tension between what's said and what's left unspoken in our conversations adds a complex layer that I'm unsure how to react to. Xander makes me feel like I'm too new in this relationship. Like maybe he's on level ten while I'm on level two.

It all leaves me feeling excited anytime I hear my ringtones for either of them. And, on top of all of this texting with Jack and Xander, Noah has been oddly quiet. It's actually making me a bit worried. After he asked me about the note, he sent some cryptic text saying:

> Noah: I totally understand. No hard feelings.

I'm not sure why he would have hard feelings toward me because Xander wrote me a note, and he didn't elaborate. But when I got that text, I had the feeling that maybe he was mad at me. Since then, I have tried to message him a couple of times, and all I have gotten back is one-word answers. I wish he was here. I wish we could go hit a bucket of balls or wake surf. Whoever said that being friends with boys is easy lied! Having guy friends is even more confusing than having girls as friends. The other day I texted Noah and asked him how his sophomore summer was going.

> Noah: Sophomore summer???? Please
> explain. We aren't sophomores yet.

> Me: Well, we aren't freshmen anymore, and
> so we have started the summer before we
> are sophomores. HENCE, it is our
> sophomore summer dummy!

> Noah: Huh. That doesn't track.

I sometimes forget that Noah and I have just become friends this past year at school, so of course, he wouldn't know Celeste. Morgan and I have always seen ourselves as a grade older the minute that school ends.

We all agreed, and since then, we have referred to every single summer based on the grade that we are about to go into. After I text all the details about technically being a sophomore since we just graduated as freshmen, Noah sends me a thumbs-up and never really answers my question about how his summer is going. Whatever, I can't deal with Noah's bizarre sulkiness this summer. I have two guys that really like me, and I can't get have another guy's emotions to try and decipher.

I think about how different this summer has felt. It's kinda embarrassing to say this, but I really feel like I'm growing up this summer. I mean, duh, aren't we always? But this time, it's different—like in your face, can't-ignore-it different. I'm here, juggling my feelings for two totally opposite guys, and it's like I'm on this emotional roller coaster that I never even asked to get on, but here I am, holding on for dear life. I'm stoked and freaked out at the same time, ya know? Sophomore Summer, man—it's gearing up to teach me stuff I'm not sure I'm ready for, but bring it on.

July's so close I can feel it; it's just one week away. While Jack's GIF-laden texts are these cute little daily joys for me, they're no match for the real thing. I can't wait to dive back into seeing him and spending time with him. I look forward to laughing 'til my stomach hurts and maybe even having moments when I look into those gorgeous green eyes like that night by the pool. We've tried phone calls, but soccer camp culture is no joke.

Jack warned me that his roommates go full savage mode on anyone trying to have a heart-to-heart with a girl over the phone. And he wasn't kidding. We barely got through a "Hey, how's it going?" before the ruckus in the background went to eleven. Jack was like, "This is too much, Noli! These guys are nuts!! Gotta go!" Annoying? Totally. But at least his daily texts keep him a constant presence in my life.

My phone erupts with the specific ringtone I've set for my girl friends. The screen flashes Celeste's name along with a message that makes my stomach drops.

Celeste: Call Morgan ASAP. RED ALERT!

Every so often, Morgan will have a full-blown crisis. It could be over a variety of issues, but during the summer, it usually involves her dad. After spending the majority of the year apart, their annual summer reunions can be a jarring transition for her. She adores her dad, but their relationship can be difficult at times. I can't help but worry about what could've prompted such a dire RED ALERT!—our group's code phrase for an immediate emergency. Without a second thought, I call Morgan.

The phone rings just once before Morgan answers. Her shaky breath indicates she's been crying. Skipping the formalities, I blurt out, "What is it? What happened?"

Between her sobs, Morgan manages to utter, "I effed up," substituting the slang for the swear word none of us dare use.

"Tell me. You can tell me," I assure her, hoping to calm her down.

She sniffles again, her voice shaky, "He makes me so MAD! He did it. He was the one. He made me..." Her words hang in the air, cryptic and tense.

I don't have enough information to know what Morgan is talking about. I am still completely in the dark. Prompting Morgan gently, I say, "Start from the start, Morg. What did your dad do?"

My best guess is that it's her dad who's upset her, and it seems I'm spot on. Morgan launches into her story. "We were having such a good time, and then he has to go and ruin it all."

Bingo. I guessed right. "We were doing so well, Noli. And then he just... ugh! I wish I could ghost my own dad! I'm just so done. I want to break up with my DAD!"

Suddenly, Morgan lets out a scream into the phone. "I HATE HIM!"

I quickly pull the phone away from my ear, wincing as her voice echoes. When the yelling stops, I cautiously bring the phone back. In a quiet, broken voice, Morgan says, FaceTime me.

I quickly push the FaceTime button on my phone, and Morgan's tear-streaked face is right there. She doesn't even say hi before she reveals, "He's getting married to some insane woman."

I'm at a loss for words. Despite the fact that summers can be difficult for Morgan and her dad, she has always cherished the exclusive attention she gets from him during these months. She once confided in Celeste and me, saying she didn't really care what her dad did the rest of the year as long as he kept summers just for her. Now it appears that her dad's personal life has intruded on Morgan's sacred summer, leaving her crushed and furious.

"Did you have to meet her?" I ask, not sure what exactly to say.

"Yes," Morgan whines. "And it was terrible. She is insane. She is, like, such a gold digger, and she has her claws in my dad with her big boobs and overfilled lips."

I try to imagine what this woman looks like. I keep picturing all of the women on the reality shows my mom hates and won't let us watch. Just then, my phone buzzes. It's from Morgan, sending me a pic of the woman who will soon be her stepmom. I was spot on.

The woman in the picture has big boobs, fake lips, fake lashes, and a ton of makeup, and she is obviously wearing so much body contouring that she is tucked, trimmed, and tapered in all of the right places. She also looks like she is trying to look younger than she is. The type of woman chasing youth who thinks that she has caught it, but everyone else knows she hasn't, and it shows.

I am trying to picture what the family Christmas card that her dad sends out every year will look like with this woman in it. It's always just him and Morgan in whatever place they land during the summer. I imagine this woman standing with her arm linked with Morgan's dad, her chest in full view of the camera, and Morgan standing off to the side, arms folded and pouting. I can't help myself; a laugh escapes me thinking of it.

"It's not funny," Morgan says, half annoyed and half amused at herself for making me laugh.

"I'm sorry," I say. "I was just trying to picture this woman in the annual family Christmas card with you and your dad."

Morgan lets out an agonized sigh. "You haven't heard the worst. She has kids—three little demons, to be precise."

Morgan once said she wished for more family, and I blurt out, "Well, you always wanted siblings."

"Noli, don't you dare," she warns, her voice threatening to crack. "These kids are hellions. Be with me, or I'm hanging up."

"Okay, okay," I backtrack quickly. "I'm forever on Team Morgan."

"And besides"—her voice softens—"I already have the best sisters a girl could ask for."

I love that she includes herself in our family and thinks of us as sisters. She pauses, and I wish she could be here with our family. Maybe she shouldn't be with her dad during the summer anymore.

"That's not the end of it," Morgan whispers and my stomach tightens, bracing for the next emotional blow.

"I had my first kiss," Morgan finally says. Her voice is hesitant, and she looks into the camera to see my reaction.

"WHAT?!" My scream startles even me. My heart flips with excitement. "Morgan, spill! We promised—a play-by-play, no holding back."

She starts crying again. "It was awful, Noli."

My heart sinks. We had dreams for our first kisses—magical, heart-stopping moments. But 'awful' had never been part of our discussions. What could be so bad that it broke Morgan?

Realizing I've prodded a sore wound, I soften. "Morgs, you don't have to say anything. I'm here for you."

"No," she sniffles, "I want to tell you. Maybe it'll save you from a disaster like mine."

Morgan dives into her tale, becoming the captivating storyteller she's always been when we're hanging on her every word. "Dad and I started off well. We arrive at this beautiful rental, and he's acting a little distant, but that's normal for us. It usually takes a week for us to adjust."

I chime in, fueling her storytelling mojo, "Right, the one-week warm-up. Classic for you two. What happened next?"

Morgan's voice strengthens. "He grows weirder over the next week, constantly on the phone, avoiding me. Then, one night, out of nowhere, he's back to being a Dad. He takes me to this swanky beachfront restaurant. We're enjoying ourselves, and I am telling him about my school year when he cuts me off and says, 'I met someone.'"

Morgan gets even more animated as she continues, "He tells me they have been dating for three months, and he proposed right before the start of summer. Then he tells me she and HER KIDS are coming to spend the rest of the summer with us in the Hamptons, and that is why he rented a big house for the summer."

She catches her breath and then asks me, "Can you believe that is how he told me he is engaged?"

I've been friends with Morgan long enough to know that in order to hear the rest of the story, I have a part to play as well. "I can't believe that he would do that!" I say, matching her disgust.

My reply clearly struck the right chord as Morgan eagerly resumes her story. "Can you believe he is such an idiot sometimes? I was shell-shocked, and he keeps going on about how incredible she is, how he's madly in love. I couldn't stomach another word. And to add insult to injury, the next morning, I was jarred awake at 6 a.m. with the ear-splitting screams of not one, not two, but THREE kids. These weren't gleeful squeals; these were shrieks. As if they were miniature agents of chaos. I went downstairs, and there she was with her three kids. She introduced herself as Auntie Michelle. I mean, come on. She's going to become my stepmother, and she wants me to call her 'Auntie'. Unbelievable."

Morgan goes on to tell me how the devil kids trash the house in a matter of minutes. Throwing things around, jumping on the furniture, and literally going out and getting buckets of sand and dumping them on the kitchen counter.

Michelle acts like it's completely normal, and her dad just stands there and lets them do it without saying a word. Morgan lost it when she later found one of the kids stealing things from her room. She locked her door and told her dad she was going to the beach and she didn't know when she would be back.

I can't help myself. I want to know about her first kiss. This is taking way too long. I blurt out, "So when and who did you kiss?"

Morgan knows I have been patient. She dives into the kissing part of the story.

"So I left the beach house and went to the beach. I was so mad at my dad. He does the dumbest things sometimes. I have always just thought he would date while I was away and keep our summers for just us, but I guess I was wrong."

She exhales deeply, "I was at the beach, and I felt like a crazy person—furious one moment and sobbing the next. I tried reaching out to you and Celeste, but neither of you answered. So I went on that app—yeah, the one your mom banned. It connects you with people nearby. Anyway, a cute guy pinged me; he was just a mile away."

I feel uneasy about where this is going, but I keep my thoughts to myself.

Morgan continues, "He was super cute and was asking me tons of questions, and then he asked me if I had kissed anyone before. I thought it was kind of odd, but it was such a good distraction from my dad and the domestic circus back at the house."

My mind races. Where is this going? What happened? Did he hurt her? Is she safe? Before I can ask, she starts again, "I told him no, and he suggested we meet up somewhere. He gave me the address of the hotel he was staying at."

I can't help but interject, "No, Morgan, you didn't." How many times has my mom talked to all of us girls about being smart with boys, especially strange boys that we don't know? We always make fun of her because she talks to us like we are going out with guys all the time when in reality, none of us has ever dated or kissed a guy.

When Morgan is silent, I realize she doesn't need my judgment right now. She needs her friend that has her back no matter what. I tell her, "I'm sorry, it doesn't matter now. Tell me what happened."

"I know your mom always tells us to be so careful and what NOT to do—" It's like she is reading my mind. "But I wasn't thinking. I was so mad and hurt by my dad. I walked over to the hotel and met him in the lobby. He asked me if I wanted to come to his room."

This feels like too much, and I am so scared of what Morgan is going to tell me about what happened to her. I mean, I know we are teenagers, but really, none of us have even had our first kiss. And now, here is Morgan telling me about meeting a guy in a hotel. I don't know if I want her to go on.

She continues, "Your mom would have been proud of me. I told him no and that I was totally fine to hang outside by the pool with him. He was a bit weird about that but then seemed to be fine. We hung out and talked, and he seemed like a really nice guy. He asked me if I wanted to have my first kiss, and it just felt like such good timing to meet a sweet guy and have a bit of a distraction from my ruined summer vacation. I told him okay. He leaned in and kissed me, and I was so excited to tell you guys about it. I even thought that maybe I could get a picture with him and send it to you to show you the cute guy I had my first kiss with."

Morgan spills the beans before I can even ask her why it was such a disaster. "Just when I thought it was a magical first-kiss moment, his cousins burst from behind the bushes with freaking confetti cannons and cameras. They shot them right in our faces, and suddenly, the pool was a mess of paper shreds, and I had confetti all over my hair and clothes. It turns out this guy and his cousins had set up the entire thing, cameras and all. He stood up, flashed this infuriatingly smug grin, and said, 'Hope your first kiss was explosive!' Then he looks at his cousin holding the camera and says something about 'liking and subscribing.'"

As Morgan recounts this, my free hand shoots up to cover my gaping mouth. I've seen some absurd pranks with confetti cannons online, but nothing this heartbreakingly humiliating.

A mixture of horror and relief floods over me. I'm terrified by the thought that Morgan actually kissed a random guy who turned out to be such a creep, but I'm equally grateful that she didn't get hurt. The situation could have escalated into something far more dangerous. My mind doesn't even dare venture to the 'what-ifs' that follow.

"I'm just so relieved you're okay," I manage to say.

Morgan sighs, "That's not the worst part. The video the cousins recorded was up on YouTube almost instantly. Colby from school even messaged me with the link, asking, 'Is this you?'"

The thought of that video going viral at school leaves me nauseated. Morgan could forever be stamped with the cringe-inducing nickname of the "Confetti Kisser." I can feel my own cheeks flush with secondhand embarrassment.

Just when I think she's on the verge of tears, she flips the script. "Lucky for me, my dad isn't just an idiot dad who wants to marry crazy women; he's also a big-time lawyer. I rushed back to the beach house and told him what had happened. Despite Michelle's objections, we got into the car and drove straight to that hotel. I wasn't there for the entire confrontation because Dad had me wait in the lobby. But what I do know is that the video has been taken down, and the hotel kicked that whole obnoxious family out."

A sigh of relief escapes my lips. I can't help but wonder how many people had seen it before it was pulled down. A small, morbid part of me is curious to watch it, too. Shaking off that thought, I realize the significance of what Morgan went through.

"I don't think that should count as your first kiss. You totally deserve a do-over," I try to console her.

She laughs softly, regret coming through her words. "That's the thing about firsts, though. There are no do-overs. They're a one-time-only deal."

I know she's right. I know there aren't any do-overs for first kisses, first loves. I wish I could be there right now and hug her. I tell her that. She says, "I do too. But more than a hug, I need your help figuring out what to do about the whole Auntie Michelle situation."

We talk for another hour. As much as Morgan wants to come home and run away from being there, she knows that if she does, it is almost inevitable that her dad and Michelle will get married. But, if she stays, she can do her best to show her dad what a huge mistake it would be.

We trade some half-hearted schemes about how to "Parent Trap" Michelle, but Morgan says she wants to marinate on the ideas and also hear any zany plans Celeste might cook up. I tell her to also binge a couple of the *Gossip Girl* episodes where Blair and Serena cook up their own schemes, and she promises to rewatch them again. Just as we're about to say our goodbyes, Morgan's tone changes.

"Noli," she says solemnly, "your first kiss doesn't have to be perfect, but it should belong to a perfect moment. Don't cave to any sort of pressure. It should happen with someone you genuinely like, whenever you want it. It shouldn't be a checkbox to tick or a trend to follow."

As our FaceTime ends and I lay the phone aside, Morgan's advice doesn't just linger; it resonates. I find myself engulfed in a silence that fills the room. I can't shake the feeling that Morgan's parting words were more for me than they were a general piece of advice.

She must have sensed my secret envy, my itch to join her and Addy in the 'kissed someone' club. I've been silently wrestling with this growing fear of being the only one left in the sandbox while everyone else moves on to more grown-up playgrounds.

I ponder how easily I could let my first kiss be an accidental slip, a stumble on the path of growing up, rather than a genuine connection. Should it just happen in the spur of the moment as an answer to peer pressure and FOMO? Or should it be as meticulously planned as one of my mom's extravagant events, each detail contributing to a larger-than-life experience?

Caught in my thoughts, I can't help but wish for a guide, someone who's been through the maze and come out the other side. And that's when it hits me; perhaps I do know someone like that.

Instinctively I start texting.

Me: What was your first kiss like?

The instant I hit 'send,' regret floods over me. If only texts came with an 'undo' button! Time ticks by slowly, and a part of me hopes that Jack will overlook my text altogether. Just when I think I'm off the hook, those three ominous dots pop up, signaling he's typing a response. How could I have been so naïve? You don't casually text your crush to ask about their first kiss. Except, in that fleeting moment, I'd somehow forgotten my feelings for Jack because I merely wanted to ask my friend.

Jack: My first kiss was with a girl named Claire at my friend Tim's birthday party. Her friends had told me that she liked me, and my friends were egging me on to kiss her. I found her at the party and asked her if she wanted to follow me. She did, and we kissed in Tim's parents' bathroom. It was ok. She had really dry lips and braces.

I don't know why, but I feel a twinge of jealousy rising in me. This isn't the first time I've heard about Jack kissing a girl, but for some reason, it feels different this time. I think back to when we were kids, and I remember Jack telling me about kissing Claire. I read the text a couple more times and then respond.

Me: Would you do it again? If you had your first kiss to do over would you choose to have that same first kiss?

Jack: Yeah. She was nice and honestly it was cool to be the first kid in our friend group that kissed a girl.

I am bothered by his response. He kissed her just to look cool in front of his friends.

Me: Did it mean anything to you?

Jack: IDK what you mean??

Me: Like was it special?

Jack starts to tease me, and I can't tell if he is trying to be flirty or if he is trying to dodge the question.

Jack: Little lady, are you looking to find info
so you can have your FIRST kiss?

Jack: Who's the guy?

He texts fast.

Jack: OR girl, no judgment! ;)

I can't believe I came to Jack about this. He is dodging my question, and at this point, I don't even know if I want to hear his answer. It seems like kissing isn't a big deal to him. I wonder if that's how he would feel if we kissed. Would I be just another girl to go and tell his friends about?

Me: Never mind.

It takes Jack about ten minutes before he texts me again.

Jack: kind of weird to text about it. Let's talk
when I get home.

I roll my eyes. Of course. He doesn't want to text about it, and when he gets home, I know he won't want to talk about it either. I don't know what I was looking for, but that definitely wasn't it. I toss my phone on my bed. Just then, it pings again. It's not the tone for Jack or my besties. I go over and grab my phone again to see who it is. It's Xander.

Xander: Hey cute girl! Just finishing up
camp.

Xander: Can I come and see you when I get
home?

I smile. Xander has been texting me quite a bit since he got to soccer camp. He is always sending me funny pics of him doing crazy stuff. It feels like texting Xander is my class in learning to flirt. He is cheesy and sends cute things, and since reading his note about liking me, this feels like the first step to maybe something bigger. I send flirty, bold texts back to him because, honestly, it feels a bit like I'm getting back at Jack for something, not sure what. Of course, Xander is so cute and knows exactly what to say to keep me smiling and interested, and I have to remind myself that we aren't anything right now, just a possibility.

I can't believe I do it, but I send a text back to Xander. I don't answer his questions; I ask my own question.

Me: What was your first kiss like?

He responds instantly before I can start to be mortified that I asked him.

Xander: My first kiss was with Kennedy in
the math building one day after school last
year. It was awesome.

I'm surprised that Xander is being so candid. I'm unsure if he is being honest, but it seems he is. As much as I hate hearing that he was, in fact, hooking up with Kennedy last year, it's cool that he is being honest.

Xander: We were just sitting there waiting for our teacher to come back from the bathroom to grade our tests. We were goofing around, and I said something about how pretty Kennedy looked. She leaned over and kissed me.

Xander: It was fast, and the teacher came back right after that. After our tests were done, we went outside and kissed behind the math building longer.

Xander: I like it so much I ended up kissing Kennedy, McKinley and a couple of other girls quickly after that. Just NCMO you know.

Xander: Kissing's fun but I realized I want to be kissing girls I am interested in, not just kissing to kiss.

Xander: What was your first kiss like?

I am taking all of Xander's texts in. He is being honest with me. I don't know if that makes it better or worse. Maybe what Celeste said about Xander just being a guy that wasn't ready for a relationship was real. Maybe he is hinting that he is ready to be in something more than just making out with people.

In our friend group with all the guys and girls, we never talked about dating or kissing. It just wasn't something that came up when we were all together. I knew, of course, that Chris had kissed Addy, but really had no idea if Evan, Xander, or Noah had ever kissed anyone. I decide since Xander is being honest with me, I should be honest with him.

Me: Haven't had my first kiss yet

> Xander: I know someone who has a huge
> crush on you. I think you should have him be
> your first kiss. ;)

> Me: Really? Who?

> Xander: Let me see you when I get home,
> and I will tell you in person.

> Xander: I'll beg and plead with you if I
> have to!

I smile. I'm texting Xander back when my phone pings in Jack's tone, and a text from him comes through. I have to switch gears. What am I doing texting Jack and Xander about kissing at the same time?

> Jack: Noli, your first kiss should be amazing.
> It should be fireworks on the fourth of July. It
> should feel like the time you hit a hole-in-one
> on the golf course. It should be a mixture of
> complete elation and excitement. I want that
> for you.

> Jack: It doesn't matter what my first kiss
> was. It matters what you want. I want you to
> be adored by whoever he is.

For some reason, this is the response I was wanting. I wanted to hear that it was okay for me to want fireworks. I wanted to hear that it wasn't about hooking up in your friend's parents' bathroom or behind the math building. I wanted to know if I shouldn't expect my first kiss to end up on YouTube or get a confetti cannon shot at my face. I just wanted my guy friend to realize how important first kisses are, even if it wasn't that way for him.

Me to Jack: thank you Jack. That is exactly
what I want.

Me to Xander: I think you should come over
on the Fourth of July. The fireworks will be
epic. ;)

After I send out both texts, I question what just happened. Did I send the wrong text to the wrong guy? Isn't Xander the guy that should be making me see fireworks on the Fourth? Liking Jack was just a weekend thing, right? These texts are just flirty fun between friends. I start confusing myself about what is supposed to take place this weekend. I decide it can't be settled right now, but whatever happens over the Fourth, I tell myself, will be exactly like Jack said: complete elation and excitement with the right guy.

7

My eyelids flutter open well before the sound of my alarm can pierce the quiet of my bedroom. Jack is coming back from soccer camp today. I wish that I could be there to pick him up with my mom, but I can't miss the golf tournament that Dad signed me up for. Coach Gus, my private golf coach, is adamant about me arriving early to warm up, so there is no way I can see Jack. I even daydream of sneaking away to see Xander really quick, but there is actually no way that will ever happen. I have to be patient and wait for the Fourth.

As I splash water onto my face and coax a toothbrush across my teeth, I find my mind calculating how long the tournament will last and how much time I'll miss with Jack at home. If everything goes according to plan, Jack will be home two hours before I'm able to come home and see him. I keep telling myself that is the perfect amount of time for my sisters to see him and have my mom spoil him. By the time I get home, Jack will be excited to see me, and we can start our fabulous Fourth of July weekend.

My phone buzzing interrupts my thoughts, causing a jolt of

excitement. Is it a dumb GIF from Jack? Or maybe one of those very flirty texts from Xander? I have no idea what to expect. I freeze mid-brush, my toothbrush dangling from my mouth, as I reach out for my phone and swipe the screen.

It's not Jack. It's Xander. Last night was so much fun texting Xander. I had been so much more flirty than I ever would have in person. I wonder if I can be that bold when I see him over the Fourth. Do I want to? I just keep going back to the note he wrote and put in my yearbook. He likes me. I feel like I don't have a crush on Xander anymore. What would I call it? Maybe infatuation? Yes, that's what it is. I am infatuated with Xander. I want to be with Xander in person and see what happens. See if there is that flirty intensity that I feel in our texts.

His raw, honest texts about his first kiss has me more intrigued than disgusted. I think about all of the selfies he has sent me over the past couple of weeks. The boy knows his good side! I haven't told my friends anything because I don't want them judging me. I feel like I am still keeping my promise to Morgan, but I also haven't wanted them to know that our texts have gotten. Well, let's just say I still haven't sent nudes. But here I am, feeling like I am right back to the feelings I had for him at the beginning of freshman year and really needing my friends to weigh in on what I should do. Unlocking my phone, I open the message.

> Xander: Hey Noli girl! I went to bed thinking about you.

> Xander: Can't wait to see you on the Fourth.

He sends me a pic of him doing a kissy face at the camera. I can't help but roll my eyes. Oh, Xander. Such a charmer. For a quick second I wonder how many other girls received the exact same set of texts. But I push that aside. That's not my Xander anymore.

I swiftly screenshot the messages, wanting to share it with

Morgan and Celeste. They would die laughing when I ask if I should kiss Xander right when I see him. Right before I hit send, I remember that I won't send this message out until after the fourth, just like I promised Morgan.

I place my phone down and return to brushing my teeth, contemplating what to reply to Xander. I wonder if I should be flirty back. Maybe the right move is to act like I don't care if he shows up or not on the Fourth or say something about how much I want to see him. I don't know! The more I think about it, the more confused I get. Maybe I should text Morgan and Celeste and let them know what's going on.

The thought of Morgan calling me to yell in the phone has me decide against it. I text Xander back.

> Me: Hey handsome! I can't wait to see you

I feel a surge of pride for being so audacious in my texts with Xander lately. Initially, it felt like a counterstrike, a silent declaration of, "See, I can play this game too." But, as I reflect, I realize it's really been about me learning to navigate the world of flirty texts and male attention. I'd likely clam up in person, my voice drowning in the allure of Xander's smile. For now, though, I can relish this digital courage. On a whim, I snap a goofy selfie, puckering up for the camera with a ridiculous smattering of toothpaste on my lips. It's not flirty; it's fun, and that's exactly the note I want to hit.

> Xander quickly responds: HOT!

> Xander: you know how fireworks light up the
> sky? That's kinda how I feel when we text.

> Xander: What do you say we turn this spark
> into a flame?

I laugh out loud in my bathroom. It is so cheesy. Like so bad. I send him a quick reply with a firework emoji and decide to leave him hanging until I see him. I have to focus on golf.

Xander sends me a question mark, then a pleading emoji, followed by a selfie of him making a pouty face. Why does he have to be so dang cute? I am just about to silence my phone when another text comes through. It's from Noah!

> Noah: Why did the golfer bring two pairs of pants?
>
> Me: I don't know…why?
>
> Noah: In case he got a hole-in-one! HAHAHAHAHA
>
> Noah: CRUSH the competition today!

I can't believe that Noah remembered my tournament today. And with how things have been so weird between us this summer, I thought he wouldn't care at all. It makes me so happy to see that he remembered and texted me. I text him back.

> Me: I can't crush anything today. I have a dumb friend who distracts me with dumb jokes. I have lost all motivation to golf.
>
> Noah: OH NO! I will be over in 4 hrs to revive you.
>
> Me: I miss you!!!! thx for the msg.

I don't hear back from Noah, and now I am worried that telling him I miss him was the wrong move. The thought has my stomach in knots. I don't know what I did, but it seems like I just can't get it right with him this summer. It reminds me of Jack last summer, and my heart drops.

My thoughts shift fast from Noah to Xander and Jack. It suddenly hits me that I will be seeing both Xander and Jack on the Fourth of July. Why had I not thought that through before this moment?! I have never had any of my school friends over during the Fourth party. They are all out at different places, so it had never crossed my mind. Plus, I have never had any guy friends that I would even consider asking to come to the party.

When Xander mentioned hanging out over the Fourth, I completely spaced Jack being here. Xander doesn't know we've got family friends over, and Jack's never seen me hang out with any guy friends. I think about Jack. I think about Xander. The last thing I want is to juggle my two guy friends and have to play hostess to both. All I want this weekend is to have the best Fourth of July holiday that I have ever had. Unsure of what to do, I glance at the clock and see I am running late. I can sort this all out after the golf tournament.

Coach Gus is going to be irritated that I'm not on time. I see him waiting patiently in his car outside as I rush downstairs. Clutching my golf clubs, phone, and purse and practically tripping over my own feet, I make my way out the door. I must look like a total disaster. Coach Gus pops the trunk open, and as I struggle to load all my gear into his car, he yells out from the driver's seat, "Winners don't fumble. They maintain impeccable care of themselves and their equipment."

I push the button to shut the trunk and hop into his car. He doesn't miss a beat and continues, "Winners are punctual to achieve the right mental and physical state."

Knowing that no excuse will appease him, I don't even bother to try. Instead, I aim for some comic relief. "Sorry, I was busy texting a boy who I thought would be my first kiss. Now I'm not so sure he deserves it."

I don't even get a smirk. Coach Gus swivels around to glare at me. "None of them will be worth it," he grumbles before starting the car and steering us toward the tournament.

The initial minutes in the car are filled with his customary pre-game lecture. It's a speech I've heard so often I could probably recite it verbatim, but I keep my focus. I know if I get lost in my phone, there's a real possibility he'll snatch it and fling it out of the window. So I listen attentively, mentally mirroring his speech, nodding at all the right moments. Once he's finished, he says, "Now get in the zone!"

This is his way of saying that it's time to listen to my custom Spotify playlist. Coach Gus and Dad are always discussing the optimal training strategies, which led them to compile a Spotify playlist for me. It's the worst. It's full of dated tracks from Gus's younger years, a handful of strange motivational speeches, and one section that's simply the sounds of wind and bells. I listened to it once right before a tournament and had the most atrocious game of my life. I tried to explain to Coach Gus that the playlist actually hurt my game, but he told me it was a secret that only the best did and knew how to tap into the music to make it unlock their next level. I call bullcrap. But, not wanting to have that conversation, I let them think that listening to their insane playlist is my "pregame routine."

I put in my AirPods and switch to my own handpicked list. I start to scroll through my phone, browsing pictures, texting my friends, and occasionally checking the single social media platform my parents permit me to use. It's hardly thrilling, but it provides a tiny window into the everyday lives of my friends. I send Celeste a selfie and tell her I am headed to a tournament. She sends one back and says she just finished killing off a character in her novel and that it was "delicious." Sometimes I wonder about her. But hey, she's an award-winning writer.

We arrive at Glenwild Golf Club, today's tournament venue. This is one of my favorite courses in Utah, but it's also one that demands a considerable chunk of my mental energy to perform well. I realize it might have been a better use of my time to mentally prepare during our drive up to Park City. But that's water under the bridge now.

We're here, and I've got barely ten minutes before I need to be out on the green, warming up.

Golf and I, well, we've got a complicated relationship going on. I didn't exactly get into golf because it was my dream or anything, but because it was my great escape from all the other sports my parents tried to stuff me into. When I was just a little kid, like five or six, Mom decided dance was my thing. It turns out that I was so bad that the lady running the studio ended up giving Mom her money back for the whole season, hinting that maybe I should give Cheer a shot. Yeah, cheer wasn't much of a hit either. Over time, I got tossed around different sports like a hot potato, but none of them clicked. Team sports just aren't my jam, and stuff like dance, cheer, or ice skating—yeah, not my cup of tea, either.

I even tried horseback riding lessons, but horses are so scary. This one time, during a lesson, my horse just decided he was done for the day. Out of nowhere, he went from walking to lying down for a good ol' dirt roll. Lucky for me, my quick-thinking instructor saw the horse's mood swing, darted over, and yanked me off the saddle just in time. That episode pretty much slammed the door on any future horse lessons.

My golf career started one random morning when I was ten. Mom had to dash off to Jazzy's dance competition, and our babysitter totally bailed on us. With no one to look after Poppy and me, Dad decided to take us along to his tee time at the country club since he wasn't going to pass up his golf game.

Poppy spent the morning chasing butterflies and playing with golf balls while I just sat there, watching Dad tee off the first couple of holes. Curiosity got the best of me by the third hole, and I asked Dad if I could give it a shot. He and his golf buddy laughed, thought it was adorable, and set me up with the kid clubs the clubhouse girl had given me "just in case" I felt like swinging.

And what do you know? I smacked that ball straight down the fairway from the men's tee box. My dad and his friend were shocked.

They figured it was just a lucky swing, but I kept whacking that ball with decent accuracy for a little kid who'd never played before.

Dad came home super pumped that day, telling Mom about his newfound golf buddy. The attention was nice, and hanging out with Dad was all I really wanted to do. So I didn't have the guts to tell him I found the whole golf thing pretty boring at first. Of all the sports they tried to shove me into, this was the one I hated the least. So I just went with it.

Today I am the reigning top girl golfer in the state. Heck, if they let me play against the boys, I'd still be in the top ten. But of course, they won't. Golf comes naturally to me, and quite honestly, I have learned to love it. I love being outside, and I love that each course and hole is like a new puzzle that I have to figure out. And the puzzles are always changing based on the conditions outside, the equipment you use, etc. This is my sport, and I know it, but there is a downside to it.

I used to get all caught up in competing, and I would let it turn me into a crazy person. Tournaments made me all jumpy and jittery. Some girls even try to psych you out during the games just to mess up your performance. This one girl named Juliet had this long blond braid, and she always freaked me out. Her dad was some sort of pro athlete, and she'd always brag about how he taught her to drain her opponents mentally. I was always on edge around her.

Then, at one tournament, we were paired together. I saw her and her dad off to the side just before teeing off. They didn't see me, but I heard him shouting at her, saying really awful things. It hit me then that no game is worth that kind of stress, and I would be broken if my dad spoke to me that way. I couldn't help but think, "Where does all this intense pressure and competition have us headed? Going pro?"

Maybe for a couple of us, but not for most of us. And as I sat there and listened to this former pro athlete rip his daughter to shreds, I realized I didn't want to be part of this full-time. So I made up my mind to just chill, enjoy the game, do my best, and not sweat the small stuff.

I played coolly and confidently in that tournament because I realized it was all made up. It wasn't real life, and this one tournament wasn't as intense as everyone made it out to be. Even when Juliet tried pulling the same stunt her dad did on her with me, something changed in me. I felt sorry for her, not intimidated by her. After I snagged the win, she walked up to me and said, "You play a really good game. I'm sorry about the things I said."

Once she realized she couldn't shake me, she never tried again. After that, she was my favorite person to get paired with, but this summer, she has been absent from all of the tournaments, and I wonder if she quit playing altogether.

Dad and Coach Gus wish I'd take it more seriously. They've got a chunk of their pride hinging on my performance, but that's their issue, not mine. I'm here to play the game my way and to remember that, in the end, it's all just pretend anyway.

I'm on the practice putting green, with headphones on. Coach Gus believes I'm vibing to his eclectic playlist, but actually, I'm listening to Taylor Swift crooning about regrettable romances. My phone pings—a new message. I know if Coach Gus sees me pull out my phone, it's game over.

Yet, the curiosity is killing me. Did Xander text some cute message? Is Jack home and wondering where I am? Did Noah text me back? I know I won't be able to focus until I find out who it is. I glance around—Coach Gus is nowhere in sight. I saunter over to my golf bag, where my phone is stashed, and retrieve it. It's Jack! My face lights up as I lift the phone to unlock it.

Just then, I hear, "What do you think you're doing?" Coach Gus is standing right beside me, hand extended for me to surrender my phone.

Reluctance pulls at me; I don't want to give up my phone. I lie. "The playlist ended. I needed to rewind it." I struggle to keep a straight face as I feed him this line. Of course, it's not a thing to rewind a playlist, but I remember that back in Coach Gus's heyday, they actually had to rewind their tapes.

He misses my fib, yet he remains unyielding about the phone. "You shouldn't need to rewind. I designed that playlist to last fourteen hours."

I let out a small pout. "Can I just check my messages?" Clinging to my phone, I hope for a rare moment of leniency from Coach Gus.

His stern gaze pins me down. "Absolutely not. I won't let the outside world and its happenings disrupt my player's mental state."

How do you convince a seventy-year-old man that the 'outside world' will indeed disrupt your mental state if you don't check your phone? How do you explain the impact of not knowing whether a certain soccer-playing boy is casually lounging around your house shirtless while you're trying to concentrate on hitting a tiny white ball into a hole in the grass?

Well, you don't. I exhale deeply and surrender my phone to Coach Gus. It seems I won't know where Jack is lounging around shirtless until I get home.

Coach Gus says, "I need you on your A game today. You are paired up with Juliet."

To Coach Gus, this means I have to prepare for war. Juliet and her dad are Coach Gus's least favorite players. He hates seeing Juliet's bulked-up dad on the sidelines at each hole, yelling something or another to her. He used to caddy for her until he got banned for life. Juliet said it was the best day when that happened because she could get her actual coach to be her caddy.

I smile, thinking that it will be nice to catch up with Juliet and see what she's been up to this summer. She has been absent from the recreational tournaments this summer, so I haven't seen her since high school golf got over. I knew the high school season was hard on her, but because I practiced on my school's boy's team and are in different school circuits, we never played together.

I got the number one spot for my school circuit and even got an article written about me being included in the boy's team. Juliet didn't even finish in the top ten on the girl's list. So when I didn't see her show up for summer tournaments, I worried I might never see her again. I'm excited to see that she is here and we are paired.

We're almost up, so Coach Gus and I move toward the first tee. Coach Gus is decidedly traditional. Whenever I play in a tournament, he's my caddy, and he insists on wearing the classic white jumpsuit that few caddies don these days.

Consequently, we stand out like a beacon. All the other girls' caddies are attired in standard golf shirts and shorts. Meanwhile, here I come, accompanied by my caddie decked out in his crisp, bleach-white jumpsuit. I spot Juliet and give her a wave. She returns it, but when she notices Coach Gus, she can't contain her laughter. She once told me that he looks like a mechanic in his jumpsuit.

Coach Gus shoots her a glare, then turns to me, warning, "Don't let her get into your head with her mental games. Maintain your distance. Only engage in conversation about the golf course. Don't let her lure you into thinking you two are friends."

He is always so dramatic about playing golf and the other players. I respect Coach Gus, and I would never do anything to be disrespectful to him. But I am also here for the next several hours, and I am going to play and speak however I want to. I simply give Coach Gus a head nod and make my way over to Juliet with Coach Gus behind me. I give Juliet a big hug and say, "Hey, girl! What have you been up to?"

She hugs me back and tells me she took a break to get away and just chill for a bit. As we chat, I catch a glimpse of Coach Gus in my peripheral vision, uttering a low growl—his signature signal of disapproval. I assure Juliet we'll catch up later and then position myself next to him.

Juliet takes her turn first. As she lines up in the tee box, I can't help but notice a distinct change. I've watched the girls in this state play so many times that I've become intimately familiar with their individual swings.

But Juliet's is different now. Her stance has become more

assertive, her alignment with the ball more precise than I've ever seen before. With a swift stroke, she sends the ball sailing down the fairway. The modest crowd gasps in admiration at the impressive distance she's achieved. Her dad yells encouragingly, "That's it, baby girl!" Then, turning to face me, he throws out a taunt, "You've no idea what kind of storm you're in for."

Coach Gus swiftly turns on his heels and retorts, "Be careful, John. You've already lost your privileges as a caddy. You wouldn't want to be booted from the course altogether."

Juliet's dad merely laughs and dismisses Coach Gus with a wave. As I move toward the tee box, I pass by Juliet and give her a smile of approval. "Great shot."

With a smug smile, she responds with a simple "Thanks" before striding off the tee box.

I set myself up and take my shot, landing on the fairway roughly where I usually do on this course. Noticeably, though, it's significantly behind where Juliet's ball ended up.

Juliet surges ahead by three strokes as we proceed through the first few holes. Her game has transformed drastically, and she's playing unlike anything I've seen from her before. She's demonstrating increased strength and superior accuracy, and if she keeps up this pace, she's likely to crush us all by a substantial lead.

She thunders the ball down the fairway at the third tee box, nearly landing a hole-in-one. The small crowd, which has been gradually swelling, goes wild. I see more golfers leaving the clubhouse to come down and watch Juliet's performance.

As we cross paths, Juliet nonchalantly drops, "Hope you're prepared to relinquish your golf queen status." She moves closer, lowering her voice to a whisper. "Oh, did I forget to mention? I took time off for an intensive golf training camp... specifically designed to annihilate you." She strides off with a smug tilt of her head and a smirk.

My previous feelings of simply having fun and not taking golf too seriously vanish instantly. I can feel a wave of nervousness crashing over me, and my blood begins to boil. I thought Juliet and I were friends, but it appears she's been pretending all along. This no longer feels like a simple round of golf, like I've been telling myself. Instead, it feels deeply personal, and I can't believe I've been ignoring Coach Gus every time he warned me not to trust people on the course.

I have to pause and gather my breath. I know if I try to swing right now, it won't get me where I want to go. I signal Coach Gus to come over with my water bottle. He immediately senses something's off. He hands me the bottle, and we turn our backs to the crowd. Taking a swig of water, I manage to mutter quietly, "She played me. She's been training all summer just to knock me off my game."

Coach Gus heaves a big sigh. "I suspected this. When she didn't show for the first two tournaments, I figured she'd quit or be out training somewhere else." He takes a moment to collect his thoughts. "Here's what we do: You play the best round that you can today. You observe her. See what's changed about her game. Keep meticulous mental notes. You might lose today, but we'll regroup and devise a new game plan."

It stings to hear Coach Gus already predicting my loss, but that's one of the reasons I respect him. He's brutally honest and is renowned for his game-planning abilities.

Coach Gus gives me a solid nod as he looks into my eyes. In that moment I realize I have taken him for granted. All these years, he has been training a bratty little kid who has natural talent and ability but who has been too stubborn to treat the game with the seriousness it deserves. Of course, I've listened when he instructed me on my golf swing, but I've largely disregarded all the advice and training he's imparted about the mental aspect of the sport. I can't help it. I am frustrated at being played. A tear slips out and down my cheek.

Quickly, Coach Gus intervenes. "Don't you start crying now. That won't do you any good, and if Juliet sees it, she'll think she has already won." He points down the fairway as if we're strategizing where to hit the ball.

He instructs me, "You play the game you know to play. You have a love for this course, and you know it well. Don't focus on Juliet's game; you play your game. Now, I want you to act like you are sneezing and wipe your eyes. Let's get through this day."

I do as he says and pretend to sneeze several times and dry my eyes I guess Juliet and I won't be catching up and dishing about our summer crushes anytime soon.

8

The rest of the tournament is brutal. Juliet is the worst. She reverts back to what her dad taught her and taunts and teases me when only she and I can hear it. Worse than that, she plays amazingly well. I stay a couple of shots behind her, but it is a challenge. I am exhausted by the sixteenth hole and just want to go home. But I have to finish this game.

We are waiting at the sixteenth hole for the group ahead of us to finish up when I hear Juliet say, "Who's that hottie in the crowd? He's definitely not here to golf."

Funny thing about girls' golf. There are only two types of guys that ever show up to watch us golf: boyfriends of someone playing in the tournament and retired golfers who are probably set to tee off after the tournament. We never get crowds of cute guys our age who decide to spend their days watching girls golf.

Hearing there is a cute guy. He is probably following a girl in front of us, but after they finish up hitting off the tee box, I hear Juliet say, "He must be here for me." She smiles in the direction of the guy and waves.

I can't help but be intrigued. I look in the direction she's pointing. At first, all I see is the usual gathering of spectators, but then my eyes catch sight of a familiar figure. My heart leaps into my throat as I recognize him.

He's definitely not dressed for golf, clad in a soccer jersey, board shorts, and slides. It's Jack. When he sees me, he gives me a huge smile and waves. Jack is standing next to my dad, who looks concerned. He probably got the rundown of my play today from someone else, probably Juliet's dad, and he doesn't look too pleased.

I smile weakly at Jack, give a head nod to my dad, and turn back around. Juliet is glaring at me. "He is here with you?" She is pissed. I can't contain my excitement and nervousness that Jack is here watching me golf.

I may not be able to win the tournament today, but maybe I have won something even better. I smile at her. "Yep, he's my boyfriend. He came to watch me play."

I lie just to piss her off more. It just doesn't sound as good to explain to her that Jack is a family friend. She scoffs, "Too bad he came to see you lose."

She turns around and makes her way up to the tee box. I roll my eyes and realize she is right. Jack has come on the worst possible day to watch me golf. Jack and I have played with our dads at the club course, but Jack has never watched me play in a tournament. I am mortified that he came today. Juliet smashes the ball, and I look over to see both my dad's and Jack's mouths open in astonishment at how far it goes. We switch places, and Juliet says, "At least one of us can give your boyfriend something to be impressed by."

Now I'm the one who is pissed. I take my place in the tee box, but instead of squaring up like I always do, I match Juliet's stance to the golf ball. I have been studying her since the first hole, and I think I understand why she is standing the way she does in relation to the ball. I hear her dad laugh in the crowd and say, "Good luck trying to hit like that on your first try."

I tune out their voices, my focus narrowing to the ball in front of me, the club in my hand, and the fairway ahead. For a moment, I picture myself in a completely different scenario, practicing on the course back home. No taunts, no laughter. Just me, my club, and the ball.

With a deep breath, I take a backswing and then strike the ball with as much force as I can muster. There's a sweet sound of the club hitting the ball and then silence. I see the ball flying, cutting through the air. It lands on the fairway, much farther than I've hit all day. The ball has gone several yards past Juliet's ball.

The crowd bursts into applause. Juliet's dad goes silent. I can hear Coach Gus let out a noise from the side. I can't tell if it was excitement or frustration. I look at Juliet, who is wearing an expression of shock and annoyance.

Then I glance at Jack. He's grinning, his hazel eyes twinkling with amusement and pride. Suddenly, despite the challenging game and Juliet's hostility, I find myself grinning too.

I snort a laugh and turn to hand my club to Coach Gus. I realize just then that he is furious with me. He is trying not to yell, which means that his voice gets low. "Don't you ever hit like that again. Do you hear me? If I see you do that, I will quit as your coach."

The threat at the end catches me off guard. I don't know what to say. I feel embarrassed that I am getting reamed by my coach in front of Jack. My cheeks flash hot, and I simply nod at him. I want to yell back, "Don't you see what I just did? Aren't you happy for me?" But I know that would be crossing the line with Coach Gus.

I make my way down the fairway, with Jack following on the sidelines. I keep stealing glances at him, and each time I do, I find that he is looking at me, smiling and ready to laugh and say something just he and I will get. I have to remind myself I am almost done. I can talk to him afterward. With Jack there, my motivation has changed. Right now, I have to focus on winning.

On the seventeenth hole, I play to perfection. I do everything that Coach Gus tells me to. I have gone from thinking I was going to lose this tournament to having a pretty great shot at winning it all. I can't believe it! Juliet is fuming, but I don't care. We aren't friends, and I'm no longer here to be nice. The final hole is all we have left, and it has come down to the two of us vying for first place.

Juliet and I are tied. She steps up first and hits the ball so cleanly and beautifully that I can't help but be impressed. As much as I know her swing, I still am dying to know where she trained and her conditioning schedule. On top of her new golf swing, she also looks leaner and more muscular than I have ever seen her before. It's like it was a full transformation wherever she went.

I take a deep breath before entering the tee box. It has come down to this. I'm used to the pressure but am desperate to win in front of Jack. Coach Gus has always been incredible when it comes to coaching me, but today, he and I aren't on the same page. He wants me to finish; I want to win.

I know this hole. It's long, and if I hit the ball with my usual swing, I know I will be a stroke behind Juliet. The new swing that Juliet does would help me stay with her swing for swing. I think I can win it from there because I am a better putter than she is. I have a moment to pause and decide what to do.

I glance over at Jack. He winks and sticks his tongue out at me, and in that moment, I know what to do. I get up in the tee box, take a deep breath, and then line up the new way I have seen Juliet hit. I swing, and suddenly I feel a sharp pain in my arm. It feels like razor blades are cutting my shoulder. The hit was solid, and the ball has gone farther than Juliet's. My ball lands near the hole, and I can see how close I am to winning.

But the pain is immense, and I cry out and drop my club. Coach Gus rushes over to me. "Damn it, Magnolia!" he says as he cradles my arm, and I wince in pain. "I told you not to hit like that. That is a dangerous swing, and it cannot be done without putting the golfer at risk."

My dad and Jack are there now. I start crying it hurts so bad. Another dad from the crowd who is here watching his daughter comes over. I recognize him from the country club. It's Dr. Angus. He asks my dad if he can examine me real quick and see what's up. Dad agrees, and Dr. Angus moves my arm a bit. Pain shoots through me, and I see stars for a moment.

Dr. Angus's expression hardens as he tells us what he is seeing, his voice steady and resolute. "This is what I was afraid of," he says. "The way these two girls have been hitting the ball has been concerning to me. The position places an abnormal strain on the rotator cuff. It's not designed to withstand such pressure. I am worried she has torn it."

Dad lets out a curse under his breath, his face draining of color. Coach Gus storms off, hurling something in frustration. I catch Juliet and her father from the corner of my eye. Their triumphant smiles and celebratory high-fives churn my stomach. Did they plan this from the start? Did they predict that I would try to copy her swing? I can't be sure, but I do know that they're finding joy in my pain. Jack has hung back, and I find his face in the crowd. I can't tell what the expression is on his face. It looks like he is mad at me. But why would he be upset? I'm the one who got hurt.

The tournament official approaches, his question clear and cutting. "Are you withdrawing from the tournament?"

My father, his voice strained with worry, is quick to say yes, but I interrupt him. "I can still putt with one arm," I insist.

Despite everything, I'm determined to finish this tournament, and I believe I can still pull off a win.

My dad is skeptical. "Are you sure you want to do this, Noli?"

I nod. I'm sure. I always finish what I start. My dad looks around. Coach Gus is standing off to the side, his face completely blank. He picks up my clubs and starts walking down the fairway before I can even start.

Everyone follows him down to where Juliet's ball is. She is just off the green, an easy shot to get it close to the hole. She takes no time at all to hit, and her ball falls mere inches from the hole. It will be an easy three shots to end this hole. In order for me to win, I will need to make the first putt.

I walk over to Coach Gus to grab my putter. I know he is upset with me. I want to try and mend what I have done. I say, "Should be an easy one to get down."

He doesn't say anything. I know I need to apologize. "I'm sorry, Coach Gus. I just really want to win this. Don't you think I should be able to put this down with one putt?"

Coach Gus finally looks at me, "I don't coach anyone who doesn't listen to me. Whether I think you can or can't doesn't matter to you, so why are you asking? Go do whatever it is that you are going to. I'm tired and want to go home."

I'm hurt. My shoulder is burning. I don't need his sulkiness right now. I turn and go up to my ball. I am ten yards out, but I have done a similar shot before and been successful. I line up, my shoulder shoots a pain, and I inhale. It hurts. I try to push it all out and take my swing.

It's a wild swing. I overshoot, and the ball goes three yards past. I hear Juliet's dad whoop and holler. The best I can do now is tie Juliet. At that moment, it hits me. I put myself, my relationship with my coach, and probably other things on the line to win a dumb tournament that doesn't even matter. I remember how this was just a silly tournament at the beginning of the day. When did that change? When did I go into competition blindness? I wanted to show off in front of Jack. I wanted to be superior and have him want me more. I wanted him to be impressed.

Juliet quickly hits her ball in the hole. I have one chance to tie her. I just want this to be over. I line up again, ready to take my shot. I lose focus as I glance over. Juliet is standing next to Jack, whispering to him. Whatever she says makes him smile. I swing, and it feels off, but I guess it would since I am only using one arm. I watched as the ball slowed and lined up perfectly with the hole. Just as it is about to go in, it's like an invisible wall goes up, and the ball stops mere centimeters away from the hole. Juliet has won the tournament by one stroke.

I hear Juliet's dad freak out. He yells, "We have a new reigning golf queen! Juliet, go grab your crown!"

Juliet strolls over to me and says, "I'll be taking this." She raises her hands to the top of my head, plucks an imaginary crown off my head, and places it on her own. She faces the crowd and curtsies, and people laugh and cheer. Even Jack is clapping. I can't stand it. I can't be here anymore.

9

I walk over to Dad. "I want to go home," I tell him.

My shoulder hurts, but my pride hurts more, and I don't want to be here. Everyone congratulates Juliet and gives me these terrible glances of pity and shame.

My dad looks down at me, his jaw set, and for the first time, I think he is mad at me. "You know the rules," he says. "You always ride home with Coach Gus. You two have a lot to discuss."

I feel rejected. I just want my dad. He gives me a small nod and walks back to his car with Jack. I don't think I am Coach Gus's favorite person right now, and I am dreading the ride home. I look around for him but can't find him or my clubs anywhere. I make my way to the parking lot, and I am worried that Coach Gus won't be there. I spot him leaning up against his car, his white caddy outfit gone. He sees me, gets in the car, and starts it. I slink over to the car and get in.

He backs the car out and starts the long drive home. This isn't my first time losing a golf tournament. It's not my first time seeing Coach Gus upset. But this is the first time he is silent in the car. I'm not sure what to do. Do I start talking? What would I even say? I already apologized, but I don't think it mattered. I decide I would rather not talk in the car either, so I stay silent.

I check my phone to distract myself. Jack sent me a message before the tournament had even started. I finally read it.

> Jack: I get to surprise you today! I'm coming
> up to watch you play.

> Jack: I am sure you are going to kill it.

> Jack: That's what elite athletes like you and I
> do! LET'S GO!

At the mention of Jack and me being elite athletes, I silently groan. I guess he has probably demoted me in his mind. That was not the performance of an elite athlete today. In fact, it was the worst I have ever played. I wish Jack hadn't been there. I wish I didn't let Juliet get into my head. Most of all, I wish I had listened to Coach Gus. Coach Angus made me a temporary sling to help support my hurt arm on the way home. It digs into my neck, and anytime I move, pain shoots into my arm and side. I am miserable and keep trying to distract myself with my phone. Who knew that reading texts and scrolling was so hard with only one arm?

After I had read my messages, I glance over at Coach Gus. He always tells me to put my phone away when we are together, but even me reading my text messages hasn't gotten him to say a word to me. I was kind of hoping that when I got my phone out, he would start yelling about the phone. Yelling would feel better than the silence right now.

We ride the entire way down the canyon in silence. It is miserable. When Coach Gus finally pulls up to my house, I see that Dad and Jack are already home. I want to jump out of the car and run to the house. But I know I have to say something to Coach Gus.

"I screwed up big time today," I start. "I'm sorry, and I promise it won't ever happen again."

Coach Gus doesn't turn to look at me but does answer. "The safety of my players is my number one concern. As a coach, I take that very seriously. What you did today was reckless. I don't work with players that don't listen or trust me. Please tell your parents that effective immediately, I will no longer work with you. Good luck in your life, Noli."

I am stunned. How could this be happening? Coach Gus has been my golf coach since the very beginning. He can't quit. He is the only coach I have ever had. Sure, I don't always listen. But he can be so strict; it's one of the reasons we work well together. We are the yin and yang of golf. I quickly go from being stunned to being hurt, and I start crying.

"This has kind of been the worst day of my life. I really don't think I can handle you quitting too. Please don't do this," I beg.

He won't look at me. "Magnolia, you aren't the only one who you hurt today. You embarrassed me, and you defied what I asked you to do. I can't even look at you."

His words sting. I jump out of the car, forgetting completely about my golf clubs, and I run inside. By the time I open my front door, I am sobbing uncontrollably. My mom rushes to me. "Is it your shoulder?" Dad must have told her what happened.

I can barely catch my breath when I say, "CCCCCOACH GGGGGGGUSSSSSS just QQQQQUITTTTTT!!!!!" I finally get it out.

My mom gasps, and her hand flies to her mouth. "Are you serious?"

All I can do is nod. Seeing the look on her face, I realize how bad this is. I start crying harder. She tells me to go and get in the car. I don't know where we are going, but I know she will fix this. She has to. This is the worst feeling ever. I can't believe I was so stupid today out on the course. I was foolish and selfish, and all so I could show off in front of Jack.

On my way out to the car, I catch Poppy, Jazzy, and Jack on the stairs, all staring at me. They look like spectators in the stands, watching their favorite team get demolished. It feels like they are the elite superstars who are all sitting there gaping at the one loser in the house. The one person who screwed up and put shame on the whole family or something. My cheeks burn with embarrassment. I don't say anything to them and walk out to the car.

I hear Poppy as I walk out, "OH NO, someone broke Noli."

I feel that. I feel broken in so many ways. But someone didn't break me. I broke me.

Mom doesn't tell me where we are going, but as we pull out of the driveway, I see Coach Gus still sitting in his car in front of our house. Mom doesn't pull alongside him. She doesn't even wave at him. We drive off.

I'm confused. I thought Mom was going to fix this with Coach Gus. "Where are we going?" I ask.

"We have to get your shoulder checked out. Your dad said it could be a season-ending injury," she says.

I could care less about my shoulder. It is the least important thing that hurts right now. I want to fix things with Coach Gus. I want him to tell me I was dumb, I want him to yell at me, and then I want him to tell me how we are going to fix it. I want him to send me a spreadsheet of all the drills he wants me to do, and I want him to send me another lame playlist that I swear I will listen to.

I whine, "MOM, I don't care about my shoulder. Coach Gus, just QUIT." The moment I say it again, I start crying harder. This can't be happening. It feels like my favorite uncle has died or something.

Mom doesn't listen and drives me to a clinic to get my shoulder checked out. Turns out it's not as bad as they thought. I may have a small tear in my rotator cuff, or I may have just pulled it. The doctor says it needs ice, rest, and some physical therapy that will start next week. He puts me in an actual sling and tells me to take it easy during the Fourth of July weekend. He doesn't want me doing any further damage to the area.

It's a relief to hear that I won't need surgery, but Dad was right; it is a season-ending injury, and I may not even get to play for the school team this fall. None of it matters right now. I just want to go home, crawl in bed, and never leave. I keep asking Mom about Coach Gus, but she won't talk to me about it. She is staying completely quiet, but I know she knows something.

When we get home, Dad is waiting. He sits me down and says, "Magnolia, what you did today was completely unacceptable. Your actions have consequences. Sadly, your actions have led to a major consequence, and Coach Gus has quit." He stops to give me time to process what I already knew. Then Dad continues, "He won't budge on this. He is gone."

I was not prepared for this. Coach Gus has gotten irritated, bugged, annoyed, and even mad at me before. He has threatened to quit once before, and I teased him into staying. But the way Dad is looking at me makes me realize that this time is different. Coach Gus isn't coming back.

The finality of it is too much for me. I get up and run to my room. One of the most important relationships in my life is gone. That dumb swing didn't just break my body; it crushed my soul too.

I cry for hours in my room. I keep thinking about this summer. I have had the highest highs and the lowest lows in a matter of weeks. Can't life just go back to being quiet and easy?

No one comes in; they leave me alone, and I wonder if my parents are mad at me. My room feels like a cave, dimly lit and confined. I keep trying to find a comfortable position, but everything hurts my shoulder. I try holding my knees with my good arm tight to my chest to try and squeeze away the pain, both physical and emotional. This has been the worst day of my life. I don't know how I am going to come back from it.

I keep playing that 18th hole in my head over and over again. I see myself lining up with the ball in the tee box; I see the disapproval on Coach Gus's face. I imagine hearing my rotator cuff tear. I see Jack smiling at Juliet when she lands the putt. I imagine Juliet taking a real crown off my head and placing it on her own. And then, Jack claps. He freaking claps when she wins. That felt like the ultimate betrayal.

The more I play it over and over again, the more it hurts. I am getting more and more depressed the longer I am churning the day over in my head. I am just about to start down the rabbit hole all over again when there is a knock at my door.

I sniffle, and between a sob, "GO AWAY!"

Sometimes when I'm having a bad day, Poppy will come in and snuggle up to me and tell me the most ridiculous stories to make me laugh. It's annoying, but it always works.

Today I just can't do it. I can't listen to her silliness or rally to give her smiles. I want to be left alone. When there isn't another knock, I think she has left, but then my doorknob turns. I turn to yell at Poppy, and then I see it's Jack, shirtless, standing in my doorway.

"Can I come in?" Jack's voice is gentle, filled with concern, yet slightly hesitant.

"Yeah, sure," I say, wiping my eyes hastily with the back of my uninjured arm.

Jack walks in and sits next to me on my bed. Our eyes meet. I'm torn between gratitude and humiliation, thrilled he's here but mortified he's seeing me so vulnerable. I'm also so mad that he was such a Juliet fan when she won. It makes me want to yell at him.

"That sucks what happened today," he says softly. "I'm really sorry, Noli."

Tears threaten to spill over again, but I hold them back. "It's my fault. I can't believe I was being so stupid. I didn't listen to Coach Gus."

His eyes darken with empathy. "Hey, we've all been there. In the heat of the moment, it's easy to forget that coaches have our backs. I know I've made my share of stupid mistakes after I have gone against my own coaches."

His words undo me. It's another reminder that I was the one who screwed it all up. I was the one that made my coach quit. This is the last reminder that I need. Especially from Jack. My tears fall freely as I choke out, "My coach quit, Jack. He said he can't train someone who won't listen."

The regret on Jack's face is immediate. I think he realizes his words meant to connect us have reminded me of what happened today. He leans in to hug me. I brace myself for a quick, friendly squeeze, but he pulls me close instead, enveloping me in a warm, reassuring embrace. He is so careful with me, making sure not to touch my hurt shoulder.

Jack wraps his arms around my waist. We are so close I can see the pulse in his neck. For a moment, the world fades away. All that remains is Jack and me and the soothing sensation of his arms around me. I rest my head against his bare chest and hear his heart pounding as fast and as loud as mine.

He smells like he's been outside on the lake. It's a combination of water and fresh-cut grass. It's a smell I know so well because it's the smell that wakes me up each morning on my paddleboard or when I surf behind the boat, or even during my first round of the day at the country club. It is calming in the morning, but smelling it on Jack makes it electrifying to me.

I don't want to, but I pull away, but not entirely. Our eyes lock, creating a charge between us. I'm acutely aware of every point of contact: the heat of his hands still on my arms, his legs pressing against mine. Time stands still, and I feel like we're teetering on the edge of something new, something undefined but deeply thrilling.

I have to know. "Why did you clap when Juliet won?"

For a flash of a second, I see something in his eyes. Something that reminds me of last summer. I wonder if he is going to be mean or say something snarky. He doesn't.

"It's good sportsmanship to congratulate the winner." He says he is coaching me on being a good sport.

"Yeah, but it's Juliet." I shoot back like that is a good reason NOT to clap.

Jack pulls away from me, and I realize I am ruining this moment between us. I don't want to fight with him, and I don't want to talk about Juliet, even though I was the one who brought it up.

"I'm sorry," I say, "Don't listen to me. I'm just in pain."

Jack doesn't come back and hold me; he doesn't move at all. It's like we both don't know what comes next. Lucky for both of us, Poppy bursts into my room. "Noli, Mom says dinner is—Oh."

She pauses, eyes darting between Jack and me, and then she breaks into a wide grin and, in a mischievous tone, asks, "Am I interrupting something?"

Jack coughs and stands up, immediately going over to stand next to Poppy and get space between us. I can't believe I had to bring up Juliet at that moment. I could have had more time to be close to him if I would have just let it go.

"No, you're not interrupting," I say, my voice tinged with regret.

Jack messes up Poppy's hair and says, "Let's get down to dinner. I am starving."

Poppy shoots back, "Maybe your extracurricular activities in Noli's room have you famished." Being the youngest, she never backs down on calling people out.

Jack runs to grab her, and she darts out the door. I hear them both running to the kitchen.

I sit on my bed, disappointed that Jack didn't kiss me. I mean, I don't think he would have, but for a split second, I wished he did. I keep confusing myself, going between Xander and Jack and thinking about which one is going to be my first kiss. I don't know. Maybe the thought of Jack kissing me is just a good distraction from what happened today. I think back to what Morgan said about first kisses and making sure that my first kiss was special. But then I realize this is what Morgan would say is a "regrettable first kiss." I wouldn't want to kiss Jack on the worst day of my life.

This would have been a pity kiss. A kiss to distract me from the misery of the day. Jack would do it because he felt bad for me. I don't want my first kiss to be a sympathy kiss. I don't want it to be something that either one of us looks back on and regrets.

I stand up and realize I still haven't changed out of my golf outfit. For half a second I forget about my shoulder, and I go to take my skirt off using my hurt arm. Pain shoots up and down my arm, and I cry out.

I hear loud footsteps running up the stairs, and Jack rushes back into my room, concern on his face. "What is it? Did you hurt yourself again?"

I feel so pathetic. I can't believe how much it hurts moving my arm, even when I am trying to do something so simple. I can't help it; I start crying again. I sob, "I can't get out of my skirt."

"Do you need any help?" he asks.

I look up, shocked to realize what he is asking to help with, and I see that he is genuinely concerned. He hasn't registered what he just said yet, and then it hits him, and I can see his cheeks turn slightly pink. It's so cute on him. I rarely see him get embarrassed.

I can't help it, I tease him, even as I'm in pain. "You want to help me out of my skirt?" I shoot back.

I'm not sure if it's because he is embarrassed or because he is mad at me for coming after him for clapping for Juliet, but Jack doesn't take this chance to tease me back. "Uh, no. I mean, do you want me to go and get your mom or Jazzy to come and help you change."

OMG. I don't know what to say. Anytime I flirt or tease with Xander, he always flirts back. Jack also never backs down from a chance to tease me. I feel like my comment to Jack about my skirt is completely shot down. Now I'm the one who is embarrassed.

My face instantly turns bright red, and I stumble, "No, nope. I am fine. I got this."

Jack sees how embarrassed I am, and instantly, his face changes, and he lets out a laugh. "I mean, I am happy to help you out of your skirt, Noli. But you have to give me consent first."

Now he is teasing me. I realize that anytime Jack teases me, he always pushes it just to the point that I get embarrassed, and then he lightens up. The realization has me more exhausted. I feel like I can't keep up with this back and forth and trying to figure out all these emotions.

How am I supposed to know the difference between flirting and teasing? Is it all the same thing? For half a second, I imagine Jack helping me, and I instantly turn bright red. I can't stand him when he intentionally makes me blush.

I turn and retreat to my bathroom as fast as I can, not looking back. Did I really just try to flirt with JACK? I can't believe I did that. I can't even blame what I said on pain meds. All they gave me at the doctor's office was two ibuprofen. I shake my head at myself. I have been texting two boys and liking both of them at the same time. Then, to add injury to the drama, there was the disaster of today. Maybe I shouldn't be allowed to talk to anyone.

I am in my bathroom, struggling to get undressed, and I could use Jazzy's help. But I'm not about to open the door to see if Jack is still standing there. Someone knocks at the door as I try again to get my good arm out of my bra.

Oh no, Jack can't see me like this! I have one boob out, and I have exhausted myself trying to get out of the minimal amount of clothes I am wearing. I yell, "UH, what do you want, you creeper?"

I hear a snort outside the door. "You are, for sure, the creeper. Let me in so I can help you." It's Jazzy.

Thank goodness! I unlock the door, and Jazzy comes in. "Nice boob," she says, looking at the predicament I am in.

I smack her gently with my good arm. "Please help me."

We both laugh as she quickly helps me out of my bra and into a comfortable tank top. She's my lifesaver at this moment, and I am so grateful for her. My arm might be out of commission, I may have been fired by my coach, and it may have been the worst day ever, but at least I've got family to help me through it.

"Thanks, Jazz," I say as she secures my sling back in place. "You're a lifesaver."

"Anytime," she replies with a grin. "So what's the deal with you and Jack? Are you guys MORE than friends? "

I hesitate. Poppy must have said something to her. Do I really want to dive into this with my younger sister? "It's... complicated and also not."

Jazzy gives me a knowing look. "Isn't it always? But hey, you'll have the whole Fourth of July weekend to sort it out."

The mention of the Fourth of July sparks a bit of joy within me. It's my favorite holiday, a day filled with fireworks, festivals, and barbecues—a day where the worst thing that usually happens is a burned hot dog or a dud firework. I could use some of that simple happiness right now.

"Yeah, I can't wait," I say with a sigh, fantasizing about fireworks illuminating the night sky, the feeling of grass beneath my feet, and the comfort I get in knowing that all our holiday traditions will be happening just like they always do. "I really need to have something good like the Fourth in my life right now."

"Just a few more days, sis," Jazzy says, patting my good shoulder. "In the meantime, let's go eat and forget about everything that happened today."

Being a competitive dancer, Jazzy knows the stress and utter sadness that comes when you have a bad performance. I am so grateful she is here with me right now. I tell her this, and she gives me a knowing smile and tells me that life goes on even after we fail. How can she only be a year younger than me and so wise? We head downstairs, and I hope my parents aren't going to be weird with me.

The earlier awkwardness with Jack feels like it's forgotten by him. I look forward to putting today behind me and focusing on my favorite holiday. But as I sit at the dinner table, avoiding eye contact with Jack, who's sitting at the table shirtless and talking to my dad about his soccer camp, I can't help but wonder what is going on with us. There is something happening between us, and I have never felt it before. And my sisters are picking up on it, so I know it's not just me.

Jack catches my eye and gives me that coy smile he gave me earlier when he was teasing me about my skirt. I feel that familiar flutter in my stomach. Yes, the Fourth of July weekend could be interesting indeed. And for the first time all day, the idea makes me smile.

The smile drains quickly as I see my dad looking at me. He is frustrated, and I know how upset he is about Coach Gus quitting. My mom must have told him to save all of his talks for another day because he doesn't say anything. He just glares at me, and I can't take it. I try to distract him from thinking about golf.

"Mom," I start, "Is it okay if Xander comes over for the Fourth of July barbecue and fireworks?"

My mom and dad glance at each other. This is the first time I am asking if I can have a guy come over by himself. Jack is also a bit stunned. Jack actually looks mad.

Once again, I have picked the worst time to bring something up. Seriously? I was just thinking about how cute Jack is and how there may be something going on between us, and I pick right now to ask my parents about Xander. I go back to my thoughts in the bathroom earlier. Maybe I shouldn't be allowed to talk at all right now.

My mom asks, "Is Noah coming over too?"

Noah is my mom's favorite, and I am sure if I had asked if Noah could come over by himself, she wouldn't have hesitated to say yes.

"No," I say. "Noah is in Idaho with his cousins. Just Xander would be coming over. He is home alone this weekend, and then he takes off to somewhere else after the Fourth."

I try to hit my mom's motherly instincts. She hates it when kids are alone during any holiday, and Xander told me he would be alone with the house all weekend. I think he was telling me to try and hint that I should come over, but right now is the perfect chance to get my mom to say yes to Xander coming to our house.

"Mom, his family is out of town, and he doesn't have anywhere else to be."

It works. Mom says, "Of course, Xander can come over. We wouldn't want him to be alone during the holiday."

I smile, say thanks, and glance over in Jack's direction. Jack is looking at me, but I can't read his face. This was my way of announcing to Jack that I had a friend coming over. I didn't want to make it weird and ask him if it was okay or make a big deal out of it. But I realize at that moment that I am bringing up Xander to make him jealous. I want him to know that I have guy friends. I want him to know there is someone else who likes me. I want him to tell me he likes me and wants me.

"Xander is a friend from school," I tell him. "I think you will like him. He plays soccer too." At the mention of Xander playing soccer, there is a visible change on Jack's face. He is annoyed, but he just gives me a head nod and continues eating. It works. I can tell Jack is jealous, but I don't know why he looks so mad. I was hoping I would make him a little jealous, and it would lead to desire, not being mad. I tell myself Jack is being childish and that he is probably mad that I invited another guy who happens to play soccer to the Fourth. But it just isn't sitting right. It seems like, once again, I have upset one of the guys in my life.

I just can't win today. I tell everyone my shoulder doesn't feel good and go back to bed. Maybe this isn't going to be the Fourth of July I wanted. The best thing for me to do is go to bed. I have several days to reset before the Fourth. Jack's parents should be here tomorrow, and Jill, Jack's mom, always makes everything fun. That is exactly what I need right now.

10

With everything that has happened over the past week, I wake up on the Fourth of July excited to be spending today doing things that we have done for the past several years. There will be no surprises, no drama. Just our Foster Fun Fest for the Fourth of July.

Jeremy and Jill got in so late last night that I had already gone to bed before they arrived. As I wake up this morning, I hear my mom and Jill's laughs make it up to my room. They are up early and packing our breakfast for the annual hot air balloon festival that happens every Fourth of July in the town right next to ours. I love hearing Jill laugh and can't wait to see her.

I put on the annual shirt my mom has laid out for me and my favorite jean shorts. I take my sling off and gently put on my clothes. My shoulder is more sore than it has been in the past couple of days, but my doctor told me to expect this. I exhale after I get my shirt on and put my sling back on. It has only been a couple of days, and I am sick of this sling. I hadn't realized how hard it was going to be to have my shoulder out of commission for a couple of weeks. Even the smallest things, like brushing my hair, are a challenge.

I get my shorts on, but I can't do my buttons up by myself. I am about to yell for Poppy or Jazzy when I hear a knock on my door. I'm not sure who it is, but I am decent, so I say, "Come in."

It's Jack. He smiles widely at me. I guess the weirdness of announcing that Xander was going to spend the Fourth of July evening with us is gone. Jack walks over to me and says, "Do you need help brushing your hair?"

It is so sweet that he is asking. I would much rather have Jazzy do it because I know she will be gentle and also know exactly how to style it so I don't end up with a static mess on top of my head. But I can't help but say yes to Jack because he is asking if I need his help. I want his help with anything and everything because that means he will be close to me.

I say, "That would be great," and I move to grab my brush from my bathroom.

I take two steps toward the bathroom when my shorts start to slink down my legs. I totally forgot that I haven't done up the buttons because it is too hard to do it with one hand.

Jack is next to me in an instant. "I see London, I see France," he jokes, hiking my shorts back up and skillfully buttoning them.

My face is so hot. I can't figure out if I'm blushing because Jack just got a glimpse of my undies or because his hands are grazing my stomach as he does up the buttons on my shorts. Either way, my face is a heatwave.

He lets his gaze slide from my newly buttoned shorts, inching its way up to my face. It's like his eyes are tracing invisible lines on my skin, making my heart race with each inch they cover. I feel this electric zing wherever his gaze lands as if I'm suddenly aware of every nerve ending I have.

By the time his eyes meet mine, it's like I've been charged up, buzzing with a thrilling mix of excitement and jitters. My stomach does this funny little flip as if even my insides can't handle having him near.

Jack gives me his coy little smile with an edge of mischief as if he knows exactly the rollercoaster of emotions I'm going through. He is looking at me when he says, "I just saw your underpants," and bursts into a laugh before letting go of my waist and striding into the bathroom to retrieve my hairbrush.

If this were any other guy, I would be sure that what was going on between us was undeniable chemistry. Honestly, the intimacy of letting a guy into my room, seeing me in my underwear, helping me button up my shorts, and even brushing my hair is something I wouldn't ever do. But this is Jack.

I mean, this is the same guy I've seen streaking like a wild child around our summer beach house and puking his guts out after a carnival ride. This is the Jack who I've hugged tightly when his dad went off the rails on him after a soccer game and whose hand I've literally squeezed during the scariest moments of movies that our parents told us we couldn't watch.

It's complicated. He's not just 'some guy.' He's the guy who's been there for all my summer highs and lows, just like I've been there for his, with the exception of last summer. And that's what makes figuring out this whole 'us' thing a whole other level of confusing. And here I am, still clueless about what's actually going on between us. Is this just playful banter, or is this, like, a 'thing'?

I watch him as he retrieves my brush and heads back toward me, but the look on his face has shifted. Gone is that mischievous, flirty grin that seemed to get me so excited. Now he's wearing this goofy smile—the kind that reminds me of Jack as a kid. I am so grateful he hasn't brought up the Xander conversation from dinner the other night. I can't believe I brought it up in front of him and that I was trying to make him jealous.

But I still can't figure out who I like or what version of what boy I am into from one moment to the next. Take Jack. One moment, he's this heart-fluttering crush that I can't take my eyes off of, and the next, he's the wholesome boy next door who is one of my best friends. These alternating personas make it hard for me to pinpoint what's really going on between us—and if I'm falling for Jack or Xander.

As Jack begins to brush my hair, it's immediately clear that this wasn't one of our better ideas. Instead of starting at the ends, he dives right in at the top of my head, and instant tangles start to form. I try to hold back a wince but can't help myself. "Ever brushed someone's hair before?" I manage to ask through clenched teeth as another snarl takes shape.

"First time," he admits, then eagerly adds, "How am I doing?"

I wince again, more visibly this time, and he freezes mid-stroke.

"Not too great," I confess. I don't want to be rude, but the mounting discomfort in my scalp can't be ignored.

He chuckles and hands me the brush. "How about you get started, and I'll go get Jazzy for you?"

I smile, grateful that I don't have to endure any more of his brushing "Thanks for trying," I tell him, and as he leaves to find Jazzy, he turns back and says, "I'll stick with what I'm good at. Call me next time you need your shorts buttoned up."

He gives me his goofy grin and leaves. I find myself sighing deeply. It's like emotional whiplash with him—this back-and-forth between light-hearted banter and intimate moments. How much longer can I ride this rollercoaster of emotion before I need to know where we stand?

Jack has left the door open, and I take a moment to try and calm the swarm of butterflies he has unleashed in my stomach. Just then, Jill comes in, beaming from ear to ear. "Hey there, my Noli girl!"

The sight of her instantly shifts my mood. I've missed her so much, and seeing her standing here in her Fourth of July shirt, smiling like a ray of sunshine, fills me with warmth.

Given that I now know what happened last year, her being here and actually being happy feels like a big gift. I forget all about this mix of emotions I am feeling right now for her son, and I focus on being with one of my favorite adults. It's funny how you can love someone else's mom just as much as you love your own.

Jill brushes out my hair and styles it into a cute, intricate braid I've never seen before. It's the perfect style for a day packed with outdoor events, especially since the heat is supposed to be insane this afternoon. Plus, it's boating-proof, meaning I won't have to give my hair a second thought after it gets wet. As Jill works her magic, our conversation drifts to school and friends.

Jill has met Morgan and Celeste on multiple occasions, so she's already well-versed in my best friends. I fill her in on what they've been up to and tell her about the new friends I made this year at school. When I mention boys, Jill's eyes twinkle mischievously.

"So, any of these boys someone you're crushing on?" she asks, her tone playfully probing.

For a split second, I remember that Jill isn't just another girlfriend to gossip with; she's also my mom's friend. And what gets discussed here could easily make its way back to Mom.

Deciding on a partial truth, I tell her about Xander and my crush from earlier this year. I intentionally omit the yearbook fiasco and the sleepover incident, not wanting to tarnish his reputation. After all, he's my friend now. "I don't really have a crush on him anymore," I tell her. "We're just friends."

Even as the words leave my mouth, I find myself knowing that's not true. Is it even possible to just be friends with someone you had a major crush on all year? And what about the new edition of our flirtatious texts that have been going back and forth? Every time I get a text from Xander, it sends a jolt of excitement through me, and I am pretty proud of myself for my newfound art of flirty texting I feel I am getting pretty good at it without crossing any lines, even though I am pretty sure Xander has been hinting to me that he wants me to.

As Jill finishes my hair, she steps back to admire her handiwork. I am looking at my hair too. I see how Jill has taken pieces of my hair and woven them into an intricate braid pattern, and it makes me wonder if I were to take all of my feelings for Xander and Jack and try to weave them together, what would it look like? I imagine it would look something like this.

Jill prods me again about who I like and says she wants the full update on all of the crushes and flings I had during my freshman year. I tell her again that I had a couple of crushes but no boyfriends, flings, or anything else. I can't imagine opening up to her right now and trying to explain how I am falling for her son while, at the same time, being completely involved with another guy through text. I act neutral and say, "I'm taking a break from boys this summer."

Jill chuckles knowingly. "We'll see about that. The summer is far from over."

With my hair perfect, we make our way downstairs. I give Jeremy my best one-armed hug, and he tells me, "Tough break" with my arm. He starts in on a monologue about the dangers of ego in sports, but luckily for me, Jill stops him and reminds him we don't have time; the hot air balloons wait for no one.

Our group piles into cars, and we make our way over to my favorite way to start the Fourth of July day, the hot air balloon festival.

11

Fourth of July is always the same. The day kicks off at the crack of dawn—seriously, 6 a.m.—when we drag ourselves out of bed and head to the park to watch the hot air balloons. We stake our claim on the hill, unrolling blankets and setting up picnic baskets overflowing with breakfast food. Bless them; our moms have been up since 4:30 a.m., creating a breakfast spread that could rival the brunch at the country club. And, in my mom's over-the-top way, she makes sure that everything looks amazing and Instagrammable down to making sure our Fourth of July shirts are aesthetic enough to match the quilts that she has brought to sit on. She is something else.

The food is devoured in record time, mostly by us kids. Then it's time for the hot air balloon tag, which is always a frenzied game that spirals around the colorful balloons. Eventually, we end up sprawled on the ground, gazing up at the floating colors and designs. Each of us talk about which balloon we'd pick if we were ever able to go for a ride, and finally we make our way to the booths that have been set up for the festival and we beg the dads for money to buy outrageous things that we will never use after today. You know, things like puppets on strings, bedazzled cowgirl hats, and Jack and I's favorite stuffed animals that you can only win if you get the ring over an impossibly big bottle.

Meanwhile, our moms, who are basically superheroes with zero hours of sleep, usually nod off on the hillside. Sensing their dwindling energy, our dads make the quick dash to the closest gas station for a caffeine reboot—energy drinks for them, more coffee for the moms, and an insane amount of soda for the kids. I still wonder what takes them two hours to get, but they keep saying it's their secret.

Today, as soon as we pull up to the festival we jump out of the cars. Poppy races to the hill to secure our spots, and everyone else starts grabbing things out of the car to take over. I go to grab the blankets, and Dad stops me, "Can't have you overdoing it." He says.

I think he means it to be caring, but I think he is rubbing it in that I am hurt. Annoyed, I make my to find Poppy and help her secure the spot. Nestled into our favorite spot on the hill, we all dig into the yummy breakfast spread. I give Mom and Jill extra-tight, one-armed hugs, letting them know just how much I appreciate their early-morning magic.

I reserve an added squeeze for Jill, wishing I could tell her how grateful I am that she's here, especially considering what I know happened between her and Jeremy last year. But for now, a warm hug will have to speak the words I can't say. Both moms smile, and Jill nudges my mom, mouthing, *You've got a good one here.*

Just as we're about to kickstart our annual game of tag among the towering hot air balloons, Mom calls out, "Noli, I think you should sit this one out. You're nursing that shoulder injury, and I don't want it to get worse." My gratefulness for her shifts into an undercurrent of resentment. Couldn't I have just one day to forget about my shoulder and that golf course disaster? It seems like both mom and dad are going to keep mentioning it all day.

Dad chimes in before I can even voice my protest, echoing Mom's sentiments. "She's right, kiddo. Better to be safe." I catch sympathetic glances from Jack and my sisters. No one's going to fight this battle for me. I slump back onto the blanket, fighting the tears that are pooling at the corners of my eyes. I look down the hill at all of the balloons and people. It feels like I can only be a spectator, not part of all of the fun.

I watch as Jack tags Poppy, kicking off the game. From my vantage point on the hill, I can see them darting between the hot air balloons, their laughter carrying up to where I sit. The crowd around us erupts into cheers as the balloons finally lift off, dotting the sky with vibrant hues. But despite the excitement unfolding before me, a piece of my heart sinks. My dream of a drama-free, traditional Fourth of July is officially deflated.

As the hot air balloons go up, the dads disappear, and the moms, who have already put away breakfast, lie down and start chatting. I know they won't get too far into the conversation before they are both asleep.

I would sneak off to join the game of tag, but I know it's over. They always stop when the hot air balloons take flight. I try to lie down and get comfortable, but my shoulder protests each time I try. As I sit up, frustrated, I see Jack coming toward me.

He smiles at me and then glances at the moms. They are both nodding off already. "I came to rescue you from the sleeping spell that haunts this picnic blanket."

He puts out his hand to help me up. I look around for my sisters, and when I don't see them, I ask Jack, "Where are the girls?"

He tells me, "They found some dance friends and are going to grab some shaved ice at the stand."

Even at six a.m., shaved ice is acceptable on the Fourth of July. I take his hand and stand up. I assume Jack will let go of my hand when I stand up, but he doesn't. He hangs on and slips his other arm around my waist to help steady me on the hill. Jack releases me around my waist but keeps our fingers entwined. It's like he isn't even making a big deal about it, almost like it's an unconscious connection.

Jill asks us what we are going to go and do, and as soon as Jack hears his mom's voice, he drops my hand. The moment is gone quickly as Jack drops my hand. The moment is gone too soon, and I am craving his touch as soon as it's gone. I wish he would hold my hand all day. I wish he would look at me with those twinkling green eyes and playfully tickle me. But once again, it looks like none of that is going to happen.

"So what's the plan?" I ask, trying to dislodge the butterflies that have resurfaced in my stomach.

He smirks, a subtle uptick at the corner of his mouth. "How about we do the same thing we do every single year and go shopping at the booths."

I smile. He is being completely sarcastic. I think sometimes our traditions get boring to Jack, but he still puts up with it. The moms tell us to have fun and to be careful with my shoulder, and we take off toward the booths.

Just before we get there, Jack grabs my hand again and steers me away from all of the people. "What are we doing?" I ask.

"I thought you could do with a little adventure in your life Magnolia," Jack says.

The thought of detouring from our usual Fourth of July routine sends a thrill through me. Just a moment ago, I was clutching to the familiar traditions of the day and not wanting to let them go, but having Jack here, holding my hand for a quick second, and offering adventure sounds perfect. I can't say no to him. I say, "Sounds perfect. Let's go."

We weave through the festival grounds, bypassing food stalls and craft booths. We follow the path of a particularly vibrant balloon —royal blue, with swirls of gold—that seems to be floating toward a distant field. As we walk, the sounds of the festival fade away.

Finally, we reach the edge of the field. It's secluded, untouched by festival goers, covered in high alfalfa that sways in the breeze like a green ocean. There is a barbed wire fence about waist-high around the field.

Jack suggests we hop the fence and keep following the balloon. I point to the sling with my good arm and remind him I can't hop fences with one arm. Without even asking, Jack picks me up and gently hoists me over the fence. While he does this, his shirt gets caught in the barbed wire and rips a bit. I laugh when I look at him and see that he is now wearing a belly shirt.

"Anything to try and get your shirt off." I tease him.

"It's all the rage right now," Jack says as he does a spin for me to show off his new look. He is cute, but I wish he was shirtless like he always is at home. That is my favorite look on him. I mean, what girl wouldn't love to see a tanned, toned, and ridiculously gorgeous guy shirtless all of the time?

When Jack effortlessly hops the fence in his crop top, I smirk. It doesn't matter if Jack was wearing a mock turtleneck right now, he would still be adorable. He catches me staring at him and comments, "You can't keep your eyes off of me in this shirt."

I start laughing and say, "You caught me."

He comes over to me, and with that adorable grin on his face, he grabs my free hand and laces his fingers with mine. This is the first time he is holding my hand without helping me stand or playing Red Rover. His hand is warm in mine, and I am reminded again how good it feels to hold his hand. It's like our hands are meant for each other.

"This feels like a moment I will always look back on and remember. Jack is holding my hand.

We stand there for a moment looking at each other, and I think I might explode with excitement. This isn't just playing around, and it's not just being playful together. There is something here between us. Something that I know we both feel. Jack smiles mischievously at me and pulls me farther into the field. When we are close to the center, he says, "Sit down right here, and we can watch the hot air balloons."

I look up, completely forgetting what we were doing in the first place. Oh yeah! There are hot air balloons up there. I look around and spot the blue and gold balloon we were following. It is hovering in the distance.

Wordlessly, we sit down in the midst of the alfalfa, hands still entwined. Above us, hot air balloons are everywhere, and with the blue backdrop of the sky, the balloons stand out. It's a sight that words can't capture. I have been to this festival for years, and never has it felt more special and magical than it does right now. I want to say something, but I'm not sure what to say. I look over at Jack, and he smiles at me.

"You and I," Jack says as he looks at me, "We are meant to end up together."

I feel it too. It's Jack. I was always supposed to end up with Jack. Sitting here with the hot air balloons in the background couldn't be more perfect. I'm not spinning in emotions trying to figure out who I like or who likes me. I'm not bouncing between text messages and trying to decipher what anyone actually means. I am not trying to change myself to be liked.

The fact that Jack feels it and finally admits it to both of us makes me feel complete. We are meant to end up together.

As we look at each other, Jack's fingers leave mine and he leans into me. He brings his hand up to my cheek and slowly traces his fingers down my nose.

This is all new to me, having a boy touch me. As if pulled by some invisible force, our faces inch closer. Our lips are just a whisper apart, teetering doing something exhilarating when a loud shout from above startles us both.

"Hey, look out! Coming IN!"

Jack jumps up, and I struggle with one arm to get up. I look up just in time to see the royal blue balloon we'd been following coming down into the field at an alarming rate. Adrenaline surges through me as we scramble out of the descending hot air balloon path.

It's a close call. The balloon basket touches down where we'd been sitting only moments before. A ripple of shock courses through me as I catch my breath. Jack asks me if I am okay, and I nod. We both realize we were almost in big trouble sitting here in the alfalfa field.

Jack helps me back over the fence and is so gentle with me as he lifts me over. I am now obsessed with him touching me. It's my new favorite thing, and I can't get enough of his hands. I want to feel them in mine all of the time. There is something about knowing for sure that I am choosing him that makes all of it feel official. No more of this back and forth.

We start walking back toward the festival, and I slide my hand into his. But something changes. It feels like his hand stiffens. It doesn't feel the same as it did just moments ago. Jack says, "Jazzy and Poppy are coming," and he moves away from me.

Why would it matter if Jazzy and Poppy see us holding hands? Do they already think there is something going on between us? I feel hurt that he doesn't want my sisters to know. It's silly, but it stings.

Poppy starts excitedly talking to us as soon as we are close, "Did you guys see that hot air balloon go down?"

"Yeah," I say, "it almost landed on us in that field."

"Poppy keeps talking, "There was a kid that had a BB gun, and he shot it down!"

Jazzy interjects, "He was lying to you, Pops. There is no way his BB gun could reach any of the balloons in the air."

Then Jazzy turns and looks at Jack and me with a mischievous smile on her face, "What were you two doing in a field?"

Before Jack pulled away, I would have told her the truth, but now, I don't know. I wait for Jack to answer to see what he will say.

"We just went over to see if they needed any help." He says.

Jazzy knows instantly that it's a lie. I just told them that we were there BEFORE the hot air balloon landed. Jazzy takes this to be a sign that something else is going on.

"Yeah, right," she says, grinning even more. "I believe you."

This sting from before feels like it is becoming a smolder or hurt. I try to calm myself down. It's fine. It doesn't mean anything. Of course, he doesn't want to hold my hand, tell me where we are meant to be together, and then go around and confess his love in front of everyone. It's fine.

We walk back to the parents and join them just as they are starting to pack up. Jeremy sees all of us and says, "There you are. We sent the girls to come and find you. Where have you been?"

Jack quickly answers, "We were following one of the balloons, and we saw that it was in trouble, so we hopped the fence to see if we could help out."

This wasn't the response my dad wanted to hear.

"You did WHAT?" He is upset. It's probably because of my shoulder injury. I quickly start talking because I don't want Jack to be the only one taking the heat for this.

"Well," I start to explain, "It wasn't a big deal. Jack was super careful and helped me over the fence. I didn't...."

Before I can finish what I was saying my dad interjects. "Champ you have got to be smarter than that. You know Noli shouldn't be climbing fences. She really could have gotten hurt, and by the looks of your shirt, it wasn't the easiest fence to jump"

The mention of Jack's shirt reminds me of earlier today. I wish we could go back. I am bugged that my dad is putting this on Jack. I wanted to go. I wanted to be there. I want to say something and stand up for Jack, but Jack quickly says, "You are right, Gavin. I'm sorry."

Jack won't look at me, and as we pack up and head to the cars, he doesn't talk to me. It feels like he is trying to avoid me. I jump into my dad's G-wagon, sidestepping the task of choosing if I want to ride home with Jack. I want him to have to choose what car he rides in.

He doesn't choose to ride in the same car as me. I'm torn about how to handle it. Should I confront him and demand clarity about how different he has been since the field? Our relationship keeps going between moments of intense connection and periods of being just plain old friends as we have always been. I don't want to ruin the Fourth of July for myself by dwelling on this emotional seesaw. I decide to put it aside for now, redirecting my focus to the upcoming day on the lake and the huge BBQ tonight.

When I think about the BBQ, I realize that I have totally forgotten that Xander is coming tonight! Shoot! I should text him and tell him not to come. Nothing could make this worse than having Xander show up and confuse the situation even more. I get out my phone and pull up my text thread with Xander. I see that I missed a text from him this morning.

> Xander: Rise and shine gorgeous! I have a feeling tonight is going to be lit.

I'm not sure what to do now. I start typing out the message to tell him not to come, but it feels mean. I stop typing. Maybe the best thing to do is to act like everything's a go for the BBQ tonight and then act like I'm sick.

That way, I don't have to deal with all of this. I reply to Xander with a smiley emoji and turn my phone on silent. I will tell him I am sick a couple of hours before the BBQ starts.

The thought pops into my head that the person I really want here with me for the BBQ and fireworks is Noah. Noah would be all in for fun, and it would be completely drama-free. I wouldn't spend all of my time trying to decide what a glance or a phrase meant. I wouldn't worry about if he would fit in and get along with everyone. It would just be the best time goofing off, having fun, and playing.

I take out my phone again and shoot a text to Noah.

> Me: What do ducks love about the Fourth of July?

> Noah: DUH….fire-quackers!

> Me: What did the flag do when it lost its voice?

> Noah: wave

Me: What did the firecracker eat at the movies?

Noah: pop-corn

Me: OK! You win! You are the king of bad jokes.

Noah: I have always thought I would look good in a crown.

Me: Miss you

I don't get a text back. What is it with him? As soon as I mention missing him, he stops texting. I think about calling him, just so I can hear his voice, but we are back at the house and told to run in and change so we can get out on the lake.

I go to my room to change into my swimming suit. It is ten a.m. and already hot. Going out on the boat and surfing will feel amazing. I know I won't be able to surf because of my shoulder, but lately, my dad has been teaching me how to drive the boat, so I am hoping that he will let me drive today with his supervision.

I head downstairs after it takes me way too long to get my suit on. I only needed a little help from Poppy tying the backup. When I get into the kitchen, I see Dad there with his swim shorts on. He is ready to go and is packing up a cooler with drinks and snacks for the boat. He looks up from what he is doing and sees me in my swimming suit. He lets out a sigh and says, "Sorry, kiddo, you can't go surfing today."

I already know that. So I give him a small smile and say, "Dad, I know I can't surf, but I thought this was a chance for me to work on driving the boat."

Before I can finish what I'm saying, Dad shakes his head and gestures out the window. "Look, there are two neighbors already out there on the lake. You know the rule: You can't practice driving if other boats are on the lake. Today just isn't the day to practice driving the boat."

I follow his gaze to our backyard lake. It's not your typical lake; it was custom-engineered for the gated community that lines one of its banks. Spanning the width to accommodate four boats easily and stretching about as long as two football fields, it serves as a private oasis for water sports. On one side, a row of custom homes has been built, and on the other, the manicured greens of the country club golf course provide a contrasting backdrop. Two boats are already carving through the water, their wakes crisscrossing the lake's surface.

Frustration courses through me as I suggest another compromise. "So what if I just ride along? When we stop to switch surfers, I can take a quick dip to cool off, then climb back in." This seems like a reasonable solution to me; it's the same thing Jazzy does when she's not in the mood to surf.

Dad's already shaking his head again before I finish my sentence. "I don't think so, sweetheart. You might be able to hop into the water just fine, but climbing back into the boat could strain your injured shoulder. We can't take that risk."

"Ok, I say," my irritation is growing. "What if I just sit in the boat and I can dip my feet in the water."

Dad is done with the back and forth. "Noli, you aren't coming on the boat today. No compromise. This is what happens when you make poor choices."

The fact that he is hinting at the golf tournament hurts. It feels so passive-aggressive. It's like he is trying to make it a worse punishment than it already is. We still haven't hashed out the issue of Coach Gus leaving, mostly because of the chaos of Jeremy and Jill arriving, and I keep feeling like instead of getting a one-time lecture and having it be over, I am getting these small micro lectures that are just too much. I'm done putting up with this. I don't yell back or say anything. I just want to be done talking to him.

"Whatever," I snap, letting my frustration fill the word. I storm off, each step pounding out my annoyance as I make my way back to my room.

I pass Jack in the hall, and the sight of him, shirtless and ready for the water, makes me even more upset that I don't get to go out on the boat. Surfing with Jack is one of my favorite things; he's incredibly good at it, despite my having more experience. He pushes me to better myself, and I can't help but regret missing out on that today. "Enjoy your time on the boat," I say, unable to keep the sulkiness from my voice.

Jack halts. "Wait, why aren't you coming?"

"My dad's got this ridiculous idea that I'll somehow ruin my shoulder by doing basically anything boat-related," I exaggerate, though it feels painfully accurate.

He sides with my dad, aggravating me further. "It's probably for the best, Noli. We don't want to see you get hurt again."

The 'we' in his sentence makes him sound like he's one of the dads, and something in me snaps.

"Oh, you don't want me to get hurt again?" My voice is laced with venom.

"If you don't want to see me get hurt, why don't you decide what we are to each other? This back-and-forth game is getting old really fast, and I can't handle it anymore."

Words spill out before I can censor myself. "You need to decide, Jack. Do you want me as a girlfriend or just a friend? Make up your mind because you can't have me as both."

The hurt washes over his face so quickly I almost miss it. He stares at me, his eyes devoid of the warmth I'm accustomed to. "I don't need you for either," he says flatly.

And with that, he moves past me, his steps heavy as walks down the stairs and away from me.

I am left with the worst feeling. That is not what I wanted. I wanted him to give me a hug and rub my back. I wanted him to tell me he was sorry that my dad was being harsh. I wanted him to offer to stay back and be with me. I didn't want him to tell me he was done with me. I sink onto my bed, my thoughts cluttered and messy. The sting of Jack's words is only made worse by my own regret. It's like I am always pushing him away by pushing him too fast.

Today was supposed to be simple, maybe even magical. Lying in the alfalfa field, hand in hand, watching the hot air balloons above us. We were in a place where 'us' didn't need defining. It felt okay to exist in the in-between. Then I had to push, to prod, to demand answers that neither of us was ready to articulate. What was I thinking?

I wasn't. That's the problem. I let my insecurities and uncertainties hijack a naturally growing moment between us. I wanted him to give a name to something that we hadn't even fully explored yet. Now, it feels like I've dug a huge hole between us that words can't bridge.

The excitement I had for the Fourth of July festivities evaporates. The BBQ, the fireworks—they all seem trivial now. The holiday feels tarnished, colored by my own self-sabotage. I pull a pillow over my head, craving the escape of sleep, wishing I could fast-forward to school starting. I want my friends. I want not to be hurt and wear a sling. But most of all, I want Jack not to be here right now.

I take a deep breath. This isn't going to help anything. Wishing this day away. I text the girlfriend chat

> Me: Breakdown of this morning…held Jack's hand

> Me: laid next to him in an alfalfa field,

> Me: he told me we were "always meant to be together"

> Me: Then I yelled at him, and he told me he needed to pick me forever

> Me: He told me he didn't want me as his GF or a friend.

Me: How is your Fourth?

Addy: Oh no! I really liked Jack. (even though I haven't met him)

Morgan: need more info on this alfalfa field

Celeste: I'm pretty sure there is a HUGE hole in this story.

Celeste: Group FACETIME!

I get on FaceTime with the girls and retell the events of the morning. They confirm what I have thought. First, Jack is adorable and so sweet. Second, I may be pushing him with all of this. I need to cool it and just be chill. Third, my dad is totally punishing me for the golf tournament.

I'm glad I got to see all of them. It helps me feel a little bit more like myself. And, even though Jack was rude to me right before he left on the boat, I know we can mend it and have a really good rest of the Fourth. I just need to remember that this thing between us is forever. He said it himself. We end up together.

12

Still in my swimsuit, I lie on my bed, feeling better after talking to my friends, but I'm still sad I'm not out on the boat. A soft knock interrupts me scrolling on my phone; it's Mom, carefully nudging the door open. "Hey, Noli, how are you doing?"

I sit up and decide now is a great time to ask her point blank, "Mom, is Dad punishing me for the golf tournament and for Coach Gus quitting."

For half a second, my mom's face tells me everything I need to know. He is. She quickly goes into her professional mode and covers it up. "Why would you say that?" She asks.

I don't need any more information from her. I roll my eyes and lay back on my bed. She comes over to me and puts a hand on my back. "Listen, kiddo, you screwed up. It would be one thing if you did this and didn't get hurt. But Dad was so worried about you. He doesn't do well watching his kids in pain. He just isn't sure how to handle all of this."

"It just feels like instead of talking about it, I am getting punished hard, and he keeps using my shoulder as the excuse," I tell her.

She listens and nods, "You could be right."

It still hurts to hear her admit that he isn't handling this the best and that I am getting the brunt of all of it. But it also feels good that she isn't acting like it isn't happening. My eyes fill up with tears. "This just isn't how I wanted the Fourth to be."

I sit up, and she wraps me in a hug.

"Don't let this spoil your day," she whispers, holding me close. "This holiday has always been special for you, and there's still so much left to enjoy."

I want to tell her that it's not just Dad not letting me go on the boat that I am upset about. I want to tell her about this morning with Jack and the encounter I just had with him in the hall, but I can't. She would get all weird about Jack and me, and I can't have that. I just nod and tell her I am ready for the day to be over.

Mom pulls away, looking into my eyes as if searching for answers I'm not ready to give. "You really want the day to be over?" I nod again, and she adds, "Even with Xander downstairs, eager to spend the rest of today with you?"

Xander? He was the last thing on my mind. He wasn't supposed to be here until five, and it's only two. Plus, I was going to text him and tell him not to come. I don't know if I can deal with him today, too.

"He's early!" I exclaim, faking excitement to hear that Xander is downstairs.

A warm smile spreads across Mom's face. "I texted him. I told him you could use some company while the rest of the crew was out on the boat. He was excited about spending time with you. Why don't you freshen up a bit, and I'll let him know you'll be down shortly?"

For a moment, I'm torn. Should I fake being sick, declare the Fourth of July festivities officially canceled, and send Xander home? OR should I embrace Mom's intuitiveness and be grateful for the distraction of having Xander here? I opt for something in between. I tell Mom thank you for texting Xander.

As I head to the bathroom to wash away the traces of my emotional upheaval, I find myself appreciating the unexpected turns life sometimes takes. Perhaps the day can be salvaged after all, and maybe, just maybe, Xander's unexpected early arrival is the universe's way of offering me a second chance at making things right with Jack. I can sit down with Xander and explain that as fun as texting him this summer has been, and I am actually with someone else now.

Feeling a little better, I make my way downstairs and find Xander wedged between Mom and Jill at the stove. Seeing him wearing an apron and diligently stirring a pot of baked beans is cute. I can't resist seeing how cute he is. Pulling out my phone, I snap a photo that I can use to tease him at school next year.

Realizing too late that my phone is on full volume, the shutter sound turns three heads in my direction. As they erupt into laughter at being caught off guard, I quickly snap another photo, capturing their smiles mid-laugh.

"So, did you come over to hang out with me, or are you here for a cooking lesson with my mom?" I tease Xander.

His grin widens, and he retorts, "Why can't it be both?"

Mom and Jill chuckle. "All right, scram." Mom playfully shoos him away from the stove as Jill swipes him off her cooking turf.

"Thanks for all your secrets behind baked beans," Xander says, exaggerating his gratitude for comic effect as he unties his apron. He washes his hands and comes toward me.

Without a shred of hesitation and completely indifferent to the presence of my mom and Jill, Xander wraps me in a tight hug, lifting me off the ground for a moment. But as he does, a sudden shift jerks my shoulder, sending a bolt of pain up my arm. I can't help but gasp loudly, shocked by the intensity of the pain.

Both Mom and Jill instinctively shout, "Her shoulder!"

Realizing his mistake, Xander sets me down quickly, his face etched with worry. "I'm so sorry, Noli. I completely forgot."

I gingerly move my shoulder to find a less painful position. Finally, I exhale, the tension leaving my body. "It's okay," I assure him, though the sting in my shoulder suggests otherwise.

Mom quickly makes an ice pack and gets me some ibuprofen, which I accept gratefully. As Xander and I head out to the pool, he turns back and promises my mom and Jill, "I'll be extra careful, I swear."

Settling into the circular chaise lounge beside the pool, I can't help but feel a small hesitation as Xander opts to sit right beside me. He thinks this is something different than it is, and I think I should clear the air quickly. I'm not sure how to start, so we dive into a conversation, updating each other on our summers.

For a moment, it's as if we're back at school, surrounded by our regular crew. Xander shares his enthusiasm about soccer camp and the upcoming adventure at the dude ranch. I fill him in on my golfing experience, conveniently glossing over the unfortunate tournament. Our conversation shifts to our friends; I update him on what's happening with the girls, and he does the same with Chris and Evan.

As he begins to move to another topic, I interject, "Wait a second, what about Noah? What's going on with him?" I ask, a hint of curiosity seeping into my voice.

Noah is usually so central to our conversations that his absence in today's update feels odd. Noah and Xander are best friends, and something feels off that he didn't mention him.

"Oh yeah," Xander says, acting as if Noah has slipped his mind. He goes on to give a very general update. "Noah is in Idaho with his cousins. He will be back in time for school."

I furrow my eyebrows. Something's up. "Why are you being so vague?" I ask. I don't want to sound like I am grilling him, but I want to know. I decide to lighten the mood, "Does Noah have some sort of secret double life that you were sworn not to tell anyone about?"

My question momentarily takes my thoughts to Celeste,

reminding me of her very real secret life that I am sworn not to tell anyone about.

Xander laughs it off, filling the air with a casualness that doesn't quite match his vague words. "Nah, there's just not much to say. He goes to Idaho every year, and every year it's the same old, same old."

I want to point out that this is my first summer knowing them, so Noah's "same old" Idaho trips are intriguing for me, but Xander changes gears before I can.

"Anyway," he says, shifting his focus and sliding his foot alongside mine in a caressing motion. "What I really want to talk about is how adorably flirty you've been with me all summer."

His words are a great way to start to tell him what I need to, but Xander has moved his feet toward mine and is trying to play footsie with me. The sensation of our feet touching is unbearable. I attempt a subtle shift, hoping to disentangle our feet without making it obvious. Unfortunately, he misreads my movement as playing hard to get and leans in further. The sensation makes my skin crawl; I can't take it anymore.

Seizing on an opportune distraction, I spring to my feet as I spot our boat returning to the dock at the edge of the yard. "Oh, look, they're back," I announce, redirecting the conversation and moving away from him so his feet can't touch mine. Xander lets out a sigh. What did he expect was going to happen? Did he think snuggling with our feet was going to lead to a full-out make-out session right there by the pool with my mom and Jill in the kitchen?

Xander lets out a slightly deflated sigh before hopping up next to me, putting on an exaggerated air of enthusiasm at the sight of the docking boat. His kindness toward my parents has always struck me as a bit too strategic, overly helpful, and excited to them, and he only gives the barest attention to my sisters. It's very different when Noah is with my family. He has always gone out of his way to get to know everyone in our home genuinely.

Jack is tying the boat to the dock, his back to us. My dad directs my sisters to lift the cooler out. The ache of not being part of their outing still stings. Xander sidles closer to me and calls out to my dad. "Hey, Gavin! Happy Fourth!"

Jack visibly tenses as soon as Xander's voice booms across the yard. His posture straightens as if jolted by an electric current. Slowly, he turns his head and locks his gaze on the sight of Xander standing way too close to me. It's like I watch something in Jack snap. In a flash of movement, Jack starts sprinting toward us.

My dad is midway through his greeting to Xander, his voice full of cheer: "Good to see you, Xander. Happy—"

He doesn't get to finish. Jack is running at Xander. As soon as he is within earshot, an unspoken history and tension fill the air. "We finish this now," Jack growls.

Xander's eyes widen in a flicker of recognition, but he has no time to react. Like a bolt of lightning, Jack barrels into Xander, sending both of them plunging into the pool with a splash that seems to put everything around us into chaos.

It's like time goes so much slower as I watch Jack tackle Xander into the pool, but oddly, my mind is racing. Just as Jack's body slams into Xander's, but before they hit the water, I realize they know each other.

The yard morphs into an insane, real-life episode of *Gossip Girl*. Time is twisted, racing ahead one moment and freezing the next. Saying the boys merely "fell" into the pool is like calling a hurricane a little rain. Xander and Jack don't just fall; they crash into the water, a tangle of limbs and fury. As Jack tackles Xander, I'm almost sure I hear them both shoot any and all expletives they know at each other.

My gaze snaps to the kitchen window. Mom and Jill whirl around like synchronized dancers, their faces twisted in identical expressions of horror as they bolt through the sliding door screaming for the boys to stop.

Behind me, the ground shakes with pounding footsteps. Dad and Jeremy are in a full-on sprint that is definitely slower than Jack's was. They race toward the pool, yelling their own cuss words. From the boat, Poppy's and Jazzy's voices pierce the air, their screams filled with frantic shouts of Jack's name, a big indicator of whose side they're on.

My gaze snaps back to the pool where the real drama unfolds. Jack and Xander are waist-deep in the shallow end, and while they're not trying to hold each other underwater or anything, fists are definitely making contact. Insults and four-letter words are exchanged almost as fast as the punches.

Dad's booming voice is almost drowned out by the commotion as he gets closer, yelling for them to knock it off. But then, cutting through the turmoil like a lifeguard on steroids, Jeremy dives into the water. He splashes up from the deep end, shouting, "Break it up, you assholes! You're gonna ruin your soccer contract!"

Classic Jeremy. Even in the midst of chaos, he's got one eye on the goal—literally.

By the time Mom and Jill reach the pool edge, they're in full-on disciplinary mode. Jill turns her stern 'mom face' on Jack while my own mom decides she's the one to set Xander straight. Jeremy finally manages to wedge himself between the two combatants, pulling them apart just as both start to bleed into the water. There is so much blood gushing from both of them that it's turning the water around them an unsettling shade of red.

Jack's eye is already puffing up, nearly closed, and there's a nasty cut above his eyebrow that's leaking blood way too fast. Xander's in no better shape, holding on to his nose like it might fall off, and blood is pouring out as if someone's turned on a tap.

When my sisters make it up to the pool, one looks at Jack's beat-up face, and Poppy loses it, dissolving into tears. It's a madhouse of girls crying, dads yelling, moms rushing around. It feels like half a horror show, half a reality TV meltdown. In the middle of all of it, I stand still, not saying anything and not running to anyone's aid. I just sit and think. It's becoming painfully clear that Jack and Xander have a history together that I am not aware of, and I am starting to wonder how this all started.

My head's spinning as the adults scramble to do damage control. This is a turning point, no doubt—a seismic shift in friendships, loyalties, and the whole social order really. The Fourth of July is all about freedom and fireworks, but today, it's an explosion of a different kind. I am swimming in questions, but I am not sure now is the best time to ask them.

Mom and Dad whisk Xander inside, probably to play nurse and patch up his gushing nose. Meanwhile, Jill and Jeremy are in pool-side triage mode, attending to Jack. Poppy and Jazzy are like stage moms, hovering and fussing over Jack's injuries. I'm stuck in the middle, a spectator caught between two unfolding dramas. I can't figure out where to go or who to be with. Of course, Jack. I should be with Jack, but Xander is my guest, my friend. I invited him here, and Jack attacked him. Before I can move to either one, Jeremy's saying something to Jack that makes me hyper-focused. "Is this the kid you told me about from soccer camp?"

Jack doesn't bother with words, just a nod. A simple nod carrying the weight of untold stories I want to hear.

"And what the hell is he doing here?" Jeremy's voice is a mix of anger and disbelief. He has no clue about my friendship with Xander or why he was even on tonight's guest list.

Guilt washes over me. Was I somehow responsible for this?

Jeremy's face takes on a look of resolve. "I'm calling the cops," he announces. But before he can whip out his phone, Dad reappears. "Noli, can you come in here, please?" Dad looks worried and, all of a sudden, very tired.

Jeremy tells Dad he is calling the cops, but Dad cuts him off. "Let's hold off on the police for now. Let's see if we can sort this mess out first." He's got a point—Jeremy's plan might backfire if the cops know Jack threw the first punch I'm not too sure it is going to be a good thing for Jack.

Jeremy pauses, considering. Then, reluctantly, he nods. "All right, I trust you can handle that kid." What he means is, 'I hope you can swing this in Jack's favor.' Because right now, all Jeremy wants is for Jack to end up on top, as always.

As I take a step toward the house, Jack abruptly rises, his eyes locking on mine with an urgency I've never seen before. "Noli, don't go in there with him. He's a snake," he warns, his words slurred slightly by a swollen, cut lip.

My gaze lingers on his face, battered and bruised from the fight. My heart clenches; I want to pull him to me, take care of him, and promise him that he's safe and that I'm in his corner. But those eyes —so intense, so defiant—he has been keeping things from me. I think there are things that have to do with me, and I'm not sure what to think of all of this.

"How do you even know him?" My voice comes out softer than intended, almost a whisper, challenging him to fill in the blanks.

Jack looks as if he's swallowed something bitter. "Soccer camp," he finally says, spitting out the words as they've soured in his mouth.

Jill tells Jack to stop talking. She needs him to stay still while she cleans up his face more. As painful as it is, I watch for a moment. Then it hits me—the elite soccer camp Xander casually mentioned earlier is the same one that Jack had been at. How did I not connect the dots sooner?

Xander had downplayed it like some community college summer course, while Jack had told me he was going to an invite-only, make-or-break-your-future camp that was going to help determine his future in pro soccer. I had never put two and two together that they were at the exact same camp. I wonder if their fight today was more about soccer or me.

The day's events are like a jigsaw puzzle, each piece slotting into place yet creating a bigger, more complex image. While the details— the whys and hows of their animosity—remain foggy, one thing becomes painfully clear. The two guys I've been texting, daydreaming about, and emotionally juggling—they know each other. And not in a 'hey, we met once at a party' way but in a deeply complicated, past-filled manner that I'm not sure I'm ready to untangle.

This is bad, really bad, and I have the sinking feeling that I'm standing at the epicenter of a collision course with no exit in sight.

"I'm just going in 'cause Dad called for me not to take sides," I assure Jack, desperate not to incite further tension.

His eye, the one I can see that isn't swollen, is still brimming with skepticism and softens a little. He nods but not without cautioning me. "Be careful around him, Noli. He isn't who you think he is."

13

Walking into the house, I notice Xander doesn't look nearly as bad as Jack, except for that noticeably swollen nose. Mom's got it under control, with tissue in hand, dabbing at the traces of blood. Dad catches my eye, his gaze a mix of concern and what seems like muted suspicion.

"Did you know these two had crossed paths at soccer camp?" he asks, each word heavy with subtext, almost as if he's accusing me of being in the middle of this mess.

"I had no idea they went to the same camp. Jack just told me," I retort defensively, my voice tinged with exasperation.

Dad sighs, his features softening. "Look, this isn't on you. We're all trying to make sense of the hows and whys."

I notice Mom talking to Xander. She offers to call his parents, but he shrugs it off, insisting he's fine and that they aren't around anyway. Mom still phones our neighbor, an ER doc who looks like he's from a Norman Rockwell painting, to come check him out.

While they wait for him to come over, Dad turns to Xander. "What's the history between you and Jack?"

Laying it on thick with the innocent act, Xander replies, "Honestly, Gavin, we met at soccer camp. As for why Jack went off on me, beats me. Maybe he just can't handle the competition."

Dad's not sold, but he lets it go, probably not wanting to dig a deeper hole. "All right. I called your folks. Turns out they are home. Your dad's on his way."

I glance at Xander, surprised. He'd lied about his parents? What else might he be hiding? He mumbles a quick, semi-plausible explanation about his parents coming back early, and I can tell he has been caught lying.

The doorbell chimes, announcing the arrival of our neighbor. After a quick inspection, he gives Xander a clean bill of health, just cautioning him about potential swelling. Mom and Dad huddle, their voices hushed and conspiratorial. They're peacekeepers but also tacticians, always strategizing. What's their next play here?

This has been an eventful Fourth of July afternoon. As I try to sift through the chaos, one thing's for sure: Whatever's going on between Jack and Xander, it's far from over. And I can't shake the feeling that I'm entangled in a much more complicated web than I'd ever anticipated.

Our neighbor doctor passes through the house saying that he needs to grab some sutures from his house to stitch Jack's face up. I notice that Xander looks genuinely pleased at having done damage to Jack, and I don't like it. I am starting to wonder how I ever had such a huge crush on this guy. I can't believe I ever liked him for so long without seeing this side of him. It seems to me like my crush clouded my judgment because my friends saw it, and it sounds like Jack saw it, too.

My thoughts are interrupted as Dad wraps up the conversation. "Well, Xander, your dad should be here soon. We'll wait for him in the living room."

Xander gives a nonchalant shrug as though this whole afternoon was a minor hiccup, not a glaring spotlight on hidden layers of personality that he has exposed about himself. "Thanks, Gavin. I appreciate it."

We move to the living room, and I realize I have misjudged Xander so badly. What else have I misjudged? Is my radar so off that I can't distinguish genuine kindness from manipulative charm? What about the note in my yearbook? How could that be from this guy that I find so repulsive right now?

A car pulls into the driveway. It's Xander's dad. The relief I feel knowing Xander is leaving washes over me. My dad goes out to the car and talks with Xander's dad, and Xander gets up and extends a hand to my mom. "Thanks for everything, Lily. Sorry, it turned out this way."

His voice lacks sincerity. He turns to me and smirks. "Sorry about your boyfriend. See you around."

I don't know what is more annoying, that I spent time texting and flirting with him or that he just nonchalantly called out the one thing I have been wanting with Jack all summer.

As he walks out to the car, I can't help but feel like we're closing a chapter I never really understood. What was it about that soccer camp? Was it really a matter of competitive rivalry, or was there something deeper that brought about this confrontation?

After Xander leaves, my parents turn to me. "Honey, I think it's best you distance yourself from Xander for a while. We don't know what's going on, but it's clear he isn't being entirely honest with us."

I nod my head in agreement. "Yeah," I reply, my voice tinged with regret. "I get that now."

I tell Mom and Dad that something was off with Xander since he came over. I mention how he wouldn't talk to me about Noah and kept trying to play footsie with me by the pool. The mention of footsie has my mom and dad laughing as Dad says, "He must not know you very well if he tried to touch your feet."

I say, "Yeah, dead giveaway that he is a psycho."

We all laugh, and my dad comes and puts his arm around me. "Hey, I'm sorry that I accused you of being in the middle of all of this. I haven't been nice to you since the tournament, and I'm sorry."

I snuggle into him. It's easy to forgive him when he is calling himself out.

"You're forgiven." I say, and then add, "I'm sorry for how I acted at the golf tournament, and I'm sorry for all of it."

Dad kisses the top of my head and tells me that I am forgiven and that we still have a lot to talk about but that it can wait until after the holiday. It feels good to finally get some of this out of the way and move on. I hate the way Dad and I have been acting toward each other.

Just then, Jill brings Jack inside his eyebrow, newly stitched by our neighbor. He looks worn out and weaker than I have ever seen Jack. I'm not used to seeing Jack busted up or hurting.

"Jack, how are you feeling?" I ask, trying to gauge his emotions.

"I'll survive," he says with a weak smile. "Just glad Xander's gone."

I nod, understanding him completely for the first time. "Me too, Jack. Me too."

The atmosphere is strange, like the calm after a sudden storm that nobody had seen coming. We've still got the party ahead of us, the holiday not stopping just because of the drama that unfolded. It's like we all feel the need to reset time to take us back to two hours ago when we didn't know what was coming.

But Jeremy isn't about to let it go. His approach is almost forensic, trying to figure out what just happened and why. He wants to gather all the fragments, dissect conversations, and retrace steps. He's like a detective, determined to solve his son's sudden lapse of judgment so it never happens again.

"All right, I want to hear it from the top," Jeremy begins, pacing back and forth in the pool area, now transformed into an unofficial investigation scene. "You aren't the type of kid to start fights, Jack."

Jack sighs heavily. "Dad, I told you, he started it back in camp.

He's just one of those types that boast about everything and can't back it up"

Jeremy pauses, giving Jack a scrutinizing gaze. "But why? Why did it get under your skin? What happened that made you snap?"

Jack hesitates, weighing how much truth to unload. "It's complicated, Dad. Competition brings out people's true selves, and let's just say Xander isn't who he pretends to be."

Jeremy's not satisfied, but Jill tells him to back off, at least for now. I think she is ready to be done with this. "Fine. But this isn't over. We need to get to the bottom of this."

Mom is supporting Jill with her need to move on and calls out, "Come on, everyone. We've got a party to host, and I don't intend to let one moment of madness ruin the whole evening."

It's just the thing my mom and Jill need to forget about what happened. They instantly shift gears and get back to making food. Mom calls Jazzy and Poppy to help, and by the grace of something, they don't call Jack or me. Jazzy and Poppy make both come and give Jack big hugs, and Poppy tells him, "Your face doesn't look as bad as it does on Street Fight when I kick your butt. I think you're gonna be okay."

Jack snorts a laugh and tells Poppy, "I will be better soon and will kick your butt any day in Street Fighter."

Poppy and Jazzy retreat into the kitchen, and Jack asks me if I want to go outside for a minute. We go outside and sit on the grass near the dock. I don't know where to start. This whole thing had me completely forget about my outburst in the hall before Jack went out on the boat, but now that we are sitting alone together, I can't help but think I owe Jack an apology for earlier.

I look at Jack, and even though his face is swollen, he gives me a small, familiar look. It's a look that says we both are sorry. I scoot closer to him so the sides of our bodies are touching.

Jack is shirtless, the dried remnants of blood still staining his shorts. His mom has focused so intently on cleaning up his face that she must've overlooked the rest. My mind reels, trying to take in this beaten version of Jack with the boy I've always seen. I attempt to recall what Xander looked like as he emerged from the pool, but my memories are a blur; all the vivid details from the fight are focused on Jack.

I remember the urgency when Jeremey pulled Jack from the water after he'd already pulled Xander out, instructing him to sit poolside. Jack's breaths came fast, his eye so clouded with blood I could barely see the pupil, but still, I could see Jack's gaze that kept darting between Xander and me. The haunting vision of his face swelling and blood trickling down his body still unsettles me so much I feel nauseous. I hated seeing him like that. I never want to see Jack hurt like this again.

I don't look at Jack, but I am close enough to him that I can feel the air going in and out of his body as he breathes. I'm not ready for the breakdown of what just happened, but then Jack speaks. "I found out at soccer camp that you and Xander knew each other."

This is news to me. Until now, Jack has remained cryptic about the poolside showdown, and whenever his dad probed, Jack would say it was about competition or Xander being a jerk. Also, Xander never once mentioned meeting Jack at soccer camp. Once again, I am seeing how Xander has kept things from me. But I guess Jack has too.

Not wanting to overwhelm him with a flurry of questions as Jeremy did, I grab his hand and turn his palm upward. I start to trace the lines on his palm with my finger like we used to do as kids. I wait for a moment before I ask. "Was this fight about me?"

If he answers just this one question, that will help me understand.

For a moment, he's quiet, still absorbed in looking at my finger, tracing the lines on his hang. Then he looks over at me, meeting my eyes, and whispers, "Yeah."

Our eyes lock, and I am reminded how bad his face looks—his swollen eye, the stitches, the cut on his cheek. I wrestle with the revelation that I somehow caused this ugly incident. "Thank you for telling me," I say softly, taking my time.

Patience has proven not to be my strong suit, but I am starting to realize how crucial it will be, especially with Jack. We hold each other's gaze, allowing the tension to dissipate. Finally, Jack opens up.

"One night, all the guys were talking about girls back home. Xander starts boasting about all these girls that he has hooked up with at his school, from social apps to his neighborhood; I mean, he made us all doubt him with how he was carrying on. I didn't like him before this, so him going on and on about hooking up with girls and being very descriptive about it just made me hate him even more."

I need to make one thing absolutely clear. "Jack, I've never kissed Xander," I say, needing him to know that information right now before he says anything else.

He nods. "I know."

When Jack came for the June weekend, we didn't talk about crushes or anything. We were so focused on just having fun and reconnecting after the drama of last summer. But Jack did ask me if part of my "glow-up" was getting my first kiss, and I had told him no.

Jack fidgets and grabs a clump of grass with his other hand, clearly wrestling with what to say next. "Another guy called Xander out, saying he was lying about all the girls he'd supposedly been with." As he talks, he keeps his eyes on the grass clump he's playing with, avoiding eye contact with me.

"He starts naming girls from his school, and I realize he goes to the same school as you because he mentioned Celeste and Morgan. But I knew he wouldn't mention you because you have never kissed anyone."

I once again stop him totally outraged that Xander would say anything about my friends. "He NEVER kissed Morgan or Celeste. What a jerk!"

Jack snorts a laugh. He loves it when I get so protective of my friends. "I know that too," he says.

Jack takes a deep breath before continuing. "Xander starts showing pictures and texts from all these girls. Then his phone buzzes; he tells everyone that the text is from his next 'target.' It was from you." I am mortified. Xander showed people our text messages. I am so grateful now that Jack still won't look at me, but I wonder what else he isn't telling me.

I want to stop Jack and tell him my side of the story. I want to tell him it was a crush that it didn't mean anything, that I would never have kissed Xander. But I can't. Because, honestly, I don't even know if it is true. I was falling for Xander. I did have a huge crush on him, and he did write me that letter telling me he liked me. Until this weekend, I was still toying with the idea that Xander could be my first kiss.

Jack waits for my response. I take a deep breath. "I had a crush on Xander freshman year. We were in the same friend circle, but it never progressed beyond that. He wrote a really sweet note that he put in my yearbook, and I thought maybe..." My voice trails off as I ponder how the guy who wrote such a sweet, honest note could also be the one who turned out to be so gross.

At the mention of the note, Jack looks up and meets my eyes. "Yeah, I heard about that note," he says, his curiosity piqued. "You know that it wasn't really from him, right?"

Confused, I ask, "What are you talking about?"

"He didn't write it," Jack says this is information I already have, but this is the first time I hear anything about the note not being from Xander.

"Xander's best friend asked him to give it to you because he was too nervous to give it to you himself. Xander took the note, copied it in his own handwriting, signed his name, and tucked it into the back of your yearbook. He found it hilarious. Xander kept telling everyone how he screwed his best friend out of being with the girl of his dreams."

My shoulder starts to sting. Maybe this pain is phantom pain happening, so I don't have to think about the shock that Jack just hit me with. The sweet note that made me start to like Xander again wasn't from Xander at all. I have to have Jack explain it again because what I think he is saying can't be true. "Wait, go back. What are you telling me?"

Recognizing the shock on my face, Jack exhales loudly. "I knew it," he mutters under his breath. "I knew you couldn't have known that it wasn't from him. You would not still be texting him if you knew."

"Are you saying that note—the reason I even considered having feelings for Xander—was actually from NOAH?"

I still can't process this. I have to ask again, "Jack, are you saying that Xander stole that letter from NOAH?!" I feel sick.

Jack sees how this is having an impact on me. He winces, seeing that I am not taking this well. Why did he not say anything before this?

"Yeah, the note is from Noah. I guess your boy Noah wrote it and asked Xander to give it to you because he was too nervous." I know Jack has just said all of this, but it's like I am hearing it for the first time as he slows down and explains it again.

"Xander read it, rewrote it in his handwriting, and put it in the back of your yearbook. I guess he got jealous of Noah liking you. He said something about wanting to be the first for all of the girls in your group and then laughed and told everyone that Noah could have his sloppy seconds."

I'm swimming in shame, reeling from my naivety. How could I not see that the letter was so uniquely tailored to me, noticing things only Noah would say? It all falls into place—the way the words echo Noah's subtle hints of our shared memories. The way Noah is so outgoing when it comes to our friendship and then so shy when it comes to telling me how he really felt.

I think back to our summer texts. There were times when I felt like I should call or FaceTime him, but I never did. Sure we would occasionally text dumb jokes, but I let these other two guys completely flood my thoughts. I have been a terrible friend.

Overwhelmed, I drop Noah's hand and touch my face with my hand, teetering on the edge of a full-on meltdown. Before I can dissolve into tears or release a scream, Jack continues, "Xander is a snake; he ran this whole game without a second thought about what it would do to his friends."

"There's more," he says reluctantly, almost as if he's afraid to let the next words escape his lips. "That first day I was at your place— you snapped a selfie in the kitchen. I was in the background." He waits for me to remember. The picture surfaces in my mind; I had taken it to avoid dealing with being so nervous around Jack and my new kindled infatuation with Xander and his note. But how could that photo matter now?

Jack hesitates, then goes on. "Xander recognized me in your photo. Realized I was your out-of-town friend. And he used that to taunt me, constantly bringing you up. Every text you sent him, he'd read it aloud to everyone, talking about how naive you were and how he was going to show you a thing or two when he got home."

A new wave of humiliation washes over me. My personal messages, those messages that I felt like I was learning how to be cute and flirty, were all read out loud at soccer camp, and who knows who else saw or read them? I'd been manipulated; my feelings were part of some twisted joke for Xander, while Noah's sincerity was stolen and Jack's friendship was exploited.

The heat floods my cheeks as I grapple with the realization that Xander has made a spectacle of my private texts, especially to Jack. A sudden thought surfaces, sharp and insistent: Why hadn't Jack told me any of this sooner? My eyes blur, and tears start spilling over.

"Why didn't you say something before?" My voice trembles, heavy with both accusation and vulnerability.

Jack's eyes lock on mine, and I see pity—sympathy layered with an understanding that only magnifies my humiliation. In that instant, I realize I can't bear to hear whatever justification he might offer. I abruptly stand, hastily wiping my cheeks.

"I can't deal with this now. I have to call Noah," I announce, my voice faltering.

I don't know if I really want to talk to Noah right now, but I know I can't sit here and think back on all of the texts I sent Xander. I can't have Jack tell me a play-by-play of what he thought or what was said about me. It feels like the ultimate betrayal from both Xander and Jack. I notice that Jack's face read a mixture of relief and regret washes over Jack's face; he's off the hook, at least for now. "I'm sorry, Noli," he murmurs, his words tinged with an undisguised sadness.

As I begin to walk back to the house, I glance back at him. Why wouldn't he tell me? What would have been different about this summer if I had known the note was from Noah or if Jack had told me what Xander was doing at camp? I just can't stand the thought of talking to Jack anymore. I know I should feel sorry for him with his busted-up face and that he did that for me. I should be grateful that he was trying to spare my feelings during camp, but I am so mad at him.

There are layers to the mess that's been made, layers I'm only just beginning to understand. But for now, one urgent thing has to be done and right now. I need to talk to Noah. I need to set at least one thing right. I have to let Noah know that I didn't know

14

Ignoring the crazy preparations for the BBQ downstairs, I make my way to my room. I feel like crying, but it seems like my body is revolting against me. Because as much as I want to cry, nothing comes. I am left wondering what to do about Noah. I worry that if I don't talk to him, Xander will call him and spin some lie about what happened, and I may lose Noah as a friend forever. I can't let that happen.

My fingers twitch nervously over my phone. I'm not sure how to start. I'm not sure how I feel toward Noah, I haven't had time to think about it. I know that what he wrote was so sweet, and I love him for it, but I just don't know if I like him like that. One thing is for sure: I wouldn't want him ever to think I would ignore something so sweet.

I start to type a text but then reconsider. This isn't a conversation to be had in bite-sized sentences and emojis. I need to hear his voice, and he needs to hear mine. I take a steadying breath and dial his number. After two nerve-wracking rings, it goes to voicemail. I freeze as the beep sounds, signaling my cue to speak. But I can't think of what to say. At that moment, I can't find the right string of sentences to tell Noah my regret, my apology, my explanation. Eventually, I hang up without leaving a message.

Almost immediately, a text notification pops up. It's Noah. A sinking feeling in my stomach tells me that he likely sent my call to voicemail intentionally—probably because he didn't want to talk to me.

Noah: Hey Noli, What's up?

The message isn't the cheery goofy Noah message that I am used to getting. He is getting straight to the point.

Me: Hi, can you talk?

I can see he has read my text, but I don't see the three bubbles pop up. He is sitting there trying to decide if he wants to talk to me. It kills me. I hurt him. Not on purpose, of course, but I hurt him. Finally, he sends a message back.

Noah: I can't talk, but I can text.

I want to hear his voice. I want to see him. I want to tell him everything and have him wrap me in one of his famous hugs and tell me that everything is going to be okay. I still haven't processed through how I feel about the note being from Noah, but I also know that I can't leave this entire thing alone. I need to be brave. I quickly text.

Me: I really need to talk to you about your note. The one you gave to Xander to give to me. I didn't know it was from you. Xander forged it and said it was from him.

I may be throwing Xander under the bus with his best friend, but at this point, I don't care. Jack was right about Xander. He is a snake.

It feels like forever before Noah texts me back, and I wish I could just talk to him.

Noah: I'll call you in twenty minutes.

It's a relief to see that Noah is willing to talk to me, but I don't think I can wait twenty minutes. It seems way too long to go without resolving this thing. I think through the messages I have sent him this summer. I have been such a terrible friend. Going back and forth between Jack and Xander and ignoring my friendship with Noah. My heart sinks as I think about all the ways I sucked this summer. I shouldn't be able to call it my sophomore summer; I should have to call it my screw-up summer.

I am trying to think of all the ways to distract myself. I think about cleaning my room or going downstairs to help with party prep, but I just can't focus. I know what I can do for twenty minutes until I can talk to Noah. I text my friends.

Me: RED ALERT for me! FaceTime me!

I instantly get Morgan, Celeste, and even Addy on FaceTime. Even though they are all in the middle of their Fourth of July celebrations themselves, they all show up for me. As soon as I see them, I burst into tears. I tell them everything. I tell them about not going out on the boat, about deciding to tell Xander I wasn't into him anymore and wanting to send a fake sick text to him so that he wouldn't come to the BBQ. I tell them about him coming over early and the disastrous fight in the pool. They all listen, completely shocked about what has happened.

I see Morgan smirk when I tell them about Jack tackling Xander into the pool and the brawl that happened.

Celeste even gives a self-satisfied whoop when she hears that the note isn't from Xander but from Noah. "I KNEW HE DIDN'T WRITE IT!"

It's almost like she just solved the "who done it" from a book, and we all laugh that she is so stoked to hear that Xander was lying about it the whole time. When I finally tell them that Noah should be calling at any minute, Celeste asks me, "What do you want Noah to say?"

I hadn't really thought about it. I just knew I wanted to get the truth out there. I didn't want to excuse being a bad friend all summer, but I did want him to know all of it. I say, "I don't know," but as soon as it comes out of my mouth, I know it's a lie.

I call myself out, "Actually, that's not true. What I want is to be friends with Noah." When I say it, I know it's true. I don't want to date Noah or be his girlfriend. I just want my friendship to still be strong after I tell him everything. I want him to forgive me for this summer and tell me he still thinks I'm awesome. Before anyone can say anything else, my phone rings. It's Noah.

I tell my friends Noah is calling, and they all give me heart signs and blow kisses to me. Just before I hang up, Addy says, "Call us back when it's over." I don't know if I will, but I nod and hang up.

I slide my phone to answer and say, "Hello?"

I don't get my bubbly, crazy friend on the other line. I get a hesitant, quiet version of Noah. I can't exactly read the tone in his voice. All he says is, "Hey, Noli."

I worry that I have already lost him. I may never have my friend back, and the thought of this instantly creates a lump in my throat. I shake my head to try and push through. I have to do this. No matter what happens. I have to tell him everything. I remind myself about Noah's goofy smile on the last day of school and his warm hug. This instantly has my nerves melt away, and I have a moment of courage when I start the conversation.

"Noah," I start, "I have been a terrible friend. A terrible human, really." From there, everything spills out. I let it all out, sharing the convoluted story of Xander and the letter, the ensuing text messages, the fight between Jack and Xander, and everything else in between.

Until this point, it feels like a recounting of a story, but now comes the difficult part. The part about us.

A knot tightens in my stomach as I take a deep breath. I could lose one of my best friends in the next few minutes. It's a high-stakes confession, and my anxiety is off the charts. But I press on, laying bare how I neglected our friendship while getting caught up with Jack and Xander. Then, I start telling him how I found out the note was his.

"As soon as I knew the letter was from you, it made sense. All of the sweet things you said, the way you talked about seeing me and getting excited each time. It all clicked together that it was you, not Xander." I brace myself for the hardest part of the conversation, but before I go on, Noah stops me.

"Noli, before you say anything else, I just want to say thank you. Thanks for calling me and letting me know what was going on. It takes guts to admit you were a jerk, and I appreciate it."

It feels good to hear him say this. Who knew someone agreeing that you were being a bad friend would actually be a relief? I wonder why I would have thought for a second that Noah would be mean about any of this. I want to continue and get the hardest part over, but Noah goes on.

"It makes sense that you didn't get the letter from me and why I never heard from you about it. But before you say anything else, I think you should know... I have a girlfriend." Noah stops talking.

Noah has a girlfriend? This is great news! I don't have to break his heart and tell him I just want to be friends. We CAN be friends if he has a girlfriend. My body is betraying my mind. As soon as he says he has a girlfriend, my stomach drops, and the lump in my throat returns. I keep thinking that Noah having a girlfriend is a good thing, but everything inside me feels crushed. I realize Noah is talking, and I have to refocus.

"...we met a couple of weeks ago on the river. She is from here. She's great; you would really like her."

I want him to know I am his best friend. I swallow and try to get the lump in my throat to leave. With fake enthusiasm, I say, "She sounds great!" I am not sure what else to say, but that isn't what a best friend would say. I imagine that I am talking to Morgan or Celeste, and I say, "I hope you are so happy. I can't wait to hear more about her." As I say it, I realize I mean it.

All I want is for Noah to be happy. I want the best for him. I still haven't figured out why it hurts so much, but I am grateful that I don't have to break his heart by telling him I just want to be friends. There is a lull in the conversation, and I'm not sure what else to say. Everything that has happened today instantly catches up to me, and I am exhausted.

Noah quickly says, "Oh hey, that's Hannah on the other line. I better go."

I realize I must have missed hearing his girlfriend's name. I am assuming it's Hannah. I'm so tired I'm not sure what to say. "Oh, okay."

Before he goes, Noah says, "Noli?"

I sound quiet even to my own ears, "Yeah?"

"Thanks for calling me. I just had a spot as my best friend become available recently, and I think you just filled it." His voice sounds genuine and sincere, and hearing him makes the tears start again. I laugh and say, "You got it."

" And Noli?" Noah says.

"Yeah?"

"Do you know what elevator jokes and our friendship have in common?"

I think for a moment and then say, "Because they work on so many levels?"

"Exactly." Then he hangs up.

It's the perfect Noah way to end our call and let me know that we are good. I don't know what it is about what Noah said, but I lose it. I break down for what feels like the millionth time that day. Why do hard things always leave me in a puddle?

As I lay on my bed and cry, the scent of grilled meat and charred vegetables wafts through my window, a reminder that the Fourth of July barbecue is underway. I also start to hear more and more voices in the backyard. The party must be in full swing, but I can't bring myself to go down and enjoy it. My favorite holiday seems to have passed without being that enjoyable at all.

I ponder the complicated dynamics of my life at the moment. I have a childhood friend, and we have this weird but exciting chemistry that hangs between us, and I don't know where we stand.

I have had a crush for almost a year on a gorgeous guy who ended up being a total sleaze and a really bad friend. And, I must say, I should have known better as soon as he tried to play footsies with me. Gross.

I have my favorite guy friend whom I've carelessly ignored, who, in reality, ended up being the guy who had a crush on me for a year, and yet—ironically—might be the one who's slipped through my fingers. But he's taken now. Which should be okay because we can just upgraded to being best friends.

Wow. Even as I think about all of them, it sounds like a lot. Why do relationships have to be so complicated? Why can't I be like a regular girl who has one crush and sees it through?

I sit and process through the day, starting with Noah. It's a good thing I called him today. I am glad he is happy and has a girlfriend. Most of all, I'm glad we are still friends and that I apologized for blowing him off this summer. When I think of Xander, all that I can think is, "Don't let the door hit you on the way out." I was entrenched in my very own *Gossip Girl* episode with him. UGH.

I have to forgive myself for getting involved in sending him flirty texts and thinking that he was different than he really was. I think if I've learned anything, a relationship that needs to be kept secret probably isn't a good one. Also, some guys are jerks.

Now, my thoughts shift to Jack, the one puzzle I've yet to piece together. I probably need to apologize for leaving him sitting on the grass by himself after he told me everything about Xander and the soccer camp. I still don't fully understand why he wouldn't have just said something, but I know Jack; he would never do anything to hurt me intentionally. I have to let that one go because I have more pressing things to think about Jack.

Where do we stand? We are definitely more than friends. There was undeniable chemistry between us at the balloon festival this morning. Yet, I can't help but think maybe the chaos of the day has soured things. I wish I could know without worrying, wondering, and waiting.

There is a knock on my door, and Jack opens my door with a crash and sticks just his banged-up head through my door. He does an impression of my dad as he asks, " Hey, Cowboy, can I come in?"

I haven't heard my dad ever call Jack Cowboy, but I also wouldn't put it past him either. The impression makes me laugh. "Of course, come in," I reply.

As he steps into my room, I catch another glimpse of his bruised and stitched-up face. It seems almost surreal that all of that happened today; it feels like an eternity ago.

He sits beside me on the bed, turns to face me, and looks at me with his one good eye. The other is so swollen it's practically shut. Normally, the color of his eyes offers a clue to his mood, but today, with one eye bloodshot and the other concealed, they're unreadable.

An urge overtakes me—I want to reach out and gently touch the places where he's hurting. As if my touch could somehow speed up the healing process or at least convey how much I care. The intensity of my desire to touch him makes my cheeks flush.

Shifting my gaze away from his face, I look down at my hands. "I spoke to Noah," I start.

Jack nods, not pressing for details, but I feel I owe him some context. "He's a great guy, nothing like Xander. I told him about everything. He's seeing someone now, which is good. I have only ever liked him as a friend."

I deliver each sentence as if rattling off a weather report, unsure of what Jack actually wants to know. I notice Jack exhale; it's not like he was holding his breath during my account of Noah, but the relief washes over him. It makes me think that maybe Jack was worried that I had feelings for Noah.

This revelation sends a chill down my spine. If Jack didn't care about me as more than a friend, it wouldn't have bothered him if Noah and I were together. He may have even been encouraging me to go for it with Noah, but he never did. Seeing how relieved he is that Noah is just a friend makes it more clear to me where I stand with Jack. He likes me.

I decide to lay it out clearly. "I've never liked Noah, you know. Even before finding out he has a girlfriend, he has always been a friend. Apparently, after Xander pulled the stunt, he kicked Xander out of his best friend's spot and gave it to me."

Xander doesn't even warrant a mention; he's a closed chapter, but I thought that telling Jack what Noah said would help show him our friendship. I hope Jack gets where I'm coming from. We lock eyes, and for a moment, it's as though we're the only two people in the world. I give myself a mental push, and my courage surfaces for a brief moment.

Taking a deep breath, I go for it. "So, um, Jack, the thing is... I really, really like you."

As soon as it comes out, I regret it. It sounds juvenile. Not how I feel at all. It feels like something a sixth grader would write on a piece of paper, "I really, really like you. Do you like me? Check the box, Yes or No" My face flushes, and I want a do-over.

The Fourth of July celebrations beyond my window suddenly seem miles away, the music and laughter a faint backdrop to the silence enveloping my room. Now I wish I were outside by the lake, swirling sparklers in the air if only to escape this nerve-wracking embarrassing moment. I wanted Jack to know, but I am so afraid that maybe he is going to pull away. That his words from earlier today at the balloon festival have somehow expired, or that he has realized maybe I'm not worth all of this.

The silence right now instantly makes me a ball of fear and doubt. I feel like I used every ounce of courage I had to say what I did, and now I can't think of anything else to say. , I remember this morning and how Jack's hand felt in mine. I want more of that. I want more of all of him. And now I'm freaking out a little. What if this is worse than that awkward Noah situation?

What if he laughs at me and tells me I'm childish or that he was only teasing me this morning? If he's not into me, what will all of our summers look like knowing that I confessed my feelings and he rejected me? Suddenly, I'm regretting being all brave. Maybe I should've just kept my big mouth shut.

I stand up and walk to the window to distract myself. Jack still hasn't said anything. I have to believe that this morning wasn't nothing. Jack isn't like Xander. He doesn't play games. Or does he? I realize I don't really know. The truth is, I don't really know him in this way. He lives a whole different life on the opposite side of the country, complete with his own friends, his own world, and his own crushes. We have never had this type of chemistry between us.

As I turn to backtrack everything I've just confessed, I find that Jack has quietly moved closer to me. We are facing each other. No words, just a moment. He gently brushes my hair away from my sling, his fingertips lightly grazing my collarbone. His touch starkly contrasts the aggressive hug that Xander gave me earlier.

A shiver courses through me as his fingers gently touch the gold chain necklace that rests against my skin. When he pulls away, the necklace settles back against me, and I'm filled with a sharp longing for more. More of his touch, more of this closeness.

Our eyes meet, and it feels as though the world freezes. He finally breaks the silence. "Noli, your first kiss should be perfect. Kissing a guy who looks like he got into a bar fight isn't exactly that."

In that split second, I get what he's saying. He'd kiss me if it weren't for his busted-up face. But right now, I don't care. I don't care that I can only see out of one of his eyes or that his face is all swollen. I don't care about his swollen lip or the stitches on his face. I don't care that we are standing in my bedroom and that our families are down, living it up at the BBQ. I don't even care that

I'm stuck in a sling and wearing a worn-out pair of my comfiest PJs.

None of that matters. All that matters is this moment and the guy standing in front of me, as imperfectly perfect as it is. All that truly matters is this moment. All that matters is that we like each other. His words from this morning when we were lying in the field come back to me, "We were meant to end up together.". With a small smile, I take a step toward him and our bodies are touching. This is what I've yearned for. It is what I have been craving from him. I want to feel the electrifying moment of Jack's lips meeting mine, as flawed and perfect as the moment itself. This is what the perfect moment feels like to me.

He slides his hands around my waist, careful with me and my shoulder. He is mirroring my smile, and our eyes meet one final time as if asking for silent permission. In a heartbeat, that distance vanishes. Our lips meet, hesitantly at first, like two magnets finally giving in to the pull they've been resisting. The world around us— the loud music, the laughter from downstairs, even the teddy bear on my shelf—fades into nothingness.

The sensation surpasses all of my fantasies. My lips against his, our bodies pulled together by a magnetic energy. Just when I think it can't feel any better, Jack's hands slowly make their way up my back. He draws me into him, getting me even closer, and I melt.

I don't know how long we kiss, but we are startled apart when the first explosion from the fireworks goes off. Out of my window, the entire night sky lights up as the fireworks show from the country club starts. We laugh at how we both jumped at the same time when the fireworks went off.

As soon as we are apart from one another, I feel even more unsure of myself. What am I supposed to do after I kiss someone? Should I thank him? Give him a high-five? Fist-bump and call him Tiger? I mentally flip through romantic scenes from *Gossip Girl* for guidance and quickly dismiss them as profoundly unhelpful.

Fortunately, Jack isn't weird. He leans in, kisses my forehead gently, and says, "I have been wanting to do that for a long time."

I smile at Jack's confession that he has wanted to kiss me for a long time, and before I can say anything, he says, "It might be a while before I kiss you again with my lip all swollen, but I promise you I will do a lot more of that with you."

I realize that kissing probably didn't feel amazing with the state of his face, and I furrow my eyebrows, thinking that maybe he didn't like kissing me as much as I liked kissing him.

He laughs, and I can tell he knows exactly what I am thinking.

A smile stretches across my face, crinkling my nose, I joke, "Was it that bad?"

I still can't see his eyes very well, but I imagine they are sparkling, or maybe they have changed to the color of green he gets when he is mischievous or teasing. I think he is going to tell me that it wasn't great or that I should get more practice, but instead, he says, "It was perfect."

I grin up at him, very aware of how much taller he is. This would have driven me nuts before, but I adore Jack being taller than me now. I love how I fit with him and how he leaned down to kiss me.

He smiles down at me now and says, "Well, little lady, can I escort you to a Fourth of July party?"

I don't want to leave. I want to kiss him again. I want to stay here longer. I pout my lips and shake my head. This moment is something I've dreamt of for a long time. It can't be over yet.

Even with my pouty lips and the alluring smile I am giving him, Jack keeps in character. "Ma'am, that's not going to do. This is your favorite holiday. and I'm not going to let you miss it because of some guy."

I laugh at the mention of 'some guy.'

"As the official sheriff around here, it's my solemn duty to escort you to said festivities," he adds, maintaining the playful act.

Realizing he won't budge on this, I accept the inevitable. We slip out of my room, me still in my pajamas, and into the vibrant chaos that is a Fourth of July celebration. While everyone is looking up at the night sky, Jack slips his hand into mine, and he quickly looks down at me and gives me a wink.

Just as I'm reveling in holding hands with Jack, I catch sight of Jazzy's shocked, excited expression. It's clear we've been caught. A momentary impulse tells me to retract my hand, but I sense that Jazzy understands how complicated this relationship between Jack and me has been. She mouths a gaping, *WHAT?!* complete with raised eyebrows.

With an ecstatic grin, I mouth back, *I KNOW!* Jazzy nods her understanding, and I realize there won't be any sleep for me tonight until she hears all about it. This feels right. This is how it was always going to happen. Just like Jack said, we were always meant to end up together.

15

The next morning everyone sleeps in. Sleeping in isn't in the cards for me. My shoulder aches, and I can't find a comfortable position to go back to bed. So at six am, I am up and out of bed. I grab the book and quietly head downstairs. I make my way out to the lake and sit on the dock so I can put my feet in the water while I read. Usually, if I was up this morning, I would be on the lake on my paddleboard or going to the golf course, but I can't do either.

The cool water feels good on my skin, and I ache to be in the water. I settle for this and start reading. I'm about three pages in when I hear someone coming outside from the house. I look over and see Jeremey coming down to the dock. It looks like he has already been out for his morning run. Leave it to Jeremy to not miss his workout even after such a crazy day yesterday. I smile as he makes his way onto the dock and pulls one of the chairs over to sit by me.

"Morning," I say.

He has his protein drink in one hand and takes a sip as he sits down on his chair.

"Hey Noli. How's the shoulder this morning?" He asks.

I scrunch my nose up. "Honestly, not great. I was really hard to sleep last night."

I wait for Jeremy to launch into a lecture on how selfish I was during my tournament or a tutorial on how to work out my shoulder to get the fastest recovery time, but he doesn't. He just sits there nodding his head and sipping his protein drink. I wonder if I have dodged a long discussion when he starts to talk.

"Noli, you are really important to Jack," Jeremy says.

I'm not sure where he is going with this, but I am surprised that he is bringing up Jack. My shoulder is aching, so I stand up and slowly start to do the stretches the doctor told me to start doing.

I look at Jeremy and say, "Jack's important to me too."

I can't imagine Jack confided in Jeremy last night about the kiss, so why is Jeremy all of a sudden wanting to talk to me about Jack and me? I wait for him to say more before I say anything else.

Jeremy keeps talking, "Yesterday, the whole mess with your friend..."

He is talking about the fight with Xander. It feels like it was months ago, not yesterday afternoon.

I want to let Jeremy know where I stand with Xander before he launches into a whole thing.

"Ex-friend," I tell him. "Xander and I aren't friends anymore."

Jeremy nods his head, pleased to hear this.

"Glad to hear that you know where your loyalties should be." He says.

If he only knew how loyal I am to Jack. Especially after last night.

"Jack is going to need that. He will not only need your loyalty, but he will also need 100% of your support."

I'm not sure what he is talking about. But this is Jeremy. Always laser-focused on Jack's potential and future. I nod my head, letting him know that I understand.

"More than ever, Jack is going to need the people closest to him to be all in on his future. No distractions. No drama. No reason to start fights with random guys. I need you to promise me that you are all in on Jack. Do you understand what I am asking of you, Magnolia?"

In his own way, Jeremy is telling me not to distract Jack from soccer. He is telling me not to drag Jack into an episode of *Gossip Girl*. I'm not sure what our relationship will look like long distance, but I have always been team Jack in soccer and his future. I want him to reach all the goals he has for himself.

"I get it," I tell Jeremy. You have nothing to worry about it. That won't happen ever again."

Jeremy stares at me. It's like he is trying to decide if he can actually trust me. The intense focus makes me uncomfortable. I'm not sure what else Jeremy wants me to say. I assure him, "I'm team Jack all the way."

When I say that, he lets out a deep breath, takes a sip of his protein drink, and as he stands up, he says, "Remember that. I either need you to be all in on supporting him, or I need you to get out of the way."

Jeremy walks back to the house and goes inside. What did he mean when he said get out of the way? Does he know about last night? I still find it hard to believe that Jack would say anything about us. But the intensity that Jeremy just came out of me makes me wonder. I have to remind myself that sometimes he's just intense like that. Usually, I have one of the other parents around to calm Jeremy down or tell him to change subjects. He's an intense guy, and I think this was him being protective of Jack and not wanting anything to jeopardize all of Jack's hard work in soccer. I chalk up that whole conversation to that and go back to reading.

I must have read on the dock for hours because I soon hear the rest of the house waking up and smell breakfast. The day after the Fourth is the one day Jeremy and Dad cook breakfast a year. I can smell the traditional biscuits and gravy with bacon cooking, and all of a sudden, I am starving. I stand up, stretch, and make my way back to the house.

I walk into the kitchen, and suddenly my stomach flips. Jack is shirtless on one of the barstools, with a pair of board shorts on. I can't see his face, but I take in his back muscles and how tan he has gotten this summer. He looks good, and I can't help but smile.

"Earth to Magnolia!" Poppy says, and she waves her hands in front of my face.

While I was admiring Jack's tanned body, Poppy must have been talking to me. Count on Poppy to be the one to call me out. I look down at her and raise my eyebrows expectantly.

"What do you need, Pops?" I ask her.

"I asked you if you saw the fireworks last night." She says.

Jazzy is sitting behind us at the table, and I hear her say, "She was too busy making her own fireworks."

Luckily Poppy doesn't hear her. But I have, and my face instantly turns red. Jack comes to my rescue and turns around. His face looks so much worse today. Even from where I am standing, I can see shades of red and purple on his face. Places where I didn't even notice he had gotten hurt last night.

"Pops, Noli and I were standing right next to you last night during the fireworks, you silly girl. Remember, you threw snaps at us?"

Poppy grins wide. "OH YEAH!"

Jack looks at me with a smile that I haven't ever seen before and mouths, "Morning," just to me. Can you both melt and feel electricity course through your body at the same time? Because that is exactly what it feels like right now, standing in the kitchen with our families all around us.

I'm not sure what to do here. I mouth back, "Morning," trying not to be distracted by his toned body. How is it that I have seen him like this countless times, and it has never affected me? But now I can't stop staring.

Dad says, "Breakfast is ready," and I am pulled away from looking at Jack.

Jazzy has already eaten her breakfast, so she gets up to go and get ready for the day, but then Mom calls to her. "Hey Jazz! Can you come back in here?"

I am getting my breakfast, and Jeremy says to all of us, "Let's all sit down at the table; we have something to talk to you kids about."

This is probably one of those talks where the parents tell us what the rest of the week is going to look like. It's not unusual for us to do this, but when I look at Jill, I start to worry about what this is about. She looks nervous. I glance at Jack to see if he has picked up on this too. I realize he looks just as nervous as his mom. Oh no! Has something happened? Is this about Jeremy and Jill? All of a sudden, I don't want to eat breakfast.

We are all sitting down, and the parents are glancing back and forth at each other, probably deciding who should take the lead on this discussion. This is killing me. I can tell that something has happened by the way they all look at each other, and Jack won't look at me.

My mom says, "So, we have something we want to tell you."

She stops, and I can tell she isn't sure what to say next. It's like hot potato, my mom quickly says, "Jill, why don't you tell them. It's your announcement."

Jill is startled at being asked to take over. "Um, yes. Ok. So as you know, Jack has been working really hard in soccer this year. Well, not just this year. He is always working hard in soccer. We are so proud of him."

What is happening? I can't gauge it, and Jack isn't giving me any clues.

Jeremy takes over talking, and Jill seems relieved. "There has always been one goal for Jack with soccer: to go pro. He did well at the soccer camp this summer, and some major players noticed. He has been selected to play for a different team. It's an ECNL league team. It's the Elite Club National League."

He says this like we are supposed to know what it means. From what I gather, Jack is moving up leagues. This is great news, but I'm not sure why they are making such a big deal about it. Jack moves up leagues every so often, and they never have to announce it like this. They usually just send a text to our family's group chat.

Jazzy is sitting next to Jack, and she playfully shoves his arm, "Way to go, bro! Proud of you."

Jack purses his lips and nods at her. I watch him, aware of his movement and the way he isn't looking at anyone, even how he is breathing. Everything seems tense. I refocus back on Jeremy when he starts talking again.

"The ECNL league is a huge deal. It's the league for players right before going pro." He explains to us.

This is great news! Jack has worked so hard for this. Jack glances at me and smiles wide at him. I want him to know how proud of him I am. He gives me a tight smile and a slight nod. He doesn't seem as excited as everyone else.

Now warmed up enough with the subject to talk, Jill takes over. "Jack has been selected to play on the ENCL team here in Utah!"

Soccer is Jack's life. He practices, trains, and studies soccer like it's his full-time job. If he is playing soccer in Utah, that means that he is moving to Utah. Jack is moving to Utah. The thought of it hits me hard. Jack is going to be close. Poppy figures this out at the same time I do.

"Is Jack moving in with us?" She asks excitedly.

Jack smiles and says, "Not quite moving in with you, Pops, but close."

Now excited to join in, Mom says, "The Fosters are moving HERE! They just put an offer on the house two doors down. We are all going to be neighbors!"

At this, we all freak out. We have always talked about how much fun it would be to live by the Fosters. Our parents even talk about how they will travel together when they retire, live by each other, and grow old together. Part of that dream seems to come true before they get too old. Plus, Jack is going to be here. This morning's intense talk with Jeremy now makes more sense. He wanted my support with Jack coming here, going to school with me, and his training. I guess it was Jeremy's small hint of what was to come. I am so proud of my Jack. He has my absolute full support.

My Jack. I can't believe that we won't have to try to have a long-distance relationship. I get to have him living here, just a couple of doors away from me. Everyone is celebrating, jumping up and down, giving Jack hugs, and congratulating him. I wait my turn and then go over to him. I say, "I'm so proud of you!" He smiles, but it still looks tense. I whisper to him, "You don't seem happy."

He turns and mumbles, "I'll tell you later."

Everyone is talking over each other, and I hear slices of information. Jeremy has to leave today and get back to work. Lily is staying and finalizing buying the house and getting Jack enrolled at school (my school!), and Jack is going to be here for another week before he has to get home. He and Lily are going to head home, start packing up the house, and say goodbye to friends. Jack will stay with us for the first week of school while his parents finish up and move everything to Utah.

This is exciting. We all know how much Jack has wanted this. This is one step closer to going pro. It's basically like a league saying that they recognize how good he is and want to invest in him. We can't stop celebrating and congratulating Jack. I am pretty sure my dad uses every single nickname he has for Jack.

Everything's a whirlwind. This morning, I was convinced that Jack was leaving, that our first kiss was doomed to be our last. But now? He's staying. With us. Going to my school. I can't help but smile, the corners of my mouth stretching so wide they might hit my ears. I squeeze Jack's arm and say, "You're going to love Cascade Prep!"

Jack quietly says, "Noli, I have a life back home. I have friends. I have teammates. It's not like it's easy to leave all of that."

Honestly, I'm a little stung. Shouldn't he be jumping for joy, at least a little? But then I remind myself that Jack's life is getting shaken up, not just mine. I realize that this huge announcement means something different to all of us. For me, it's exciting and a dream come true to know that we get to be together. But for Jack, it means sacrifice, navigating a completely new school, team, friends, all of it. I take a deep breath, letting the gravity of the moment sink in. Whatever happens next, we're both stepping into new worlds. But right now, Jack needs to know he won't be navigating this alone.

"Hey," I say softly, sitting beside him. "You okay?"

He turns to me, and for a moment, I see a flash of something indescribable cross his eyes. He gives me a small smile that doesn't reach his eyes and nods. "Yeah, I'm good. It's all just... a lot, you know?"

"Yeah, I can imagine," I respond, but we both know that's not entirely true. I can't imagine what he's feeling, a life uprooted in a matter of minutes. That would be hard, but I still don't know why he isn't happy about being close to me. That should make him happy, right? I focus back on him. "It's okay to feel overwhelmed."

He sighs and nods again, more genuinely this time. "Thanks, Noli, I needed to hear that from you."

He looks back at me with his swollen face and says, "I was worried you were going to get mad at me for not being excited right at this moment, too."

Busted. Jack knows me so well. I scrunch my nose up at him. "Well...." I give him my smile that lets him know I'm busted.

He shakes his head, acknowledging that he knows me so well. I still haven't gotten him to laugh. I want to hear him laugh right now. I want to know he is going to be okay.

"You caught me, Sheriff. What's my punishment?" My eyes glint with a hint of flirtatious fun.

He laughs, and the sound makes me relax, knowing that even though this is a shock for him, he's going to be fine.

He raises his eyebrows and scoots close enough that our bodies are touching. I go hot all over. He leans in, and his lips touch my ear as he whispers, "I can think of a couple of punishments for you."

Blood rushes to my face, and the room is suddenly a thousand degrees. I can't believe Jack is hard-core flirting with me right in front of our families. I don't even know what to say. I want to turn my head and find his lips with mine. I want to kiss him hard, but we are sitting here, steps away from our parents.

Jack continues, "First thing I'm going to do to you is"—he pauses—"steal your room and move in. You can have the guest room."

I move away fast so I can look him in the eyes. He is teasing me. I smack him on the arm with my good hand and say loudly, "You can't have my room!"

I almost forget that our families are around. I want to hug him, to kiss him on his busted cheek, but Poppy reminds me where we are and who else is here, "You can share my room!" She yells.

Everyone laughs and continues to talk. The atmosphere around us is buzzing with the laughter and conversation of our families, but in our little pocket of the world, it's like time has stilled.

"I was worried about you, you know," I confess, taking advantage of our unspoken intimacy. "When you didn't react like everyone else, I thought you didn't want to be here. With me."

He glances down at our hands, intertwined but hidden. "I was just blindsided, Noli. My whole world just turned upside down, and I guess, for a moment, I forgot that this is what I have always wanted. Both you and the contract for soccer."

Jack has worked so hard for this. I am so proud of him. I feel like the stars have aligned perfectly that he got the opportunity to play in Utah. He could have gotten a contract in so many different places, but he got accepted here. It is just too perfect not to think that this was meant to be.

16

Summer unfolds in a way that is both unexpected and utterly beautiful. Jeremy heads back to their home, leaving Jack a rigorous workout plan, and promises to check in daily to ensure he is ready for the next chapter of his soccer career. Jack and his mom are scheduled to go home in just a couple of days, and I am dreading seeing Jack leave, even if it's just for a couple of weeks. All these transitions are happening so fast, but one constant since the Fourth of July remains—Jack and me.

We have both started to heal. Jack's face is almost back to normal, and all that is left from his fight with Xander is a small scar where his stitches used to be. I am out of my sling and going to physical therapy every day. Even though I don't look hurt, my shoulder still aches every day, and my doctor won't clear me to start playing golf for another couple of months.

Jack has been sticking to his dad's training schedule, which has him gone all day. I miss him, but I'm also so glad that every evening he comes home, and we get to spend time together.

During the day, I spend time in therapy or catching up with friends. I've been texting Noah every day. I even got to meet his girlfriend, Hannah, over FaceTime. Noah was right, she is super sweet, and I like her a lot. Noah seems to be loving his time with her, which I love. Morgan hasn't been able to talk his dad out of marrying the crazy woman. I have felt terrible for Morgan. It sounds like she has had a terrible summer. I just got off the phone with her, and she is coming home early. She is at the airport now. Addy has been crushing all of her comps, and she even got a huge modeling contract for a dance wear company, which is a big deal. And, best news ever, she broke up with Chris. They are staying friends, but she said she wanted a fresh start when she starts school. Morgan finished her book in record time, and it is at the publisher's getting edits done. She is thrilled with how it turned out. I can't wait to read it. It seems like all of us had pretty crazy summers, and I am counting down the days until we can all be together.

I am sitting in my family room reading the rest of my book when I hear something that makes me stop reading and look up. I see Jack staring at me with a smile playing on his lips. I am surprised to see him here. He should be training. I also wonder how long he has been sitting here watching me read. My book is getting really good. I was just smiling while reading about the main character in the book kissing the hottest guy at school. It was just getting good.

Jack comes toward me, "You have no idea how much I love watching you read." He says.

I am shocked to hear that he loves to hear me read. Who likes watching someone else read? I ask, "You watch me read?"

"Absolutely," he says as he comes and next by me. "You get this secret smile when you get to the good part of your book. It's like you have an inside joke between you and the author or characters."

I feel the heat rising to my cheeks, "You notice that?"

"I love getting to know parts of you that I have never seen before." He says as he reaches up and touches my gold chain.

I love the way he touches my gold chain so that he can be close. I love the way his fingertips wander to my collarbone. His fingers are making their way up my neck when he asks, "Want to go paddle-boarding with me?"

I sigh. "Dad won't let me with my shoulder."

I'm annoyed with my dumb shoulder and a little with my dad and how strict he has been about it. We had a really great talk about the tournament and everything that happened with Coach Gus. But I still had consequences; staying positive about it has been hard.

Jack smiles while still tracing his finger on my neck, "I already asked him." He finally looks at me. "He said as long as I take good care of you, I can take you wherever I want."

It feels like Jack is a knight in shining armor saving me from a tower of boredom. How is this boy real? The way Jack looks at me, his fingers on my skin, all of it. My heart feels like it's trying to escape my chest, beating wildly as if it knows something incredible is happening. For the first time, I truly understand what people mean when they say time slows down. Jack's eyes lock on to mine, and it feels like he is looking right into me.

"I'd love to go paddleboarding with you," I finally manage to say, my voice barely more than a whisper.

The corner of his mouth turns into a real, genuine smile that makes my stomach do somersaults. "I was hoping you'd say that."

We sit in comfortable silence for a moment, and the atmosphere has a new kind of energy—intense yet comfortable, like the air before a summer storm. Jack's fingers stop their tracing, and he moves his hand down to mine. I think he wants to hold my hand, but instead of interlocking our fingers, he stretches his fingers out over mine slowly. He says, a smile playing at his mouth, "Look at that. Even my fingers are taller than yours."

Before, I would have smacked him and told him he was dumb. But all I want to do is lean in and kiss him. I don't dare to do that here in the family room. I lean closer to him and let my lips make their way to his ear. I don't say anything for a couple of seconds. Just let him feel me breathe. I feel him shiver. Mission accomplished. I smile and whisper, "Let's go paddleboarding."

I stand up and go to get my swimming suit on. I glance behind me and see Jack looking up at the ceiling and letting out a big sigh. Good. I can tease him like he teases me. I go change, and Jack gets the paddleboard.

Jack holds the paddleboard still for me as I climb on and sit in the middle with my legs crossed. He pushes us off and, kneeling, gets three strokes in before he stands up. He takes a couple of steps forward, and we are touching, me sitting cross-legged, looking forward out at the lake and golf course, and him behind me paddling us out.

We make our way to a secluded part of the lake, a hidden nook not visible from the house. Jack hands me the paddle, and I put it to the side. Jack sits down close and straddles me so I can be close to him. I lean back against his chest.

We stay like this for a moment, but it's too hard to be this close to him without kissing him. The urge to kiss him is overwhelming. I tilt my head up, and it's as though he read my mind; his lips meet mine with a fervor that hasn't been there before. The angle is awkward, but the intensity of the moment leaves us both a bit reckless. I didn't realize that kissing could be so different, even with the same person. I am getting into this just as much as he is, but my neck is at a weird angle. I go to turn around so I can kiss him better. I shift my body around, and we flip the board in a flash.

We both go flying one way and the board the other. Jack pops up fast from the water and yells, "NOLI!" I pop up laughing because of how hilarious we must have looked, but I stop as soon as the pain in my shoulder comes back. "Ouch," I say.

Jack is worried, but I tell him I'm totally fine because I don't want him to worry. Jack swims over and grabs the board. He tries to help me, but with my arm out of commission, I struggle. Usually, getting on a board is as easy as walking, but trying to navigate getting on the board with one arm is a challenge.

We try several times, each time flipping Jack off it. We laugh each time because it is just too funny. What if we had to explain to my dad how we flipped the board and why I couldn't get back on?

Finally after the eighth try, we get it. Jack has to be in the water and give my butt a boost to get me on top of the board. Jack has his hands on my butt when he says, "I don't care if this takes us a hundred tries. I am committed to getting this lift right."

I have to stale fish onto the board and then slowly roll myself all the way on. I swat him on the head when I am finally on the board. "You pervert." I tease.

"You liked it." He says and winks at me.

When it looks like I am secure, Jack pulls himself up easily. We lie with our heads next to each other and our legs going in opposite directions as we catch our breath. The silence feels more intimate than any words we could say. Jack's eyes meet mine, and sitting here with him like this feels so good.

"Today was perfect," he says softly, "Even though I almost had to tell your dad I flipped you off the board while I was kissing you and couldn't get you back."

"I would love to hear that conversation," I say to him as I get lost in his eyes.

Jack smiles. "You know we are eventually going to have to tell the parents.

I smile back, thinking of all the stolen moments to come, the secrets we'll have to keep from my parents, and the limitless joy of spending time with someone who was once just a friend and is now so much more. "Yeah, maybe when school starts," I suggest, not wanting to ruin our secret life.

We lie there on the paddleboard, floating in a part of the lake, invisible to the rest of the world, and I realize that sometimes the best things are those that remain unseen, tucked away in the hidden corners of our lives and our hearts. We don't need an audience to validate what we have. It seems crazy to me that we are going to be sophomores. Maybe we are too young to fall for each other, but then

I remind myself this is part of being a teenager. Learning how to flirt, kiss, love.

Finally, we decide it's time to paddle back. Jack stands up, and I manage to wiggle around and put my head on the top of the paddle board. I stay lying down, and instead of looking out at the lake, I watch Jack paddle us back in. As we glide through the water, our laughter ringing in the air, I can't help but think how incredibly lucky I am. I look up at Jack, his eyes focused and concentrated.

The future is uncertain, but I realize I'm not worried or anxious as I look at him. With Jack here, whatever comes is going to be worth doing.

As we near the house, we both get quiet. Maybe it's not wanting my family to hear us, or maybe we are both thinking about what is ahead in the next year for us together and individually. As we step off the paddleboard and onto solid ground, our eyes meet one last time before we join the world again. No words are needed; our smiles say it all.

We ended up together. That's all that matters.

JUNIOR SUMMER

I open my yearbook at our annual yearbook sleepover and already the tears threaten to start. I'm not worried about finding a note professing love or what McKinley has written. It's what I know I won't find in here that has me feeling so emotional.

How is it that the person I spent the most time with all sophomore year, my person, my boyfriend wouldn't write anything in my yearbook? I take a deep breath and remind myself that ex-boyfriends don't sign the yearbooks of their ex-girlfriends.

Junior summer just won't be the same without Jack.

ACKNOWLEDGMENTS

This has been such a fun project to work on. Thanks to the team over at Stormy Ocean Publishing. Thank you for allowing me to keep my work special and for being my biggest support.

I had a pretty rare opportunity to work with a teenager who loves to read and wanted to see the behind-the-scenes process of writing a book. Having a sixteen-year-old mind help me with the writing process was a blast. Ocean Marshall, you are rad. Thank you for being my teen editor and for being so open to learning. Keep working toward your own writing dreams and goals.

Lastly, thank you, reader. I think so much about what is going to delight you and make you love reading as much as I did at your age. Thanks for picking this book up, and please reach out and tell me what you would love to read!